Out of the dusk a Shadow,
Then a Spark;
Out of the clouds a silence,
Then a lark;
Out of the heart a rapture,
Then a pain;
Out of the dead, cold ashes,
Life again.
†

Evolution

John Banister Tabb 1845-1909

Passage to Cuba

Passage to Cuba

Quest for the Masque of Gold

A Lana Victoria Bell Adventure-Suspense

Penelle

LANA Victoria BELL Adventures

Paperback publisher: CREATE SPACE - A division of Amazon, Inc.
Copyright 2015 by Penell-Braida Skinner
Lana Victoria Bell Enterprises, Sarasota, Florida

For information, or speaker's bureau, address the author at:
www.PenelleOnTour-books.com (Contact page)
www.LanaVictoriaBell.com (Blog site)

Written and manufactured in the United States of America

ISBN-13: 9781512077339

ISBN-10: 151207733X

Library of Congress Control Number: 2015907367
Createspace Independent Publishing Platform
North Charleston, South Carolina

Cover Image – El Morro & Cuban Flag; Masque of Gold. Courtesy of Istock
Interior map - Republic of Cuba. Courtesy of National Geographic

Interior pictures – Boats at Key West. photograph by Penelle. Havana; Tilling; Trinidad; Santiago de Cuba; Jazz-Musicians; Malecon night; Stamp. Courtesy of Istock

Logo by PENELLE - courtesy of OM ART DESIGNS

LANA Victoria BELL ENTERPRISES – A sole proprietor endeavor.

To DON

~&~

For INGRID, KYLE and MARSHALL

THE REPUBLIC OF CUBA - 2015.

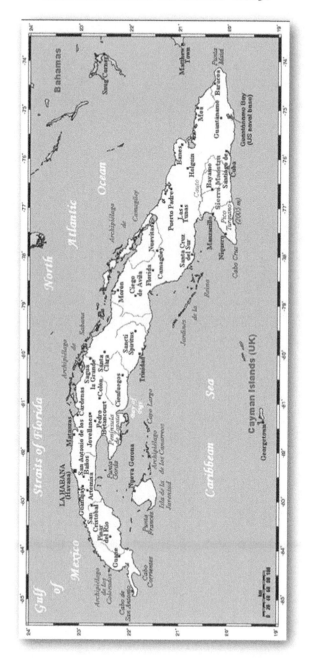

Chapter 1

*T*he wet blades – slipping between his fingers were difficult to hold underwater, and the propeller tried to move. However, he had a mechanic's skill, so even in the dark night the saboteur could handle the shaft and yank out the cotter pin. Then he manipulated the restraining nut, clenching his jaw as if it did the work, and forced it loose. His lungs were aching for oxygen, but he remained underwater, pulling the brass propeller assembly off the ship's shaft, and dropping the parts to a sandy-seabed beneath him.

Kicking with vigor, he shot himself above the waterline. Gasping and drawing in long breaths, he absorbed the damp marina air. He muttered, "*One more propeller,*" resuming his full submersion under the transom of a Marquis 420 motor-craft to inflict more damage to the sleek motor-craft. He made the second and last propeller suffer the same fate as the first. Then, raising his head above the salty water the saboteur refilled his lungs with air, and ducked down for the third time. However, this time he kept his eyes above the water's surface. They were round and very black, shining with an intensity to match the glow of a passing satellite.

Wary, the swimmer's eyes performed a languid slide left to right, scanning the area for onlookers or enemies, like an alligator hunting prey. Floating off a quiet Florida island, at the late hour, the saboteur felt unrestrained. With stealth, he pressed hand over hand against the vessel's port side pulling himself in silence from stern to bow. Treading water, he passed below the ship's lavish endowment of five portals, stopping at each dock line. With a knife lifted from his holster-belt, he drew a brutish edge along the three-quarter-inch braided hemp. Soon he had severed bow, stern and spring lines – now left long and lose hanging from their shipboard cleats. The other ends slunk into the water, dangling uselessly from the dock pylons.

If someone had been nearby, the ripple and splash of collapsing lines might have feathered their ears, but as it happened, Lana Victoria Bell and Federal Bureau of Investigation Agent Dusty Kern Cody were sound asleep in the *Esmeralda's* separate staterooms. No light shone inside the vessel, and the heater droned on. The swimmer smiled to himself over the irony of their repose. *Well, their sleep is prophetic. A lot more sound will not reach them this Christmas. They think they will reach Cuba and bring power to my people, but I am the one who will have power. At Last!*

The smirk on his lips broadened and made him wonder, for just a moment, who he had become. He knew that he had never been a true Calusa Indian; he was not their model child. His father's cruelty had put an end to those loyalties years ago. Tribal members had ignored his fears and festering loneliness so, as he became an adult, he felt little tie to them. He did not share their vision of an empowered tribe; he had his own vision — a chance for wealth and sweet revenge. His recruiters preyed on that, and he was happy to oblige. Who cared what goals they had? Let it be international chaos! Soon he would have the *Masque of Gold*, and make things right for himself. He would retreat, rich, into a far and safe pocket of the world.

Paddling, he reached the dock's ladder, and sprung up onto the planks. Lana awakened to his footfall on the loose boards as he darted away to the woods. He stopped for a quick look back at his floating handiwork, rubbing at a familiar throb in his elbow. For Lana there was little to see from her porthole in the darkness, just a figure moving away in the trees, rubbing his elbow. The only sound there was to hear came from marsh frogs echoing in the night.

Lana had no reason to expect foul play. She was aboard the boat of friends and their mission was about friendship. She dismissed the disturbance and returned sleepy-eyed to bed. As the tide receded, it gently rocked the vessel and Lana pulled up a cover and fell asleep.

Above the saboteur, heaven seemed dispassionate, draping stars across the vast Gulf of Mexico. Orion with its starry club was the prime winter witness to the figure's crimes, but the constellation had no power to help the besieged Bell and Cody; neither did the vessel *Esmeralda*. As the gentle lapping of the sea pulled at her bow, the *Esmeralda* became impatient.

"Fishing is not her goal, she is for cruising," Cody had told Lana when they boarded the *Esmeralda* earlier. "She carries no fancy head-gear to slow her progression. She is designed for action."

Even so, it took the *Esmeralda's* bulk a subtle; rear-end adjustment before her thirteen-eleven beam moved from the dock. Hefting gently to the west and moving into the wide Gulf of Mexico, the hull lightly grazed its loose lines against the pier. As she shifted, the craft's burgundy painted sides trembled with anticipation. Her face became seductive in the nightglow. Flashing long, eye-shaped, side windows and lifting pert portals at the nose, she flirted with the sea. Then, drawn by the forces of wind and water, she accelerated with the speed of a prize-catch to its lure, the bow snatching the tidal current. The *Esmeralda* was gone, unaware that even if she survived her freedom, she would harm the kindred spirits within leading them to foreign lands and into dangers of a new kind, from serving justice into a flight for life.

Chapter 2

Ten hours earlier Lana Bell and Agent Dusty Kern Cody had arrived in Florida excited about helping a friend and sharing their first vacation together. They were headed to the once restricted destination of Cuba. Restricted, if not forbidden to Americans long before Lana's birth in 1984. It was difficult, for young people not around during Cuba's coup-d'état in 1959, to fathom the varied emotions surrounding the beautiful country then, and even over the last five hundred years. Political and social changes in the country drove the many "isms" of politics until one day a revolution replied to the din of downtrodden voices. Emancipated or subordinated, people share emotions, and Lana understood the scope of that. She recognized her own feelings too, especially the deep hurt of abandonment.

One long past, snowy afternoon, rushing home from classes to prepare a special New Year's Eve supper, months after her mother's death, she bounded into the house excited about the leg of lamb her father loved. Her brother had already returned to his college out of state, so she juggled the groceries and brushed away the white, wintry flakes from the door lock. She pushed quickly inside, hitting the stereo music on and hurriedly dragging in the groceries. She called to her father about their fun evening ahead. She put the champagne on ice, and called out to him again, with no reply. Moving quickly through the house, knowing that he was still distraught after his wife's death, Lana entered his room. A lump welled in her throat. The goodbye note on the dresser was clear. He had disappeared, heading to Canada, choosing to escape his painful memories. "Someday I'll be in touch," the note read. At sixteen, Lana learned that loving people too much came at a price. Thereafter, she preferred not to pay it.

The weeks had turned into years, and Lana had become self-sufficient and happy. Then recently, her absent father came back. Lana's life had morphed into a family again, but she still felt uncertain about holding deep affection for others. Her father had been back two weeks and she still felt nervous to trust him. Therefore, she continued to focus on her job. Being a tour director was a wonderful life style, and staying on the traveling road was her tonic. Today she would be on her way to adventure again, only this was a trip to help a friend, to help right a wrong. Being useful and helping others drove her forward. She tended to ignore the dangers of that until it was too late.

As farewell, the little Vivie barked, wagging her short tail, making her poodle disposition clear. Lana picked up the small dog, and smothered her with gentle whispers. Then embracing her father a farewell too, she collected her bags and moved to the hallway.

"I'm so happy you've come back to us, Dad. Will you be comfortable here while I'm gone?"

"Very, my dear, don't you worry about me while you are away. New York is an exciting city to be in after so long an absence. I'll be fine, but I'll look forward to your coming back to us."

She turned her glance away and moved toward the door.

He reached for her arm, "I hope you will enjoy your sunshine vacation," he said with hesitation.

"This trip is really to help a friend, you see? It isn't just a vacation."

"Then what about that young man who calls you here so often?"

"Oh, Cody...?" She said softly, unsure of an answer.

"Well, stay away from dangerous people," he continued. "I don't like what you went through with that maniac last year in the Rockies. You come straight home if anything is a threat to you. Do you hear?"

It was a little late, after thirteen years' absence for her father to be so protective, but a warm feeling struggled for footing in her heart. It was not the same ache she had for DK—the one she tried to suppress.

"Don't worry, Dad. This trip will be a snap."

As her flight led Lana to Florida, she mused about her connection to DK. The youthful and yet seasoned adventurers seemed a matched pair, although Lana was not ready to be a pair. That morning Lana and her young man Cody were on a flight-trajectory toward each other, and the future was clearly, unclear.

Lana arrived at their destination from her New York City condominium, while FBI Agent Cody headed there from his new home in Washington, D.C. They planned to help a trusted Calusa Native family return an ancient artifact to the tribe; they were headed to help Lana's old friends, Oalachan and Luc Pio in Naples, Florida. It was billed as a vacation for Dusty Kern Cody.

Dusty had been promoted from his ranger assignment in hometown Spokane, to special duties at the Washington, D.C. headquarters of the FBI. He was looking forward to the new challenges of his position although he knew he would miss the Pacific Northwest as well as his buddies in Spokane. He shared a pride in their military past and several of them had stuck together through the years; they were active in their community for the common good. Now his life was changing. Dusty would take on a new job, a new location and perhaps family life. A vacation in the Caribbean seemed the right way to begin a new life, and to rest-up after several years of hard work. However, in the main, DK wanted to woo and marry Lana, the brown-eyed woman he preferred to call a girl.

Lana resisted all but friendship with her male admirers, and she met many. Her ten-year employment as an international tour director for Splendid Adventures kept her busy and in the company of many people. However, her career permitted her to stay on the move, going from place to place, keeping friendships light. She liked it that way. She would continue to hold her ground against emotional entanglements, even Dusty. He was a man she could admire even with his decisive personality. She recognized that he tried to decide for her often, but she let that go— for the time being. She knew that his military and FBI background contributed to his leadership skills, but she also knew there was a story behind his drive. It was his way of staying in control. If he had been properly in control as a teen, he might have prevented his brother's death. That was his formative lesson, and it never left his soul. Somehow, his consciousness translated that terrible experience into a challenge going forward. Dangerous situations now felt like the challenge of saving his brother. He liked to face and win against the odds. Maybe one day he could do so much good that the painful memory of his brother's loss would vanish. *Maybe that is why I joined the Bureau,* he mused, watching the earth pass below from his Boeing 737 window.

A glint of red sun flashed off the aircraft's metal sheathing like the color and sharpness of a winter day twenty years previous; the day his younger brother had disappeared in the snowy Cascades. It was DK alone, aching and exhausted, who threw himself down a dozen ski-slopes, hour after hour, with the frostbite growing in his bones, and the ice crystals clogging his nose, pressing his knees and hips into a constant slalom. As the day wore on, he was tripping more-often upon the outcrops, feeling sharp rocks cut through to his flesh. He hoped, he cried, and called for Ben until the shade of night overwhelmed his spirit. Then, as the last sunrays glinted red off a distant crest, his brother came into view. Now it was always the same for D.K. when he saw sunlight strike in the same way. A memory returned; the sad memory of a daring boy lured to ski jump off an unmarked trail who lie broken and frozen against the rocks.

People said that Dusty Kern Cody was beautiful to look at, with a noble head and broad shoulders, like the Marcus Aurelius marble bust in the museums, but he did not care. He would rather be one tenth as impressive and have saved his brother. That was not possible now. So, continue he would, helping those in harm's way. He needed to fight for others, before fate's deadly snowfall, ahead of the darkness that threatens.

The aircraft began its descent.

Chapter 3

Lana was waiting at the airport for Dusty Kern's arrival and found herself at the dry-goods shop selecting a sun hat.

"No." the clerk said. "That maroon color doesn't suit your red hair. By the way, has anyone told you that you have tiny dimples, like Scarlet O'Hara?"

Lana laughed and plopped a wide-brimmed hat on her head.

"Oh that's a good one for you," the clerk continued. "The broad brim will protect your face. I would not want to see you ruin that clear complexion under the Caribbean sun, so take this scarf too. It complements your golden-brown eyes."

Lana smiled at her new acquaintance, "Yes, good, a scarf. I love its pale green color—so cool and soft. Thank you so much for the compliments, and for the advice."

Lana paid the clerk and slipped her change into the collection can for the Red Cross. They chatted goodbyes, and Lana walked to the flight arrivals' board. She paused, unwrapped a dark chocolate candy and savored its soft center with a smile. After a minute, she moved on. Her tall, slender frame gave little resistance to her light dress, which scalloped around her with every speedy step. People watched her breeze by, but she only nodded to the families. Vamping was not of interest to her. She was not seeking men—she could take care of herself. Life was all up to her, every responsibility and every challenge.

A blame deep inside her propelled her that way—the blame of not being better prepared for her mother's passing. If she could be prepared for the unexpected, Lana could soften the shock of pain for people, as she wished she had done for her father. He might not have been so distraught years ago—if only she had prepared options for him. Instead, her dad ran away from her and her brother. She had not been better prepared to help them.

Nowadays, she did her best to prevent and outwit pain, for herself and others. When Luc asked her to help his tribe, she did not think twice about it. *I can help them. I have led travelers on tours around the world. Most of the time, I know how to stay ahead of the unexpected.*

Most of the time.

Lana estimated another ten minutes for the passengers to disembark and make it down into the waiting area. She looked around the terminal space. It seemed that everything was in order except for a clacking and tapping of footfalls. They echoed over the wide marble floor as rumbles of conversation billowed under the large room's arches.

"Sound and fury signifying nothing..." she remembered from Shakespeare. *Perhaps Macbeth felt that way because he would not forgive others, could not look to the future, and move on for the common good.* She wondered how often people were caught in that sorrow. Perhaps this related to Pio's quest too. Maybe the family just could not leave the past and move on. All she and DK could do was respond to the call. She knew that they both would go to the end of any challenge. It would have to be the Pios to decide the end.

Passengers were heading toward her from DK's flight, and Lana began to fidget. She felt excited to think that after a year of short airport meets and long telephone calls, they would be together for three weeks. Yet, would that be too much? Would she have to make commitments?

Agent Cody's eyes always startled her at the first glance. From the blue of them, a sense of broad, quiet meadows spread to her. They seemed to reflect his Rocky Mountain home with its vast natural beauty. She loved that place too, and his eyes would twinkle at the talk of it. Sometimes, however, other topics took his expression far away. If his eyes went level and his irises tinted gray, it seemed to her that a mental offensive went into play. However, for now, as the couple approached each other, nothing threatened them, and the mountain meadows were at peace. Lana's golden-red curls bobbed noticeably amidst the crowd, and seeing them, DK's face widened in relaxation, as if he himself had found home.

Lana waved the straw hat with vigor, laughing, and when they were two feet apart, time and space evaporated. She flung herself up and wrapped her arms around him, not letting go, very surprised at herself. His eyes went deep blue.

DK never admitted to Lana that his romantic alliances were rare. His looks did not stop him; his attitude did. He was not cavalier about people's feelings and did not give affection casually. His upbringing had been in the mountains of the west, close to nature, and he respected the natural order with its reliance on family. In those past cases of relationship he had entered and failed, the selfish or immature woman did not last. He found that they bled the oxygen from life. In Lana, he felt a sturdy soul, a boundless one, a fresh breath of life. In addition, he trusted her. Truth be told, DK missed her between phone calls, and he hoped for something permanent after a year of friendship, but he was losing patience.

"You look good, Missy!" He planted another kiss on her cheek as they walked arm and arm out of the airport to the van park.

"Congratulations again on your promotion, DK. Now that you work for the Crime Investigation Department out of Washington, you'll probably be exposed to more and different dangers than before, right?"

"Yes and no. There are teams of us sharing research and challenges. Therefore, it will not be all new to me, but there will be more challenges, I'm sure. I'll have new partners and maybe more bureaucratic support."

She sighed, "I'll bet that Sky and King will be happy to see you travel less. That makes you a better parent than I am. Poor Vivie sees me so little."

"Would you like her to come live with me? My dogs would love her."

Lana stopped in her tracks. Somehow, she had not ever thought to give up Vivie. Would it mean seeing DK exclusively? She was trying to avoid such deep emotions.

"Thanks," She blurted, moving fast down the corridor.

He perceived her confusion, and changed subjects. "You look in great shape, Lana. Is that arm all muscle?"

They laughed. "Yes, I'm still lifting suitcases, and they are as good as gym weights."

He gave her another hug at the airport curbside, and then looked up to see a young man approach them. Younger than DK he had a stocky build, the physique of a baseball umpire. DK accepted the broad hand, shook it and handed over his suitcase. Lana made a theatrical extension of her arm to introduce the two men.

"DK this is Luc Pio. Luc, I'd like you to meet my friend, Special Agent Dusty Kern Cody."

"Call me Cody or DK," he said, returning a powerful handshake.

Luc produced a generous smile. "And this is my cousin Gusta," Luc introduced the burly man, patting his relative on the back. "He's coming with us since he's the skilled sailor, although Lana tells me you've got experience in boating too."

"Some."

The men made a rapid assessment of each other. DK's wavy, dark brown hair cut in the agency's smooth, professional style, more medium length than long, made him look older than his age of thirty-three. Luc studied the man whose mouth was even and eyes level. He noticed the small crease, which sat between his uneven brow bones. Luc figured that this young man had already seen a lot of life. He admired the physical presence of his new friend; the long, lean man with an unremarkable nose and set jaw. Later he would learn that Dusty Kern Cody's irises could change from deep blue to ice gray.

"You'll be a great help during our journey with your professional expertise. This team should be able to handle everything thrown at us," Luc said lifting his car's trunk.

DK put the duffle bags in place and then turned to Luc. "I want to be clear, Luc, that as an agent of our federal government, I cannot act officially during our visit to Cuba. I don't know what plan you have to collect the tribal *Masque* you seek, but I am not willing to overstep our permissions or break laws of the country."

"No. Don't worry. Gusta and I have no such plans."

"But you hinted at dangers, Luc. I didn't know we had any dangers ahead?" Lana queried.

"Aw, well, you know that one cannot predict what might come up on a long journey," he said jovially.

Lana looked at Dusty. He took a deep breath, exhaled and raised his brows at her. She remained expressionless, hoping that he would drop the subject. She wanted the trip to continue and to be useful and without discord. "There can't be much intrigue to track down this old *Masque*, can there?" She asked.

Gusta sat in the Subaru's driver seat, and Luc sat beside him, both ignoring her question. Once they had pulled from the curb, Luc teased Lana about their last tour together, and then chided her. "I didn't know that Lana dated such a handsome man. You remind me of the marble busts of great Roman emperors that I show my tour groups at the Metropolitan Museum."

Cody put up his hand to fend off any flattery. "Are you trying to butter me up for something unexpected, Luc?" he joked. "I may be bossy but I never thought of myself as an emperor."

"Sorry DK. I didn't mean to offend."

"Don't worry Luc, He is really easy to get along with aren't you, Dusty? He is honest about his feelings, like you and me, and he is just teasing you."

Agent Cody said nothing more accepting that this trip was his host's show. He decided to go with the flow. He turned to the passing scenery and drank in its complex and secretive beauty.

"Anyway," Lana continued, "I've always teased Luc, calling him, *cute Buster Brown*."

Luc patted his broad nose, sat tall, and broke into a satisfied smile. "I like that name…yep, and I like that image. Did you hear that Gusta? Cute goes a long way in this world. And if I can make people have a good time by being a comic strip character, then let it be Buster Brown."

As they drove onward, DK reached to the front seat, "Thanks for picking me up, Luc. This treasure hunt sounds very interesting."

Luc lifted his chin and turned a cheerful expression to DK and Lana. His very large black eyes were made darker by the shadow of his pageboy haircut, cut at the jaw line. Gusta's was cut the same way, but his hair was woolier, and his build was much larger.

"You are more than welcome. We should reach my father in a few minutes and they we'll all go to dinner. You will not need anything at the restaurant because you are our guests. However, be sure to keep that windbreaker with you because it is December, and the Florida temperature at night is lower than most people expect.

"Do I understand that your father does not want to make the trip with us in the morning? Lana tells me that it was he who obtained the vessel and all our legal documents."

"That's true. This trip to recover the *Masque of Gold* is his dream. He waited all these years to fulfill the dream of our ancestors and, now in his remaining years, he cannot travel the excursion personally. His health won't handle such a journey, but he is content for us to go for him."

Lana interrupted, "We'll try our best to succeed for him."

"He loves Lana. On previous visits, the two of them have taken long walks on the beach discussing philosophy. She knows how much he believes in restoring our tribe to glory. You see, he believes the *Masque* will bring us wisdom. He is anxious to meet you and grateful for your help."

"It suits me to help you," he sighed. "This way I don't feel guilty to be on a vacation in Cuba."

They all laughed.

They drove on, driving south on Tamiami Trail. Above them, the swaying palms and feathery pines tickled the sky. Colorful flowers peeped through the roadside brush. During their conversation DK un-knotted his long legs into a comfortable stretch, and reached for Lana's hand.

He loved his work for the succor it provided real people and the justice it tried to serve. Now he would have a break from the complexity of intelligence gathering, from the rush of street assignments, the constant watchfulness and stealth, from gun practice and new procedures, from piles of paperwork and other technical aspects. Ultimately, it felt good to have this tropical vacation and relax from the law enforcement.

Chapter 4

The Subaru had room for its fifth passenger, Oalachan Pio, the father of young Luc. He bore a proud carriage in spite of his proclaimed age. His face revealed leathery skin from a life under the sun, but his eyes had the welcoming glow of a lighthouse. He loved to meet people, and shook hands genially with DK. Then planting a brief kiss on Lana's check, he maneuvered himself into the front car seat while Luc moved back.

Cody warmed to the family patriarch, "It's an honor to meet you sir," he repeated.

"Posh! It is an honor to meet you, young investigator. I see you are well suited to the task. You and Lana are cut from the same durable jib," he confirmed with a chuckle. "Speed it up, Gusta. I'm anxious to see the *Esmeralda,* and I'm sure you are all as hungry as I am."

An educated man, now beyond his former temptation to sail the seas, Pio was comfortable with his life bound to the land. He pointed out the passing sights with pride, noting the great river of grass that swayed southward. "Those grassy veins reach back into our tribal origins," he said,

"The great Okeechobee Lake drains continuously east and to us in the southwest, merging its fresh waters with the Gulf of Mexico."

DK looked at the complex habitat, excited to visit the area. "Yes, I saw this vast stretch of wetlands from the aircraft. Seen from above the waterways splay out like a fan. However, from this level I can enjoy the amazing wildlife. He pointed to the surrounding forest with enthusiasm, "Look at that great bird nest up there."

"Yes, you can see why our people love it here. It seems like a blueprint heaven-made, just for wildlife and man to play. Herons, Egrets and a host of other birdlife live together with bear, panther, raccoon, squirrel, alligator and more. Well, I should say they live and dine as they must."

DK did not join in the good humor. Instead, he was absorbed by the passing views of communities tugging at glamourous golf greens, strips of shopping stores and hints of coastal mansions.

"You prefer to live inland, don't you father," Lana stated.

"My people prefer the privacy of the woods, now that fishing isn't our only livelihood. The Pio clan inherited a large tract of land just outside the town, and since the ownership is grandfathered to us, we are happy there in our privacy. Most of the Gulf waterfront properties were taken from my people long ago."

"It's very beautiful here Luc," DK complimented. "Now what about our voyage? Will you brief us tonight?"

"The ship is sound DK, and all our government documents are in order. You should have an easy run of the voyage, and only have to follow my clan's old map to find the *Masque* in Cuba. You'll have privacy and comfort your first night on the *Esmeralda*. Then Gusta and my son will board in the morning, bringing all the ship's stores with them. All the equipment should work, including the heater, so you will be fine."

DK pressed on, "Luc, how are you planning to obtain the *Masque of Gold*?"

"Just ask for it. Our government permissions say we may search the locations indicated on my family map, throughout Cuba. However, father does not want us to intrude on people's personal lives or force anyone to help us. We just travel on asking about knowledge of our artifact. We show our documentation to prove provenance and then see if someone can take us to the *Masque*."

"I understand. Aren't there any clues now?"

The elder Pio spoke up, "I'm sorry DK, no. The challenge is exactly that. We do not know which family or town has it. You must follow the map. We do not want to steal it. If the price is too high for us now, perhaps we can pay for it later. If the parties are unsympathetic to our cause, mention the curse of the *Masque*."

"Ah." DK said, sitting back again. Amusement played on his features. "A curse, huh?" Well as long as we have the legal documents, I guess someone may be happy to offload an old cursed artifact."

"Oh yes, I'm hopeful," the elder Pio replied.

The group sat at the restaurant's waterfront table and enjoyed a simple dinner of fresh caught fish. They enjoyed their dinner so much that quiet reigned for ten whole minutes. Then the elder Pio dropped a casual command. "Any water adventure has risks. Just keep each other safe, the boat too, and secure the *Masque of Gold*. That's all I require of this adventure."

"What do you mean about risks, Oalachan?"

"Lana, we have received some threats not to continue this search. Whoever it is may oppose my expenditure, preferring it go to some immediate tribal need. However, I think the future is important and in the light of the future, our culture must be reinforced. The *Masque* could benefit the tribe by its intrinsic value and the potential tourism it suggests." Pio sighed looking at his guests with a jovial, disarming smile. "Don't let it worry you. You will be at sea and far from any dissident here. There is always dissent to something in life. The cause is noble for the end is noble."

"How was the *Masque* lost?" Cody asked.

The old man plucked a final forkful of fish from his plate, but spoke before he lifted it. "My tribe, the Calusa, lived by grace of the sea after coming north from southern continents and their Arawak origins. Here they grew into a rich culture with a language of their own. They were able to devise tools from bone, wood and shell. They had an architect's skill designing entire villages and homes completely made of shell glued with natural fibers. Their villages stood high up off the sand. They even achieved artistic abilities, revealed to us today by digs which unearth quality items. Unfortunately, anything not made of bone disappeared over the centuries. Nonetheless, the tenor of our tribe was greatness. Our ancestors maintained strong family units and a satisfactory social structure. They followed the spirits of the universe and paid them honor, living in peace without aggression. They always followed their leader, a cacique who led them with wisdom."

Luc picked up the story, gently telling of the evil, which befell all the tribes of the area. "My people were forced to fight the conquistadors because they denied us our way of life, trying to enslave and convert us. Their brutality changed our heritage. It was Ponce de León, a great Spanish conquistador who stole our most important spiritual icon, our *Cemi*. Its special name translated from our ancient language reads in English, *Masque of Gold*. Those words do not equal the real meaning which go deeper and mean a string of things; all the things that a god may know, bestow or advise."

"Was there no other Cemi to replace it?" DK asked the elder Pio.

"No, none that special. Never was one made as powerful as the *Masque of Gold*. It channeled the supreme creator. That enabled us to grow, prosper and live with honor. Even now, I am not sure whether the *Masque of Gold* can return us to that former culture, which is what my family hoped through the centuries. You see, we may have changed too much over the years, but I'm not ready to give up the dream," Oalachan Pio answered.

"What makes you think it still exists after 500 years?" DK asked.

"Because it is made of bone and gold, it can survive more than 500 years! It is the artifacts made of wood or shell did not last."

"Florida is not known to have the natural resource of gold. Where would the gold have come from to make such an artifact?"

"Good question. Anthropologists believe that European caravels marooned on shifting sandbars or sunk along the Gulf Coast yielded enough wealth, and especially gold, to share amongst the tribes during the 16th century. It is assumed that precious metals had traveled from South America. Legend has it that the greatest cacique, or chief at that time, Carlos had allotted a fair distribution of booty to all the Florida clans. Our own clan received gold. The Pio clan created this special *Masque* in honor of Carlos when he passed. He would channel the supreme creator to help us forever."

"I see."

Luc saw the fatigue come over his father and put an arm around him. "You see Cody, over time our other valuables have been lost or stolen, and our individual Calusa culture has melded with other tribes. My family has always hoped that the *Masque of Gold* would return our distinctive culture to us and guide us to greater success."

Lana touched Luc's arm, and he calmed his fervor. She smiled at DK to do the same. Luc noticed the electric effect that had on her beau. Lana did not.

"I guess that our little vacation will be a quest alright," Luc concluded.

Agent Cody broke the pause with a disclaimer of his official capacity on the journey. "I am not traveling on government business, so I can't be called upon to do anything other than sight-see. I thought that our quest was meant to collect a *Masque* from some relative in Cuba. I understand now that it won't be that simple, right?"

"Right," Pio replied. "I do hope that someone has continued to safeguard it as our oral tradition says. I also hope they will give it up."

Lana looked at DK. His facial muscles did not change. Instead, his irises faded from dark blue to steel gray. She watched him excuse himself and step outside, satellite phone in hand. He did not return to them for a full ten minutes, and Pio became anxious. He was ready to leave and to set eyes upon his *Esmeralda*.When DK rejoined them, the group exited C.J.'s Fish House on San Marco Island, driving down the entire length of Collier Boulevard, and unaware of a vehicle following them, drove into a stately condominium complex facing Caxambus Pass.

They were sixteen miles south of Naples, at the edge of the Everglades, due west of the Fakahatchee Strand and the Big Cypress Preserve. Before them, several inter-coastal waterways wove through spits of sand and hardwoods, yawning at last into the Gulf of Mexico.

Gusta drove past a security gate that closed behind them. "My wife and I live at this complex. I was able to secure a long term dock for us," he said.

As the sun neared the far horizon, they all stopped to gaze at the wide and inviting world of the sea. Alongside them, a number of condominium residences stretched heavenward, edging the shoreline. The units were similar to much of South Florida coastal real estate; investments for the wealthy, pampered perches for extraordinary views, idle much of the year. A riddle of irregular islands stretched away from them to the end of the continent; ten thousand islands sparsely populated and heavily treed.

"Caxambus Pass itself spills fresh waters from a complex and beautiful mainland river system into a collision course with the Gulf Stream," Luc said. "Once we motor away from these small islands there is nothing but the vast, open Gulf of Mexico and Cuba on the Caribbean Sea."

They were all silent for a moment understanding that to admire the beauty of nature did not deny her force. Most people living in the condominiums along the Florida shores do not ignore nature's unpredictability and stormy rawness, nor do they underestimate any enemy. Everyone concerned with the *Esmeralda* would learn that too.

Once the stalking vehicle turned away from the condominium gates, it parked off to a side road, hidden. The occupant would wait.

Gusta drove to the dock. A burly man, with an outgoing personality, he showed a remarkable resemblance to his cousin Luc, but was more the outdoor man and less the scholar. At the waterside, the five of them gazed on the fiberglass gazelle that had become Oalachan Pio's prize. He grew angry that some other boater had left trash on the *Esmeralda's* dock, but Pio calmed him.

Lana whispered to Dusty, "He seems fond of the old man and supportive of the goals, but he is quick to anger."

"Ah," DK acknowledged, raising his eyebrows. He patted the hull and turned to Pio. "You certainly have a special boat here, Sir."

Lana nodded, "Amazing."

"Yes, my *Esmeralda*," Pio uttered with pride.

"She is gorgeous. I didn't know you were a speed lover," Lana said gaily. "It looks fast like one of those fast 'cigarette racers.'

Pio laughed. "It is what they call an 'express cruiser,' a Marquis, not a racer, but very sleek. No?"

They all joined in admiration, which tickled the old man. "Our clan does not fish in deep waters. We fish close to the shore so we do not need a flying bridge and we have some little boats if we need them. However, if we are to increase tourism to our new *Masque* Museum, we will have to do business promotions, at least in the beginning. We decided on securing a vessel that was good for that. We were offered this boat at a very low price. We had to take it." He smiled broadly.

"We can also rent the boat to other interests and when the time comes, we will sell the vessel and re-invest the proceeds into the museum. We won't lose our money and stand to make a decent profit."

"Really?"

"Yes. We paid very little for the vessel." Pio smiled again. "It belonged to my brother-in-law, and he sold it to us for even less than he paid, or it is worth."

Lana smiled, "It certainly helps to have generous in-laws."

Pio shrugged his shoulders. "That's my brother in law for you, generous. Besides, he is well to do, having partnership in a successful casino resort. He used the boat for business promotions too. Giving it to us gave him a good excuse to upgrade, he said, but I suspect he believes in the cause too. He made sure everything was in top shape for us."

"Except the radio," Gusta complained.

"That's okay," Luc replied. "I've bought a beautiful new Standard-Horizon™ radio, a multi-function AIS GPS. It is boxed with the supplies that I'll bring over in the morning."

Gusta had calmed down. He relaxed, noting no damage to the boat and began to trust that everything would be fine in the morning. He did a walk-around on the vessel, and then Luc invited the others to step aboard."

"Well, go ahead, Lana. You too, DK. Look around. You too, Dad. Check out your new toy."

Pio gave them a sheepish look, now a little embarrassed at his extravagance, even if he had felt good reasons for it. "No, no, not now. Maybe when all this serious business is over you can take me for a trip along our shores so I can see our ancient places again. I like to think there are still nature's hideaways left of our former wilderness." Placing his hand on Gusta's shoulder the senior Pio reassured his trusted nephew. "So! You and Luc have done well, and I like this location because it is close to our enclave." He smiled at a new thought, "We may fit in some family afternoons as much as business promotions."

Gusta reddened at the praise, looking down at his shoes with nothing to say, but he smiled too, happy with the idea of spending Sundays on the family boat.

Pio added, "Luc this spot is a wonderful starting point for your trip tomorrow. This pier is a straight shot to Cuba. Just make sure you captains don't bump into the pirate coves of the Dry Tortugas."

Everyone laughed because marooning on that remote island location would require a definite error of his or her navigation. However, Pio was not thinking about the technical points, really. He just smiled like a proud papa at his 42-foot toy. To Lana he seemed older these days, but he retained his straight back and level shoulders. His fingers bulged a bit with muscles gone gnarly and bones gone arthritic. His hair may have grown gray, but he boasted all of it, along with bushy eyebrows to match. He tired easily, but his warm chestnut colored eyes still danced to charm the ladies.

"Well, my crew, before I go," Pio said in a playful fashion, "I'd like to hear the exciting purr of that expensive Penta engine."

Gusta revved the IPS 400 motor just part of its full strength, and for a moment, the old man stood in reverence for its quick response. He would have liked nothing better than to join the young ones in an adventure of a lifetime, his lifetime: a passage to Cuba.

Pio gave a blessing to his crew and his *Esmeralda.* "We will meet another day."

"Goodbye Senōr Pio, It was our pleasure to meet you," DK said.

Lana assured the old gentleman with a hug. "We will do everything we can to find your tribe's *Masque of Gold.*"

"I thank you, but I do not push any of you to suffer danger. Be careful."

Lana felt a slight tension in her stomach. There was that hint of danger again.

He continued, "I've decided to let Luc be the judge of the best thing to do in the end since you will all be so far from home. The future will be as it must."

Moving with an increased stiffness, he reached the car. He called behind him to them, "Goodbye my children."

Sighing, Gusta watched his mentor leave. "I wish he could have come with us. I think the boating would do him good."

"Yes," DK stated deliberately, "but he knows that there is more than boating afoot, doesn't he Gusta."

The statement called for no reply for there was none. Therefore, Gusta pointed to the staterooms. "You'll find bedding and towels below. We will be back in the morning with all the other needed supplies and the radio. My wife will come down now from our apartment now and bring you some cakes and fresh coffee. Here, let me pass you your duffle bags."

Lana looked at the vessel and then at Gusta. "If we have to visit all the towns on Luc's treasure map trail, docking at any number of Cuba's 30 ports, we will run out of time, Gusta. You understand that DK and I must return to our jobs in just a few weeks."

"Luc told me you have a time constraint, so he arranged for a van and driver to take us through the island. We'll leave the boat in Havana."

"Oh, fine."

"It's only 110 miles from here to Key West. I want us to spend the first night there so we can check the entire ship over again, refuel and enact our official business with the Coast Guard. That leg should take around five hours. I will not push the systems with five of us on board. It will be a little longer to cross and reach Cuba because we will contending with the Gulf Stream, and as long as it is not necessary, I do not want to put stress on the boat's systems. Well, goodnight. I'll see you in the morning, I'm sure our trip will be an easy one."

"I wonder," Lana said to DK under her breath.

Gusta ambled down the path, started his car and drove off with the Pios.

DK tightened the mooring lines and noticed Lana shiver, her frame slender. "Getting chilly?" He asked, putting his arm around her. "Does that warm you?"

"Fine. Thanks."

Lana and DK snuggled into the transom lounge bench, feeling at a loss for words after all the planning, anticipation and excitement of being together. Together they stared out at the 180-degree Gulf panorama, enjoying it, but feeling awkward.

"Oh I feel the boat rocking," Lana said.

"The tide is going out."

"Ah," Lana answered, facing west. She realized that she and Agent DK Cody were only friendly strangers. They had put in motion a long personal journey and a mysterious quest. They had miles to go on both accounts. How many miles lay before them, how many trials might test them and what would be the result? Embraced by mild air and wilderness islands, the couple sat side-by-side, eyes to the vast horizon. Each breathed deeply, reflecting on their dreams — DK not admitting and yet hoping for a miracle with Lana, and Lana repressing such amorous hopes.

Bright lights began a peep show of color along the stretch of island piers while different pleasure craft eased by the *Esmeralda's* mooring, returning to leafy caches of other lives. In spite of the delivery of hot coffee, the couple was very tired and they fell soundly asleep. The cold night air drove them to bed and they heard nothing but the soft whirr of the ship's heater.

Midnight had come and gone. The ship's cut lines dangled in the breeze, swaying adieu. The vessel freed herself from port—anxious to ride the beckoning sea. Later it was estimated that the *Esmeralda* had attained an average speed of three knots an hour during her errant voyage. Even fully loaded, the Marquis 420 Coupé maxed at a mere one-meter draft, so she scooted right over the great sand-shelf of western Florida. She went seeking huge tankers, great oilrigs, and untended helms like hers.

Chapter 5

$\mathcal{M}$any ships had plied the Gulf waters for thou-
sands of years. Various cultures had explored
their way through the coral reefs, verdant coastlines
and islands, but of all the passages and of all the nights,
on this particular night a mystical force overtook the
Esmeralda, and she obeyed. She moved forward, but not
alone. Ghosts of the past enveloped her. In a time warp
of repentance, the crews of his ships *Santiago, Santa
Maria* and *San Cristobal* sought to save their noble com-
mander Ponce de León, again. They would make haste
to Havana and rid themselves of the cursed *Masque of
Gold.*

It is said that only the ghost of a penitent conquistador
could have shielded Lana this night from danger; that it
was time for the great leader to expiate his complicity in
sins of 16th century exploitation. With the help of the conquistador's crew, he cast a web over the *Esmeralda,* speed-
ing her straight south out of harm's way. By morning, the
waters of the Gulf turned placid and the *Esmeralda* stilled.
She was six miles out and fifteen miles south of Naples. She

was alone with Lana, DK, and ghosts of the past. By the following day, they would be twelve miles out and eighty-five miles further south.

∽∾∽

That first dawn together, Lana woke to a clear sky as light streamed through the translucent overhead hatch. She pulled up to the stateroom porthole and peered out.

Ooo calm, she thought, stretching around on the pillow-top mattress. *I slept like a rock. I wonder if Dusty's mattress was just as comfy…. Oh dear, well, at least we can enjoy cups of hot coffee. Gusta's wife is sure to think of us again.*

She pulled on her light dress and climbed to the bridge, looking at her watch.

"Good morning, DK. Is it really eight a.m.?"

He looked back at her with less than the enthusiastic expression she had expected. Her first thought was that he had not rested well, and was annoyed with her prudishness, but then she followed his stare and saw that the land mass was gone. Panic was her first thought, and she wheeled around stretching her arm to clutch DK.

"That's right, my dear. Just the sea out there." He refused to reveal his concern, planning to be Papa-San now.

"What happened?"

"I know what, but not why. We will have to get ourselves back to shore because floundering in shipping lanes will not do. I am very sorry. I thought it wasn't a good idea to be dropped at the boat last night without a radio, kind of like being baby-sat by the baby. I blame myself.

Professional instincts should have told me that even on vacation I need a foolproof plan."

"Don't beat yourself up; this was supposed to be a holiday. You were not supposed to be on duty. Everything had been so well planned for us. Something bad must have happened to Luc because I cannot believe that a good friend like him would do this to us. The ship must have broken free."

"She did break free, but not without help."

DK led her around the cockpit to the bow. "See here? The bowline hanging free? It has been clipped with the intention of sending us off with the tide."

Lana gnawed her lower lip. DK put his arm around her and led her back around to the salon. She looked at him with as much dolefulness as possible. "And there's no coffee."

She watched for his response at which time they both clamped their lips, and stifled a laugh.

"Will our satellite cellphones work out here?"

"They should, but I've had no luck getting either of them to connect."

"Oh, well someone will find us." Lana added.

He noted that she was a person who kept hope alive, no matter the odds. "Yes, eventually. If Luc did not engineer this, then he is sure to report us missing to the Coast Guard. In the meantime, we should check the vessel out and find something to eat. At least I have a bit of fishing experience, so if things go well, we will not starve. I checked the water tanks, and they are full. This boat model holds 140 gallons. We ought to be okay for a week, so that is no worry. To avoid a collision is my concern. We'll have to keep watch all the time."

"I'll make us coffee when I'm changed…oops…no coffee," She grimaced.

"Well, guess what?"

"What?" she asked with hesitation.

"No, it's a good thing. We didn't finish off the thermos last night, so if you can stand it, let's reheat the contents in those paper cups and share our morning wake-up."

Clapping in good humor she checked the microwave. "It works."

"Once the engine starts Lana, I'll be able to get us to a port without charts by using the instruments on board and dead-reckoning. Maybe the android cell phone will work as we near land and will bring up a navigation chart. Thank heaven the day is clear."

Lana handed him the stale coffee adding a hard candy from her windbreaker pocket. It was better than nothing. DK liked it bitter usually, hard core, but this time he was glad for something to smooth the stale brew.

"Can you see?" Lana asked as they sat side by side at the lounge table, sipping the tarry beverage.

"What?" He followed the direction of her hand.

"Everything besides the beautiful teak flooring is done in fiberglass, and all the fittings are stainless steel. She is just beautiful."

"Oh I see everything all right. Let me show you the instrumentation. Come over to the helm. This motor craft holds all the instrumentation we could possibly need, except for the National Oceanographic enabled radio. It does have radar and sonar equipment." He turned to her with a twinkle in his eye. "However, I really like that the stainless safety railing encircles the entire deck." His arm encircled her waist with a hug, "I don't want you to fall overboard."

Lana giggled with embarrassment, but enjoyed the playtime. "Let me down Tarzan."

He did at once and they sat back together, this time facing the instrument panel.

"This is a double wide settee," Lana noted, rubbing her hand along the long leather cockpit seat. "I can help you steer." She smiled at him like a child.

"Uh, huh," he said without conviction, yet.

"I love how the full galley, the helm, the sitting salon and a swim platform all run together like a great-room house plan."

"Pretty nice. That way I can't lose you," he answered, delighted at her delight. He continued to study the design details, his steel-blue eyes scanning everything.

"I think the Marquis manufacturer calls this steering area a cockpit instead of a bridge."

"Oh, I see." Lana commented in a hushed tone, ready to learn something new, neither of them worried very much, yet.

"Did Luc tell you what he paid for this Lana?"

"He said that a new one would run over $600,000 and they paid way, way less thanks to a generous relative. Nevertheless, Pio used most of his retirement savings, so a few members of the tribe pitched in too. He has invested a lot in a dream. I hope that it pays off."

DK nodded, and when they had finished their sparse breakfast, he started the engine, but not much happened. The boat wiggled. The more power he applied, the less happened. They were going nowhere. He shut the engine down immediately. "Something is very wrong. I'm going under to see whether we are hung-up on debris."

He pulled off most of his clothes, and Lana winked at him. "Wrong moment, girl," he teased, turning and diving underwater.

Lana flicked on the transom light to provide more visibility for him and did a quick look into storage areas. Then she stood above the diving platform watching DK's figure moving around the ship. She began to wonder about this adventure. *How can we expect anything like a simple Masque to bring a native culture back to whole again? How can the Cuban Republic be so close to us, and yet so far?* The thoughts made her impatient. She did not like ambiguity. She preferred to create solutions. The world did not move fast enough for her.

DK broke the surface of the water, forcing up a spout of salt water. Grasping the telescoping ladder, and lifting a long leg with ease onto the swim platform he hauled his body upright, dripping wet, but smiling. "Ahh that felt good, bracing but good."

"Here take my hand, mister aquatic FBI guy." She pulled him across the Plexiglas gate and secured it shut. He feigned a fall against her.

"Brrr," she pouted in fun, "Now I'm wet too."

"Let me warm you," he offered, flinging his arms around her and kissing her on the forehead."

Lana wriggled and struggled free. Her plum-blushed lips broke into a big smile, which did, in fact, end in tiny dimples. "Stop moving. Let me dry you off, mister," she spoke in a soft tone. He let her circle him as she toweled until he felt red.

"Say you are a strong lady."

"Strong?"

"Okay, okay, *capable*. I don't want to tussle with a redhead," he laughed. Then he bent his lips to hers and left a light kiss on them.

She edged away.

"So what is the verdict, DK?"

"We've been sabotaged. The propellers are gone."

"Gone? Could they just fall off?"

"Uh, uh, no." He shook his head looking out to sea. "We are calm now but if a storm came up we could be dashed against a shoreline, although I don't see anything like that nearby. Otherwise, if we are not inundated or capsized by a storm, we can hope to attract attention. For the time being, do not worry. This boat is seaworthy." He glanced back at Lana and her steady gaze. He had half expected to see panic, but, *of course, that would not be my Lana,* he thought. Something close to panic would develop later, hours later.

"Well, while you were investigating the hull bottom, I checked all the storage cabinets. There isn't even a book on board, only a few kitchen implements."

"What about charts?"

"None. And a radio isn't a standard thing I guess."

"Didn't Luc say he was to bring a radio on board?"

"Oh yes, and he showed me the shopping list as we drove back to the airport for your flight. He is bringing plenty to meet our needs including CDs to play. Say," She added, noticing his worried look, "Don't look sad. We still can have a great vacation."

He sighed. "Well, I do feel good about the boat's exterior. It is a solid fiberglass laminate, and I saw the insignia for Knytex substrates. Since it has the water barrier coat and no cracks in the hull, I think she will withstand the elements. Pretty Brandywine color and clean it is. Don't you agree?"

She nodded in earnest. "So, we are in luxury."

"Not quite. Are you sure that no backup propellers were in the cabinets?"

"No, DK. Definitely no second pair, no loose parts anywhere. All the stowage cabinets are empty. There are a couple of closets for our gear. They are empty too. I pulled up the floor storage hatch and found only some ship's bumpers. Oh! We do have life vests. They are under the lounge cushions."

"What about the bilge?" he queried as if to test her.

"Dry as a bone, sir."

"Good. Well the *Esmeralda* is a well-designed motor craft, and its specifications card says that this model holds a thirty-one battery service with 230 volt of power. It should be plenty for a week. It's enough power to run this young colt's engine, but we are stymied on that. However, we can use the sunroof, the head, running water, the appliances and all the lighting."

"You are certainly a romantic captain. Who else would think 'sunroof', before head."

He sneezed.

"Are you dry enough?" She asked.

"I'm fine."

"Come on, you have clothes in the duffle. Please take a hot shower first, and change into something dry and warm. That water couldn't be sixty-five degrees this time of year and the wind is picking up."

He nodded, "Yes, Mama-san. Any more hot coffee?"

———◦∞◦———

Lana showered in her turn, and pulled on a fresh shift dress. She returned upstairs to see DK standing at the table drawing a rudimentary navigation chart. Lana pulled him to sit down.

"Sit. We may need a lot of strength before this adventure is over."

He joined her.

"Dusty? You don't think the sabotage is a curse from the *Masque of Gold*, do you?"

"No," he said with a firm tone. "I'm not superstitious. That gives power away, but I do believe some other power is at work—a human antagonist. I didn't feel emotionally involved in the *Masque* quest until now, thinking of it as someone else's business, but the sabotage makes it clear that a devious plot is in someone's mind; something that affects our two neighboring countries. Because harm only to the

U.S., something would have happened." He sighed. "Oh my. Perhaps I will have to take an official role. We will see. For today, we must save ourselves. Then we can try to determine who is trying to foil the quest and why."

"I'm in." She said, looking around at their wide watery world. They sat together in quiet, watching the sea, letting the soft morning caress their skin.

⸺◦◦◦⸺

The winds picked up with the arrival of afternoon.

"She's moving now and at a good clip, due south. I think we should pull out the Personal Flotation Devices. If you'll do that, I'll fill in the ship's log," DK said.

Lana pulled out two PFDs. After a second thought, she pulled out another. "What do you think of lashing one of these orange vests to the helm roof? It might catch someone's attention."

He nodded approval. They got to work on it; DK watching the radar screen to be sure the vest did not interfere with its reception.

"Now," advised DK, "Let's remove this net storage pocket from the galley wall and tie it to the bow line. We can troll for something to eat."

"Good idea," she said.

"I like sushi, do you Lana?"

"Sure. I hear it is good for the teeth."

He grinned a toothy smile back at her revealing perfect teeth. She grinned back, revealing uneven if very white ones. She grimaced like a vampire, but he ignored the danger and pecked her lower lip, "Very pretty, M' dear, but a little crooked."

She swatted him.

"I'll find something shiny in my duffle bag that you can tie to the line as bait."

By darkness, they had caught one grouper and managed to cook it directly on the stove grills.

"Tastes a little strange," Lana mused.

"Not at all. Well done, chef."

"Thank you but what I need now is a piece of chocolate cake."

"Oh that's right. You are a chocoholic. Could fool me. You can't be that trim eating cake, or maybe you work it off?" He said with a sly, knowing glance.

It was only a second that she turned to respond when he took her arm and with a gentle tug brought them face to face, his cheek against hers. Lana's eyes opened wide to protest, but he felt the stirring in her.

"Please, no, DK."

"OK then, maybe next year," he said puzzled.

She tried to ignore the sarcasm, realizing that he just did not understand her. "Let's not rush into love. I am not sure myself, okay? Perhaps we can focus on our current predicament for the time being?"

He kissed her lightly on the forehead, and turned to work again on the chart.

"Okay," he answered wistfully. "Anyway I have to work out our location. I think that the night is clear enough for me to fine-tune it. I was not in the military for nothing," he smiled and flipped the Q-Code switch.

"Look here, we only need two NAVSTARs above the horizon to come within one-hundred by a-hundred yards of our location. That's close enough out here on the sea."

"Unless there is a submarine nearby," Lana added.

He smiled and went to work. Later, when he understood they were moving southwest through the Gulf, he told her. "At least we are heading toward Cuba, but I doubt we will go the entire way without some interference from any number of quarters, big ships, the authorities and..."

"Okay," she said placing two fingers on his lips. "I get it. So, what do we do?"

"For now, we can only stargaze." DK gently lay his strong hand over hers on the ship's rail. "What do you hope to find in Cuba, Lana?"

"I hadn't thought much about it. Luc asked me to help the family a few months ago, while we shared a tour. I guess I really just thought of doing that. The boat trip is another incentive and I am anxious to learn more of Cuba; seeing more of the countryside, meeting artists. You know, just enjoying it. And you?"

He looked at her for a while. "I think I envisioned time off and relaxing too. Since I have never been to our destination, I've looked forward to seeing your tour knowledge at work as well as experiencing Cuba. However, we best be careful there Lana. There are still so many places in the world where Human Rights are uncertain. You know that they are not written by the pen of a dictator."

She kept looking at him, serious, listening, nodding. Then he added joyfully, "But I would have to say that my prime motivation to being here was spending quality time with you."

She blushed and looked out to the setting sun as they sat back on the settee together. One of them made a little sigh as the blazing, red-disk sank — erupting in a sudden green flash along the horizon. DK stretched an arm around Lana's waist and she entwined her fingers over his, each staring forward, not willing to admit concern. They had become too tired to do more than enjoy the peculiar, yet magical spell around them. They fell asleep on the deck under timeless heaven.

Later Lana woke to a midnight chill only to see DK in exhausted sleep. She slipped off her windbreaker, and tried to drape his six-foot frame with her size four jacket. Succeeding in covering only his broad chest, she smiled and retrieved one of the thin blankets from below. She kept watch for several hours, studying the bright sea under Orion's twinkling. She mulled over the types of people who would do such a thing to them and the reasons for it. She realized that Cuba was not an ordinary destination and that the saboteurs must have a political agenda. Certainly, she was not so important as to be their target. DK? Perhaps. Luc's quest? Perhaps. Political disagreements? The larger issue might be the proximity of two neighbors still not in political accord. She continued to muse over the predicament of governments with different ideologies. *They do not realize that there is no alternative to cooperation in a global age. The two countries would have to work together for many reasons: strategic for the United States, for both really.*

So, who could wish to harm both countries?

When DK shifted from stiffness, he awoke. Looking at his watch, he exclaimed with a start. "Oh, I'm sorry. Have you been awake all this time?"

"It's okay. I communed with the elements. I was wondering why the destruction of this vessel and, or, us would have an international aspect to it."

He rubbed his face. They had agreed with an earlier resolve to come through this, both to save the other. "I don't know yet. If our vessel would cause serious harm to a foreign vessel or if we collided with a tanker and caused an explosion, the respective governments could suspect aggression and respond with force."

"Humm, devious plot. Seems like we are being used, doesn't it?"

"Let's see if we can turn the tables around. When we know more we can report to the right people."

"Well we cannot report anything with our phones now. I tried them again while you slept, but neither gets a signal."

"Worry won't save us, so you get some sleep now."

He watched over them through the rest of the night as the vessel cut through the sea. Then he saw it. A distant light was moving in on them from the south. It grew in intensity until the sun rose.

Chapter 6

It was about six in the morning when Lana awoke to the frightening blast of a siren blaring like a wounded frog. She looked up through the porthole, saw a spinning colored light, and heard a male voice barking commands through a foghorn. Dashing up five stairs to the main deck, Lana had to cover her eyes against the glare of a searchlight. When she took a good look, the formidable gray object was a Coast Guard cutter.

The voice boomed again, "Identify yourselves. This is the U.S. Coast Guard. I repeat, Identify yourselves."

Cupping his hands to his mouth, DK strove to be heard over the noise of the cutter's engine.

"We are the *Esmeralda* out of Naples, stranded, and we have no radio."

Seeing no weapons in their hands, nor on the deck a voice boomed from a foghorn, "Prepare to be boarded!"

Five men wearing blue, short-sleeved shirts, navy trousers and flak jackets, looked over their ship at DK. They held machine guns, and did not look amused at an errant ship in American waters. DK threw some bumpers over the port side so the cutter could sidle-up. Two of the officers jumped on board wearing all their law enforcement gear. The *Esmeralda* gave a bounce in greeting. Then the captain of the team demanded the ship's registration papers.

Agent Cody had to struggle with the embarrassing response. "We have none. We are not the owners. We were left aboard my mistake."

This received an incredulous glance from the officers whose eyes began to travel over Lana's form as she stood mid-ship, still in bedroom attire — bare but for underwear. She caught their gaze. "Oh, excuse me!" She exclaimed. "May I go below to change?"

"Not until we have a look below, miss."

DK draped the thin blanket from the settee around Lana while an officer checked every corner of the staterooms for stowaways, for contraband and anything out of the usual.

When the officers realized that no contraband, nor radio, nor propellers, nor ship's papers were on board, they shared gestures and body language indicating this. The couple answered a string of questions. They were asked for their driver's licenses and their passports, however, these did not prove innocence of theft or terrorism. DK knew that such items could be counterfeit. Israel's Mossad itself was a master at forging them. They did so for many clients, although these were usually the *good guys*. There was nothing on board the *Esmeralda* to suggest the innocence or the guilt of the young couple, so the Coast Guard officers were left with just three conclusions: DK and Lana were alone, American and probably stupid.

"We are taking you to the Coast Guard Station where you will be detained until we assure ourselves of your identity and that this vessel is not stolen or known for contraband."

"What about the *Esmeralda*?"

"We'll have a towing company retrieve her."

The Captain signaled to the officer on the cutter's bridge who sent in the order. He told DK that the owner of the vessel would have to pay the towing or forfeit the vessel, "And it isn't cheap you understand."

"Yes officer," DK agreed. The official was in his customary and appropriate position of authority. Agent Cody would not argue.

Lana cringed too, realizing that she had brought DK into a 'vacation' that might cost him his job. "Sir, this whole thing is entirely my fault. I misled the agent."

"The officer raised his hand. "That is easy enough to understand looking at you," he coughed, "but still hard to believe, for a man in his supposed profession. Come along. Get on the cutter." He called out, "David, get the vessel attached until the tow can take her over."

"Yes, sir."

DK helped Lana onto the ladder, and once aboard the rescue vessel the other officers sat them in a corner and offered coffee. After an hour or so, Lana noticed an approaching shoreline, but it was not the mainland, it was the string of Florida Keys.

"Where are you taking us?"

"To our base at Key West."

"Key West? We are out of Naples. Do you mean we drifted that far from Caxambus Pass?"

The officer persisted, "Do *you* mean you were moored near Key Marco, the key where ancient Calusa statues were uncovered?"

Lana nodded, but DK had decided that silence was the best choice for him moving forward. It is one thing to look inept to the authorities, but DK was not going to reinforce the opinion.

"I see," the officer nodded, watching their eyes carefully.

"Are you smuggling artifacts? Is that the true reason for your journey?"

"Everything we are doing is with government approval, and we are not smuggling anything." Lana responded in a terse tone.

"Well your floundering is easy to understand without propellers, but you were very lucky. Your ship had her head and caught a current apparently. That corridor close to shore is very lonely this time of year and if our reconnaissance radar hadn't spotted you, things could have ended badly." He shook his head. "Anyway, the winter breezes would have helped too. As it is, you covered over 100 miles of the 120-mile distance from Naples to Key West. I guess that your little ship was clipping along at four knots. What was it? Thirty hours?

"Or so."

"Well you are safe now.' He gave a little grin, "If you are set free, how you return to Naples is up to you."

DK held his head and shook it.

The officer patted his shoulder, "Part of our job is to help people, not to condemn them, so if your story checks out, no worries."

The cutter was a powerful vessel and it sped them across the waters, docking with aplomb at its Key West home pier. The Coast Guard Station was not a prison, but an officer in charge made the decision to detain the two lost sailors. Once installed in separate holding areas, Lana and DK waited for news. The *Esmeralda* was moved into the boatyard, her pert bowline dragged without ceremony to its mooring for the night.

After a few hours, the officer of the day confirmed that Naples Police Headquarters had identified the runaway vessel, but they had no word from the owner regarding its absence, nor any missing person's report.

The captain summoned Agent Cody and Lana Bell to his office.

"Well, you two have a problem."

DK revealed no emotion, but Lana's back went rigid.

"The officers at the Naples Police Station say that your boat's owner Mr. Pio, and his son were struck by a vehicle the night you say your ship drifted. The elder man is in a coma, hospitalized. His son is recuperating from lesser but debilitating injuries. These men are too indisposed to provide satisfactory answers to the police. They don't know who else in the tribe can vouch for you, do you?"

"Could you ask the Naples police to find a man named Gusta?" Lana suggested.

"Gusta?"

"Gusta…Pio, I guess." He lives at the condominium where we were moored."

"Which condo building, among many, would that be?"

"Ahh, I guess we weren't very attentive, officer. Could the police contact some other member of the tribe to find Gusta?"

"Where would they find these members?"

Lana looked crestfallen. "I only know the place as the Pio Estate."

"Well, look. Naples thinks that the younger man will be able to think clearly tomorrow. They will interview him then."

"So what does that mean for us?" Lana asked.

"Little lady, you will be a guest of the state tonight, that's what it means. It may not be up to your comfort standards, but if you really are a tour director, then you must be used to adventure."

Lana grimaced. She squeezed DK's hand, concerned that this episode would jeopardize his career. He gave her a strained smile, but true to his character, he kept his own and quiet counsel. Only his blue eyes turned steely.

Chapter 7

*L*uc was unsteady on his feet. Gusta was leading him along the care-unit corridor in the hospital. "What do you mean gone, three days gone? Gusta, I've been in this hospital all that time and you didn't mention the loss of the boat or the disappearance of Lana?"

"Luc, you were too ill to hear all that. Besides, I thought they would return. The cut lines at the boat indicate they did not take the boat. If so, they would have just untied the lines. I believe they were victims like you. Besides, you've said you trust Lana, that she is honorable."

Luc pulled Gusta to let him sit down. "So?"

"So, this morning I reported the missing boat. Then, I had to go back to your home and search for all the legal documents to prove your case. I am just as shocked as you are now to learn that someone sabotaged the vessel and tried to kill them too."

"Ohhh, I'm not well enough for all this confusion. What must we do?"

"When I was at the Naples police station they confirmed that the couple is safe, in custody at the Coast Guard Station in Key West, waiting for you, the legal owner, to verify they belonged on the vessel."

"I do not know what to think of all this, and my father still in critical care."

"Lana could not have stolen your boat Luc because the ship was relieved of its propellers and left to flounder at sea. It makes no sense they would do this to themselves. No. Someone sabotaged the boat, them and you."

"Did you try to call them?"

"Their cell phone only goes to voicemail and may have gone overboard or something."

"Thank you, for doing all this Gusta. So where is the Esmeralda?"

"It's in a Key West boatyard, missing propellers and lines. They are waiting for your payment and they will do the repairs."

Luc answered flapping his hand with impatience, "Yes, of course."

Gusta set up the call and Luc spoke with the boatyard. He lay down, weakened by the stress of his situation. "I just don't know if I trust Lana anymore."

"They can't be responsible for all this if they were put in danger themselves and then spent two days adrift at sea. Someone else tried to run you over, Luc."

"I don't know. My shoulder hurts a lot and I do not like the pain medicine. I suppose I must wear this cast for several months?"

Gusta nodded yes, recognizing the stress of pain on his cousin.

"My father is in a bad state. We must pray for him Gusta." He placed two hands on his head, "Oh, my head still aches – ah me."

Gusta sat at the foot of Luc's bed and spoke softly. "You and your dad must get better now. You can decide about the trip later."

"And cancel the expedition, Gusta?"

"I'd guess that is what the saboteur wants."

"Then no," he replied with determination. "I will be here only one other day, the doctor promised. So, let us get ready to leave. Gusta will you check that all our gear and supplies are still in good shape? Get someone to help. Can you find cousin Sonoteas? His aunt came to see me and mentioned that her nephew is still out of work. He can help you load everything, because I will be useless."

As Luc sat back to rest, a police officer entered the room.

"Good afternoon, gentlemen. I am here about the hit and run attack. The nurse says we may question you now and we would like more information. I assume you will prosecute the guilty party should we determine who that is?"

"Yes, certainly," Luc stated with impatience. "The attacker has no conscience if he is willing to run down an old man. What other evil is on his mind? Can you get a lead on him based on my description?"

The officer coughed. "Well sir, we'll do our best with what evidence we have. Our forensics shows that the van that careened into you was stolen. We have found the vehicle, but dusting for prints and searching it has revealed no clues. There is a witness to the accident. She describes a slender man of medium build who wore a hoody. So, we do not have much to go on. Another witness claims the man hurt himself because he seemed to rub his shoulder as he ran away. We have sent a bulletin to all the local physicians and the local medical facilities seeking someone reporting an injury that night. So far, nothing has come of that. Can you tell me whether you received any threats recently or have any enemies?"

"No, sir. My father does not have an enemy in the world. Sometimes people in our clan have disagreements, but we are not a violent people."

"I see. Well, the witness said that after steering directly into the passenger side where your father sat, the attacker jumped out, threw down a cycle helmet and began to run, leaving you injured. He was wearing gloves the witness said. She is the one who called 911, but she could tell us nothing more. It sounds like this perpetrator was very organized. As you recover, give some thought to people you know. Perhaps someone will come to mind who could do such a thing to you. All right?"

Luc looked back at the officer with blank eyes, "Yes sir."

"We will get this guy someday, Mr. Pio."

Luc could only nod at this point. With Gusta's help, he resettled in his bed, closed his eyes and drifted off to sleep. Gusta then spoke with the officer, supplying the descriptions and authorizing a release of the young couple stuck in Key West. "Tell them to stay there until we call tonight."

As day grew into night, Gusta rang his wife, spoke to the nurses and prepared to leave Luc's room when a young man entered.

"Sonoteas?"

"I heard the story of what happened Gusta. Sounds like your boat went for a ride by itself," he said snidely. "So you want to retrieve it and my aunt says you need my help."

Luc opened his eyes to the noise and smiled weakly. "Sonoteas, I'm so glad you have come. We need you. Nothing is as strong as blood, is it?"

"Nope."

"I know we haven't been the best of cousins Sonoteas, but I really could use your help to join us on the quest my father planned. You are the only unmarried, young man in our village who could take time to help us. Could you? Are you still without a steady job?"

"That's right. Are you going to hire me for your 'quest'?"

Luc's eyes opened wide now. "Hire? Ah, well, if you like. What sort of money would that be?"

"Wait," Gusta interrupted, in an angry tone. "We are offering you a vacation all paid for. You get to be on the new vessel and see another country."

"Gusta please let me take care of this. Sonoteas you heard your cousin. Isn't the vacation enough incentive?"

"Nope. Well, are you still going to Cuba and search for the old *Masque*?"

Luc nodded.

"Well then, I guess you will need another pair of hands." He rubbed his arm, "So, I'll reduce what I need to $500–upfront." He propped a foot on a chair.

In the silence which followed and under the glare of Gusta, Sonoteas softened his tone. "Well, I guess I should let bygones be bygones. If you will arrange all my government paperwork, I will come along for half the sum. After all, I'm the best mechanic in our community." He continued popping his chewing gum.

Gusta turned to look out the hospital room window, his lip buttoned. The boy had caused trouble in the town for as long as he knew him, but Luc and Pio were kind to everyone, and it was their adventure, so it was not for him to stand in their way.

Luc saw Gusta stiffen, but only pressed his need to him. "An extra set of hands would be a big help."

Sonoteas grinned, "Upfront cousin, $250.00–upfront."

"Fine, fine. We may have two other friends to help us, but they are waiting for us in Key West."

Sonoteas looked startled. "Oh? Well I'm very fit and so is Gusta, you won't need the others, Luc. Three of us is enough to operate a boat only as far as Cuba. Didn't Gusta tell us that the ship went missing thanks to that couple's carelessness?" He paused to feel the effect of his words. "We don't need them."

Gusta remained facing the window, a look of surprise crossing his face.

Sonoteas continued to press Luc, "How can you trust them? They are not from the tribe. Besides, I have a mechanic's skill to help you, and they have nothing to offer." He wadded up the gum and, springing, he threw it into the wastebasket. "They just want the gold."

Luc's face registered confusion and pain. He leaned back, closed his eyes and tried to forget everything. Two days later the three men took off for Key West.

Chapter 8

Meanwhile things had not gone well for Lana. She had spent the night in a separate room from DK, according to local incarceration rules, not according to her own choice, as she had done on the boat. She could not decide if being forced into solitude was what she liked after all. She refused to call and upset her family asking for help because she had faith in the legal system, but after many hours in a cheerless holding cell, her spirit bewailed the emptiness. She alternated between Yoga poses and pacing, staring out the small window just to find a passing truck sign. Then sometimes a small insect would tumble from the tree outside onto her window ledge, and Lana would set him up right to carry on. Over many hours, she went in and out of meditation, then trying to recall many a happy tour, directing groups around the world. It was difficult to be sedentary when she preferred to be on the go.

Only one visitor came to see her, a local newspaperman, curious about a woman's stranding on the Gulf. He thought it was a fantastic byline story, but Lana feared the exposure would hurt DK's career or be picked up by the saboteurs: "All of Florida will read it." She protested. "The people who did this deed to us will know where we are and try again." In the end, she was powerless to stop the reporter. His assurances of safety sounded hollow, so when she read the next morning's notice she understood that both she and Agent Cody were at risk. They would have to stay alert for the stranger they had yet to meet.

Later that day when the hall clock read 1:00 p.m., a coast guard officer led her to the captain's office. She stepped quickly down the corridor, gnawing gently on her lip.

"Just for the record," the captain said, giving her some documents, "You are exonerated from any wrongdoing. I am sorry we had to detain you, but I am sure you understand the reasons. Your friend Mr. Gusta Pio did call to verify all your statements. These papers are a copy of your statements for our files. Please review them and sign."

Lana signed and then asked, "So Dusty Cody? Is he freed too?"

"Waiting outside."

"What about the boat?"

"Owner wants you to have it ready. He is still in the hospital and asked that you wait for his call. By the way, Agent Cody explained the dilemma of your cell phones, and we've charged them both for you." He handed her all her belongings.

"Thank you. Nothing further then?" she dared to ask.

"You didn't do anything wrong, right?"

"No."

"Then get going," he smiled. "Your Agent Cody has fingerprints on record and they came in handy you know. Friends in high places came through for him."

"I see," she said, relieved that the Bureau still held Agent Cody in sufficient regard to get him out of a jam.

"Thank you very much, officer, but someone *is* responsible for the sabotage on the Pios and on us. Are the Naples police working on that?"

"They are questioning the condominium neighborhood for any witnesses, and trying to find the culprit who rammed the two Pio men with a car. We have checked the boat here and dusted it for prints, but as you can imagine, if the villain had ever come aboard he wiped or smeared the prints. I do caution you both to be alert because whoever sabotaged the vessel may have additional ideas to stop you. We are here for you, but once you are in international waters and on the island of Cuba the motive for sabotage may surface again. Someone may be trying to kill you."

Lana's mouth opened, but he was not telling her anything new. She nodded and thanked him, showing herself out. As she walked the corridor to a sunny entrance courtyard, she brushed her dress, tugged on her ragged red curls and straightened up her posture with a new vigor. *Kill us? We'll see about that.*

—∞∞∞—

"Dusty!"

He welcomed her putting his arms around her and placing a kiss on her frown lines.

"It's okay now Lana, don't worry. Nevertheless, this is quite a story. C'mon! We are going to the drug store at the end of Duval Street, then straight into the Hyatt nearby. We need to get human again."

She was not sure what was happening to her; now running into a man's arms as Miss Independent. She knew that the threats of danger were real and she was worried for Pio's health. Her good friend Luc was giving them a cold shoulder and the *Esmeralda* was broken. The barriers were mounting up. Getting to Cuba was looking more difficult than ever.

"Let me cheer you." DK prompted. "We'll go for a fine dinner tonight and make our own plans for a happy vacation. We'll evaluate reasons to end or to continue with Luc."

She was grateful for his good sense and thoughtfulness, but she still felt the cloud of confusion over them. After walking a block, Agent Cody turned to notice her face. Downcast lids hid her golden-toned eyes. He restrained his emotions at her vulnerability, the one she preferred to ignore. Instead, he barked an order, "Ah well, let's get us some new toothbrushes first. The officer said Luc withheld permission for us to go back on the vessel for the things we left."

They moved in unison, stepping quickly to the shopping area. Then Lana blurted out, "What are we using for money?"

"Don't worry. I already thought of that. Just came back from the corner bank where my office had re-routed some salary."

"And so you have friends in high places?"

"There were enough people at home office to confirm our identity, yes, and to substantiate our purposes. I had left a complete trip plan with my superior. After all, I may have been naïve to come aboard a vessel without the correct gear, but when it came to planning our trip to Cuba, I knew there could be some danger. My boss had every bit of information that he needed to back me up."

"I will never underestimate you," she said relaxing her tense shoulders with a deep breath as they reached an intersection at Ocean Avenue.

DK put an arm around her and squeezed while pulling her back from a turning, delivery van. "This was a lesson for us both," he said. Then, facing her, he gave a tug to one wild, red curl, "But, I'm very happy to be with you... goldilocks."

Now it was Lana's turn to look away, avoiding his warm blue eyes, and changing the subject. "Luc and his father were injured by a hit and run driver?"

"So the Coast Guard officer confirmed. Lana, I have to tell you that the *Masque of Gold* we want must be important. From the sound of it, the auto crash was intentional and violent."

"So, there is more to this *Masque* than we have been told, huh? Maybe she is solid gold. On the other hand, maybe the *Masque* is not an artifact at all. Maybe the name represents a movement or, an idea, a place or, a valuable greater than gold?"

"Good possibilities."

"Oh, look, here is a shorts and shirt shop – just what we need. And I know there is a Fresh Produce clothing store off Eaton Street."

"Fine, I agree that it's time to put on something 'fresh'. Let's check them all out."

"Would you stop first to enjoy some Key Lime Pie? The pie shop is just over there, on Greene Street," she pointed. "And I'm tired of eggs."

"Good idea. Fresh lime and fresh duds. I like it." He rubbed his chin. "I'd prefer a steak, but then, that's for later. Let's get you your sweets." As they walked on he pointed to a dress in one shop window. "Do you like that?"

She nodded. "Well this shopping will be fun. You make quick decisions though don't you?"

"Yes," she chuckled.

"Well I'm also happy that you won't have to wear jungle shrubs."

They laughed together, feeling more relaxed, happy to laugh aloud as free people.

"I feel like an islander now," he said, patting his new sailboat-patterned shirt, no longer shabby-chic from the jail. They had showered at the hotel, and had morphed into the washed, jet setters intended—yacht in harbor and practiced seamen. Their cell phones were working, but they saw no need to contact the Pios. They would wait for instructions as they were advised.

They strolled from the hotel, enjoying Key West with its interesting architecture and exuberant, music-playing bars. It was a unique place dominated by both attitudes of relaxed lifestyle and energetic living. It offered a yin and yang of night fever versus busy, sunny, but commonplace day.

The couple joined other strollers, exuding the same daytime attitude, too relaxed to notice being followed. In a resort atmosphere with a mix of newcomers, a variety of clothes and faces, entertainment and tour buses, the sober and the not sober, the teens and the retired, who would notice two men without hats wearing regular suits? Not many. Not Agent Cody. He appeared to ignore the pursuers. He just kept strolling.

The sun sets slowly in Key West, so DK saw no need to hasten and when they had finished visiting the Audobon Museum and the Hemingway Home, it was time for that steak. He doubled back to a hotel lounge at the beach, glancing back only once. In the lounge Dusty reached for Lana's hand and ushered her into a quiet corner where they had a wide view of sailboats sailing into harbor.

DK glanced around, seeming at ease, smiling at everyone, and with a casual posture, he signaled the waiter. He ordered their refreshments, and leaned close to Lana. Shoulder to shoulder, he whispered something. Lana stood up, excusing herself. When she returned the couple huddled together again, enjoying the deepening sunset, pleasuring in each other's company, it seemed. DK nuzzled her ear while studying her phone screen with her. She dialed as he bade, the phone camouflaged in her lap, and in one concealed, swift motion, they sent a photo of the stalkers to Washington, DC.

The couple leaned closer still, seeming happy lovers, and DK said in a low voice, "We'll have to decide if Luc is on the up and up, or if he is hiding something from us. What if the threats come from another source. What am I missing, Lana?"

"Let's think. The threats may come from Cuban authorities who want the *Masque* to stay right where it is. Or, perhaps from personal interests there who don't want us nosing around 44,000 square miles of foreign territory, uncovering secrets."

"That is possible, but why would the country have granted permissions for this quest. If they had something to protect or hide, they had no obligation to grant us access."

"That sounds true, DK. This object is so beautiful we are told. It is so rare we are told. Wouldn't some investor pay exorbitant sums to have it as an *objet d'art?* The gold itself is intrinsically valuable, making it more than a family heirloom."

"The only people capable of criminal acts on such an international scale are the international art rings. You are right, but this is an unknown object as far as we've been told, so a collector wouldn't necessarily know about it yet. It is not something in demand by his competitors, so it is not an object with a ready market. In addition, a legal sale would require provenance, and I cannot see Pio granting that permission."

"How about someone who just wants the gold out of it?" Lana asked.

"No one knows how much gold is in, or, on the *Masque*. The unknown value in terms of the gold alone is a big risk for a ring of art thieves. Professionals would not jeopardize their safety without verifying the existence of the *Masque* and its approximate value. If some art ring is aware of the object, I think they would wait for it to be found, its authenticity assured, and then plan a theft. It seems more likely that a different motive is at play."

"What about foreign interests who'd like to feather their coffers; countries from anywhere in the world where fortune is desired, or maybe some interest group trying to put a wedge between our two countries," Lana suggested. She raised two clasped hands and propped her elbows on the table, musing on the possibilities. "Surely the sabotage of *Esmeralda* makes no sense if an individual in the clan wants the *Masque of Gold*. He could not get away with such a theft and remain with the tribe, his family. Someone would notice his change and newfound wealth. That thief would have alienated everyone who loves Oalachan Pio and they all do. I don't think the tribe is doing this evil. They would only hurt themselves."

"Right. If the clan lets Luc succeed with his adventure they can look forward to enhancing the tribal culture and reaping a benefit from tourism dollars. No one would be the looser or risk jail. So, if not clan motivated, the identity of a saboteur comes back to someone with an international agenda."

"Then again, Luc did say that some tribal members don't agree with the quest. They do not feel wedded to the past and see nothing to be gained in going backward. One can understand that there are those who don't care about this search for a lost object at all. They don't even want a return to glory."

"I see, but why sabotage the quest? If someone is disinterested in the outcome or the quest, why not ignore it? Why risk imprisonment or worse? Nope, all together, I do not see members of the tribe risking assets, banding together to thwart the quest itself. Let it play out and then, take over the object. It just doesn't make sense that they do all this intricate stuff to block it when they might benefit in the end," DK concluded.

"Evil," Lana said, pressing her lips together and sighing with a sad finality.

DK smiled, putting his arm around her. "Perhaps. We don't know everything yet." He leaned back in his chair and Lana saw his eyes go gray. She knew he was planning something.

"Now – Dusty Kern Cody, what have you got on your mind?"

"Nothing, nothing."

He stretched out long, looking at the sea. They each sipped from their tropical concoctions and he managed a slow smile watching Lana enjoy the sweet drink. He teased, "Umm, this fruit concoction hits the spot."

"Ya!"

"Well now, how about more of that good food we've been missing? Pie doesn't do it for me. Are you ready to enjoy a romantic supper?"

"There's that romance raising its head again," Lana teased.

He looked crestfallen.

"Now wait a minute DK. Don't be so impatient. You do not realize how fond I am fond of you. We have the same approach to life."

He stopped brooding, looking pleased, yet skeptical, "But...?"

"No, 'but', I mean it. I am fond of you. Who else but Dusty Kern Cody, an Afghanistan veteran and now a Bureau man would spend time with a girlfriend chasing legends?"

With a guffaw, he tossed his head letting an ungroomed coif take over. It made her think of him in fifty years; an old-codger living for the salty wind. She smiled in surprise at her contentment. "Always happy to create laughter," she said softly.

Standing now, making a gentleman's bow to her, he folded Lana's arm into the crook of his, "Back to a good restaurant, if you please, Miss Guide."

One of the stalkers who had followed them into the lounge had remained nearby. Camouflaged by his growth of beard and now wearing a brand new baseball cap, he lingered at the exit, turning away as DK passed. Special Agent Cody had made one serious mistake this trip, but he was determined not to make another. He paused passing the man and took a very good look at the stranger. The picture of him that Lana sent over the cellphone was just as clear.

The evening street noise in Key West always hit high deci-
bels. Streetlights and signs were boldly lit up and every
doorway beckoned the visitor. One could buy most diver-
sions, from paper alligators, beaded jewelry and ghost tours
to guitars or margaritas. People danced in bars or called to
one another as they strolled. It was a liberated place, full of
fun. Lana stopped, asking DK to wait while she ran into a
small gift shop. When she emerged onto the street, she was
clutching something small.

"Here DK, I think you should have a little gift to watch
over you in your new post." She offered it to him with hesitance, feeling suddenly shy.

He took the object, which was an odd-shaped, but flat-
smoothed stone that fit perfectly into his palm. It read,
Love all-Trust a few. He closed his fingers around it and
rubbed it, "For good luck, my dear," he said. With a peck
of a kiss to her cheek, he fingered the stone one more time
and then placed it firmly in his pocket.

As they approached their hotel after dinner, Lana's phone
jingled a tune. "Looks like our bar stalkers have an identity."

Both men on watch list of international terrorists.
Report in for details.

She showed the message to DK, and commiserated with
him. "Some vacation."

Walking slowly to their rooms, the couple was hesitant to part. A chiming noise began to follow them, and they stopped in their tracks looking back down the corridor.

A young boy costumed in a page uniform overtook them. "Call for Ms. Bell. Call for Ms. Bell."

Lana took up the message. Worried, she turned to Dusty, "At last. It's Luc."

⸺∞⸺

The resort town quieted under the dome of night. Lana and DK slept. Around them, for blocks and blocks, town revelers had folded-up their gaiety. Down at the boat-yard, the piers were locked closed. Then, hidden in the darkness, two figures inside a simple skiff slide under the security chain and rowed alongside the *Esmeralda*. One of the figures steadied the bobbing vessel while the other leapt aboard the Marquis 420. He carried a red, metal container and gently switched it for the express cruiser's $Co2$ fire extinguisher. He handed the stolen container to his partner, and then proceeded to fine-tune his replacement. He twisted a wire with such care around the head of the false fire extinguisher that it was not visible. Someone on board would have to ignite the canister he knew, and he knew who that would be.

The skiff rowed back out into the open lane, leaving no ripple to mark its intrusion.

Chapter 9

*L*ana knocked at DK's door around nine in the morning. The morning belonged to them because Luc said he would not arrive until two. He had not fired them, yet.

"Are you up, sleepy-head?"

DK Cody threw the door open dressed in his new safari outfit, replete with a six pocket vest and wide brim khaki hat. Every item was pressed and buttoned, just so. She realized that DK was seldom, or ever, undisciplined. Then he broke her thought, leaning to her and scooping her up into the air. "I'm ready and hungry as a bear!"

Landing a smooch on her forehead, he put her down, shut his door and led her to the restaurant. She just followed, not accustomed to being controlled by another person, and wondering if they could live peaceably for long, both being leaders.

"This is an interesting relationship, DK," she began, in a philosophic tone.

"Don't say," he muttered, breathing deep, raising his brows.

Lana caught the upturn of his lips however, and knew he was okay, even if they did differ in their romantic objectives. As she saw it, he was looking for a love, she for a soul mate.

Lana found them a nice spot for breakfast and DK made them put aside their concerns. Afterward, they meandered around town soaking up the natural quiet of day versus Key West's nighttime hullabaloo. Breezes crisscrossing the key from both the Gulf and the Atlantic created a fresh, expectant atmosphere. It seemed to Agent Dusty Kern Cody and Lana Victoria Bell that freedom and safety might really have chased away the shadows. The couple passed one bright shop after another, one clapboard veranda or more and conversed about everything from growing up, to friends, from foods and hobbies, to dogs. When he questioned Luc Pio's motives for the quest, Lana filled in the information.

"Only one group of 16th century island indigenous peoples we know as Taino escaped from the harsh conquerors. Some natives in Cuba were able to escape into forests and caves keeping certain cultural practices alive. However, in Florida, the Calusa who survived invasion and government programs scattered across the peninsula and were absorbed in time by other groups, losing specific cultural recognition."

DK reflected for a minute, "Yes, I know, but it isn't unique to be a descendant of many cultures. Most peoples of the modernized world are a combination of many different backgrounds."

"However most of us like belonging to a particular tribe, anyway, don't we Dusty?"

He smiled at her. "Maybe one day I'll convince you to join my own."

"Anyway, mister persistent, I suppose no one wants to lose all connection with their roots, so I don't blame Pio for his dream. Today the grouped tribes in Florida are the Miccosukee and the Seminole. Most descendants do not know much of their long lost culture called Calusa since that culture died officially 1700. They had been overrun, mistreated, demoralized and sickened. I guess that I cannot blame the earlier tribes for trying to survive by rebuffing the invaders. Ponce de León had to learn the hard way. He gave them no chance to maintain their roots and yet be useful to Spain. Natives used their only defense at that time, the bow and arrow."

"Didn't you say he died of poison?"

"Ultimately that's what did him in. The arrow itself only went into his thigh. However, the natives had rubbed the arrowhead with the juice of the local Machineel tree which is very poisonous," she grimaced.

"Interesting," he squinted at her, playful.

"Never mind," she joked back, "But I wonder why our natives didn't win?"

"They didn't have the sword nor the numbers to match their opponent. When you talk about areas of our own continent in the 1500s, native peoples had few powerful instruments to use in hand-to-hand combat against the sword. In addition to the sword, the Spanish had armor and helmets. When a battle commenced, bone knives were no match for metal armor."

"Then it was a miracle that Luc's Calusa tribe hit their mark. In the end, they did exact revenge on the former Governor of Puerto Rico and Cuba. I wonder if the conquistador ever saw that ending for himself."

"Who does?"

They stopped to chat with some of the shopkeepers who were washing down their storefronts. A large Golden Retriever stood guard at one shop, and DK stopped to greet him.

"How ya doin', fella?"

The dog wagged his tail and presented large happy eyes to DK.

"You must miss Sky and King," Lana guessed.

"Yes."

"Oh, I'm somewhat sorry that you have left that beautiful ranch in Spokane with so much room for them there. I think you must hate to leave that property just as much as I would hate to leave my Central Park home."

DK made a mental note of Lana's loyalty to everything but him, her freedom, her job, her condominium, whatever. He stopped for a second, venting a low sigh and lifting his eyes to the broad, blue sky overhead. He said nothing more for a while, thinking he had been wrong. Maybe Lana was not the girl for him.

Moving on, he and Lana strolled down pathways of tree-lined streets, banyans reaching high over entire houses, while ancient oaks ringed the avenues, dripping with moss, uprooting the sidewalks. Gingerbread designs graced the eaves of some older homes, and many dwellings were painted in soft pastel colors. Most of the houses retained their 100 to 150 year old exteriors as mandated by local ordinance. An observer could not guess in passing whether an historic home had received a stunning interior remodel. Key West was at once an expressive place and a secretive one, an outlandish place and a genteel one. The island had seen Arawak Indians come, then pirates, cigar magnates, artists, the well-to-do, the beach people, the regulars and the foreigners. It had stood up to invasions of all these, including the occasions of deadly weather. It was a place with more than its share of odd stories. One need only listen at the bars.

Lana realized her remark to Dusty re-affirmed her continued resistance to him, but she was not ready to mend the fence she had broken. Her feelings were still confused, and she could not breech the gap between temporary friend and long-term love. She had not trusted love ever since her father left her and brother Des. Being warm but distant from others was a thirteen-year habit of hers. Therefore, she brushed aside her companion's snub. Maybe she had played the flirt with him and then retreated. It was not very nice of her, and she knew it, but she still felt captive to the old wound, not in control of it, in spite of her desires. She breathed rapidly several times to fill an emptiness that over-took her stomach. Then to overcome the silence from Cody, Lana pointed in the direction of Cuba from the *mile-marker-one* outlook. "Maybe we'll be there in a day or two."

He seemed to ignore her and then spoke his thought. "Sometimes we make choices to move forward, Lana, just like Pio. You know that more good can come from that, than hanging with old ways. The world is moving too fast to stay behind." He moved away from her.

"Change takes time," she whispered to the wind.

⤙⤚

DK did not speak during lunch either. Lana stared at him, wide-eyed, no longer hungry. Suddenly Dusty dropped his fork on the plate, faced her and blurted; "I've known other loves, but never felt any of those matches were right. Not all women share my adventurous ideas or the values I cling to, like faith and family and integrity." He stopped and looked at her full on. "Not all women offer the looks and chemistry I love."

At this declaration, Lana glanced all around her like a rabbit running from the fox. DK turned away, paid the bill and walked on without her. They would sightsee, he decided, but from then on, he would keep his own counsel. He led the pace with his long gait as Lana scurried to keep up. She stole glances at his strong head and began to miss his tenderness. He was like her after all. He did not like to be controlled. She decided then-and-there that it was time. It was time that she must break from the past fears. It would be hard, but she would try. Tomorrow he might win the tug of war but not before she showed some backbone too. Lana smiled to herself and said aloud, "Oh by the way, you'd like visiting the Armory Museum."

Chapter 10

The next morning each was busy with the pre-departure duties assigned by Luc. Lana went to schedule official release from the Coast Guard because five passengers would be on board; Luc, Gusta, DK, Lana and another Pio cousin—a young man named Sonoteas. DK went to prepare the vessel for departure and move the Esmeralda. The group would meet up at Mallory Square pier.

Concluding her last minute assignments, Lana paid a visit to a local and fragrant cigar store where the Cuban proprietor welcomed her. "Hello. That's cherry tobacco scent coming from your doorway, yes?"

"Si, senorita."

"When I smell that cherry note, I wish I could be a smoker too, senōr."

"And why not? Women do you know."

"My lungs. Makes me cough terribly."

"Oh," he said, his face registering concern.

"It's okay, but thanks for your understanding. I wonder if you can help me with some information about Cuba because I am going there today."

A big smile crossed his face, and he moved his own chair from around the counter. "You sit here, señorita! Let me tell you about my little town of Trinidad, on the southern coast of Cuba." He spoke with quick, energized hand movements, describing the hills of his peaceful childhood fifty years ago. Then he shook his head, "I wish that the revolution hadn't gone sour. There was so much evil under the former dictator, and we thought the revolution would make things better. Over the years, the recent regime did some good improving lives, but it hurt many too. Then it failed to move forward, and brooked no criticism. There were many who suffered imprisonment and torture, fear and want. So many people fled, or were annihilated, and now my people must keep their lips sealed." He shook his head.

"Don't you believe that things can change?"

"Yes miss. They can, but it will take time. We all must stay vigilant when it comes to leaders with a sword, leaders who brook no compromise. I pray that my family will see a freedom from oppression..." He paused casting a shy eye to her, "as well as from profiteers."

Then he scurried behind a curtain and called out to her; "Wait one minute, will you?" When he returned, he handed her a small box. "Señorita, if you are going into Trinidad, would you leave this little box with the priest of the church? Just tell him it is from Tomaso, for my sister. You see?" He showed Lana the contents of the box: a pretty ring, a few tubes of antibiotic cream and a box of Band-Aids. She imagined that money was tucked under the little cushion. She would peek to be sure that it was no more than that, but was glad to do something personal for someone—to help a beloved sister.

"Yes, I will make a point of it. I'm sure they could use everything," she answered. "Perhaps you can help me with something also?"

He nodded, "Assuredly."

"I want to find an ancient artifact. Are there any tips you could give me?"

He gave her some clues to the proper courtesies she may not have known before. "And remember, it is human nature the world over to praise one's own country because we are attached to it, even if it isn't perfect. Likewise, people can complain about their own country to others, but no one wants to hear a stranger do it. Do you understand?"

"I understand."

"A visitor anywhere need only leave a footprint of respect. Do you see?"

"Yes, senõr, gracias. Thank you so much for your wisdom."

"Thank *you*, señorita. If you need help in Cuba, do not fear to speak with the people. If they can, they will help you. They are not mean or selfish people, they have just become accustomed to oppression."

Lana set out for the moorage location, taking along with her the little box from Tomaso as well as another one she had filled with items from the drug store. A last call from the hotel to her father and to Des provided a travel update to their message machines. Then she collected the latest clothing at the hotel and placed the items into a small tote for her and DK. She settled their account at the front desk and hurried to join DK and the Pio team at the appointed hour.

Chapter 11

Luc had been in too much discomfort to enjoy the drive from Naples to Key West. He lay across the rear seat and ached until he fell asleep. He stayed that way for the ninety minutes that the heavily laden car took from the hospital to Miami. Once on the famous Overseas Highway, where the road narrows to single lanes in each direction and heavy traffic moves southward, Luc took more medicine and fell back asleep. Gusta and Sonoteas said nothing.

The road to Key West paradise is peppered with foliage, gas stations, tackle shops, eateries, supermarkets and tiny house fronts. Everything seems dated but whitewashed inviting travelers to what was once the only tropical vacationland connected to the mainland. Vacationers from North America and abroad were often travelers on the Overseas Highway lured by the slender, sandy spits since 1861. Flagler even built them a train line down the coast. People sought Key West even more, after 1961, after prohibition against travel to the rocky shores of Cuba.

The string of small islands from Miami to mile-marker-one have been a challenge to Coast Guard authorities for a century. Regular boaters, criminals and those seeking asylum had pulled into the Florida's inter-coastal coves ever since the time of pirates. However, in the recent age of satellite surveillance, electronic devices and public awareness, illegal traffic has been controlled.

Sunrises and sunsets still decorate the double horizons of east and west; tourists still flock down the highway seeking either excitement or privacy, and anglers seek the thrill of a catch. Many come to sit on paint-peeling porches, rocking to the tunes of 1970 hits, while others choose family camping and others the package deals of hotel or vacation home. Accommodations are well maintained, or not. It does not seem to matter, for even a humble edifice has its visitors. The islands have a mystique about them, and people flock there anyway. Glitz is not usually what they seek, or find.

"It's a busy weekend," Gusta muttered looking at all the traffic, "Probably a classic car fete or another major show on Key West's Mallory Square."

As the islands finger their way to their tips, time passes. Luc Pio arose from his stupor and watched the van slip from developed spaces into a great open panorama. There, where the ocean and sea collide, comes Key West.

Luc spotted his *Esmeralda* moored in town and grew excited. He pointed it out to Sonoteas.

"I'm glad you told Lana that we'll board the vessel upon our arrival because these crowds are sure to have booked all the hotel rooms, and we don't have time to fuss for lodging. We should go out to sea as soon as we are loaded," Sonoteas commanded.

Gusta did not like being told what to do by the young upstart. He argued with him just for the sake of it, but he knew the idea made sense.

"It's just what we'll do." Luc said closing the argument. Sonoteas smiled.

Their car found a temporary parking spot, just down the street from the appointed dock. Gusta asked if Luc could make the walk.

"Yes, yes," he said, moving slowly.

Gusta left the van keys for the rental agent, and made Sonoteas help him unload. They pulled out the two-wheeled suitcases, each full of medical gifts for delivery to Cubans. Gusta propped all their duffle bags onto the suitcases, and they each put on their backpacks.

From their seats at the boardwalk, DK and Lana spotted the camel-loaded trio, and jogged off to help Luc.

The *Esmeralda* stood by, bathed clean, burgundy and shiny. Luc was overtaken with emotion to find his wayward vessel. There was no sign of damage. "She looks ready to go!" He said, his chest forward, resuming his first upright posture in days. Lana gave him an enthusiastic greeting, but he held back, moving away from her. She knew that this was the moment to explain what had happened to them and to Luc's boat.

"So, that's your explanation, huh?" Luc said in a low tone.

Lana laid her hand on Luc's trying to renew their mutual trust. "DK and I are here to help. I guess you feel anxious with us over what happened."

"You bet he does." interrupted Sonoteas.

She ignored the boy's rudeness.

"Look Luc, there is no reason we would sabotage ourselves, risking death. What would we gain? However, if you have lost trust in us then we would resign. You have Gusta and Sonoteas to help you now, and this quest is family business anyway. You don't need us."

Luc rocked his sore head, and then with a glance of understanding, he acknowledged Gusta. The latter realized that Luc had made a silent decision: They would keep the couple with them. The trip onward would present many challenges, so Gusta felt relieved that DK and Lana were there to help. From Luc's stories of Lana, he had come to trust her, certainly more than the difficult cousin he had known a lifetime.

Gusta taped the new boy on the shoulder, "I need your help, Sonoteas. Let us move our goods around the boat to make room for the Coast Guard officers. We can't leave until they sign-off on our route." His eyes met DK's and a silent smile passed between them.

"Put your new tote on board DK."

As the men shuffled belongings below, Lana watched Luc. "You look in pain, Luc. Will you be all right?" she asked.

Luc nodded, "Yes Lana, and yes."

"We'd be willing to take the ship back to Marco Island until you and your father are fully recovered. It is just an option. Would you prefer to do that than travel on in pain?"

Luc's face clouded in confusion.

Sonoteas stomped a foot, "We aren't following *your* ideas!"

Luc glanced at Sonoteas and Lana caught the undercurrent. The eighteen year old was a troublemaker, but why?

DK also saw Luc caught in the middle of the dispute and hoped to redeem Luc's belief in Lana. "We were not irresponsible with the *Esmeralda*, Luc. We had no strangers on board nor did we space-out on drugs or drink. Someone intentionally sneaked aboard the vessel to thwart the journey and harm us. We did not shirk our duty." Then to hit the truth home, he said, "We were left without the proper amenities to be alone at sea."

Luc took the sting of the remark. "Well, DK perhaps the same saboteur is linked to the attack on me and my father, so I'm sorry to have doubted you. I am not fully recovered yet and my thinking is clouded. Forgive me. Look, let the past be bygones. Shall we?"

With all in agreement, Luc directed his glance to Sonoteas, and spoke with emphasis, "I'll need all of you to work together."

----✕✕✕----

The group sat waiting for the Coast Guard to clear the vessel. Lana sat at the salon table with Luc while Sonoteas stood at the transom, facing out to sea, hands in his pockets. Lana broke the silence. "Does everyone have a Canadian credit card in case U.S. versions cause difficulty?"

"Yes," they all intoned.

Luc recalled that the Coast Guard would want to see all their documents, and asked Lana to take the Department of Commerce License from his duffle bag along with permission from the U.S. Office of Foreign Assets Control. "Take out all the Pio Foundation documents too and the authorizations for medical deliveries."

Sonoteas gnawed on a fingernail. "I guess it was lucky you could add me into the permissions. Homeland Security cleared me, right?" He exhaled with relief when Luc confirmed it.

"Yes," Luc added, "I will keep all the documents including the licenses from OFAC, the Office of Foreign Assets. One can never tell these days what legality may raise its head."

Sonoteas smirked, "Legalities...humm."

Luc looked at the others, "Don't mind him. He has always been a smart one. He even used to beat us at chess as a kid. I want to make it clear Sonoteas that I am in charge of this expedition and I am the official captain of the vessel. My name is on all the documents and I will keep them. You all take charge of your passports. Everyone, please defer to me for decisions. Don't go off on your own and jeopardize our safety." Lana detected a growing tone of his desperation with Sonoteas.

"Heads up, everyone," DK interrupted. "Here comes the Coast Guard. It is the Master Chief Petty Officer leading them. Lana and I met him three days ago."

Luc limped to meet them, "Ah! Officers, welcome, let me help you step aboard."

"Stay where you are sir. We are quite used to coming aboard vessels," the CPO reproached in an even tone, not interested in being charmed. "So, who do we have here?"

Once everyone was introduced, the CPO sat down at the long, smooth teak table with Luc and reviewed everyone's documents. His associates searched the ship, looking into everything with care. This was their third search since the ship was rescued and their first since the latest goods were boarded.

"I see you applied to the Treasury Department, and you met the registration requirements under the U.S. Federal Codes. You are licensed under section VIII."

"Yes, sir," Luc answered, "We are traveling in support of the Cuban people according to 515.560."

"Was it necessary to include section 515.575 – permitting medical supplies now that certain restrictions have been relaxed?"

"Yes sir. We wanted to be sure that those items were not taken away so we could be helpful to the people."

"Then why did you also apply under 515.576 for foundations?"

"Ah yes. My father and I are principals in a non-governmental organization to strengthen civil society through greater knowledge of the fraternal link between Taino Natives and our own Calusa tribe. We want to identify the cultural similarities of our ancient tribes. We hope to find cultural artifacts and be allowed to return with a few. So, we want to be sure that it is sanctioned."

"Humm. Well having all those licenses seems a bit of overkill, but if the higher-ups granted them, then proceed as expected. Mind you, this vessel will be searched again upon return. You may not conduct commercial business under these documents. You know that. The Masque you listed will be the only item of value permitted back in the country. Now when it comes to behavior on the journey remember that if you are detained, we may not be able to bail you out. So watch your P's & Q's," he advised, looking each of them in the eyes.

A faint reply came from Luc, "Yes, sir."

"Do you have access to Cuban Pesos, the CUP money, in case it becomes necessary to use local currency?"

"Yes sir. Each of us has tele cash debit cards for Bank Financiero in Havana."

"Whatever cash you use, be sure you keep your spending at specified limits, retain all your purchase receipts and keep cash for exiting Cuba."

"Yes."

"Good luck then," the Chief Officer said with stoicism. He handed Luc the signed Travel Service Provider form, along with accompanying forms the group would need at Cuban customs and upon re-entry to the U.S. Then he looked at his two officers. They acknowledged the absence of firearms or contraband, and followed him off the vessel.

Lana sighed. "They never acknowledged you DK. Do you suppose that means anything?"

"Don't you think they learned enough about both of us when we were in their holding rooms?" he said in a cool tone. "Well let's get moving."

"This is exciting," Gusta said, feeling at last that the journey was in motion. "Dinner in Havana?"

"Oh yes. I hope we can dine tonight at a private Paladar called La Cocina Lilliam. It is along the Miramar," Lana told the crew.

"A flavorful Cuban meal was exactly what I had in mind," Luc said. "I hope they serve the famous Ajiaco Cubano."

As everyone chatted about the adventure and busied himself or herself around the vessel, Sonoteas fingered the fire extinguisher.

Chapter 12

The *Esmeralda* slid out of her mooring and eased past the onlookers who lingered along the Mallory Square boardwalk; each one looking wistfully at the latest vessel to head sea-ward; each tourist surmising some great adventure. Amidst the crowd, two men glared at the striking and determined *Esmeralda*. She had defeated them, *only so far*, their eyes said.

Sonoteas looked back from a porthole, and with a wave of his cap, he confirmed his mission. He would have to get rid of the others on board and gain the *Masque* himself.

Above deck, Gusta managed the helm first, drawing them past the stone jetties as DK updated the motoring plan, "We have about six hours ahead of us and will maintain 15 to 20 knots an hour to reach Havana just after sunset. Since we are fully loaded, we do not need to put unnecessary wear on the boat up by pushing fast. So everyone relax."

DK then adjusted the new radio and set it to the soft tones of the National Oceanographic & Atmospheric channel. "No one else has heard a weather warning for today, right? We would go back and delay the trip if bad weather was likely."

"No, DK," Sonoteas stressed loudly. "I saw the dock's weather sign and it said clear sailing until midnight."

Gusta confirmed the report adding that he had listened to news during their drive down. "There is a storm entering Georgia but predicted to go out over the Atlantic quickly. It is just a brush-by of heavy New England winter."

"Yeah, exactly," Sonoteas agreed.

The day gave way to late afternoon. The wind shifted. The two men at the controls ceased their banter, becoming aware of an increasing crosswise-tug from the Gulf Stream.

Lana was busy preparing foods while Sonoteas ignored everyone, sitting idly by, whistling now and then. Then he stood to bother Gusta at the helm.

"Say, Gusta, do you know who our guide company is through the island and how we'll proceed once there?"

As Gusta scratched his head trying to remember, he called to Lana.

Sonoteas sauntered to the radio controls. "Lower this thing. A person can't hear you with that noise." He lowered the volume. "Now what was your answer Gusta?"

Gusta repeated, "Lana?"

She called back to him, "Havanaturs!"

"I see, and what's the route we will follow?" Sonoteas asked, sliding an arm over the console and distracting Gusta.

"Lana?" Gusta asked again, as Sonoteas let his fingers move the radio dial off mark.

"Well anything can change, but at the moment we will follow Luc's treasure map by starting with Havana and then go on to Viñales in the Rio del Pinar region. If we don't find any clues by then, we will travel south east down the entire country until we obtain a clue."

"The entire island?" Sonoteas objected.

"Until we run out of time," she answered with a smile to him. "We'll only go to the places marked on the Calusa treasure map; Cienfuegos, Trinidad, Santi Spiritus, Camaguey, Baracoa. As far as I know, the main contingent of Taino lives in the hills of Punta da Mais. We hope to get that far in any case so that Luc can open a dialog with the natives to share cultural history. So, with or without the *Masque*, the entire trip won't be a loss."

"Do you really think we should skip important locations like Santiago de Cuba because that is a very old city and Holguin offers a vast landscape. So do the forests of Sierra Maestra in Granma Province, not far from Guantanamo?"

"Oh you'd like to go there? Well, Sonoteas, if they are not on the Calusa treasure map we may not have time to visit it. Do you have a special reason?"

He dismissed the question with a wave of his hand, but pulled out a small pad and made some notes. Then he plopped down on the transom settee. Lana went to him offering a dish of grapes from the galley. "Would you like this cushion for your back?"

His eyes were wide and unresponsive. Lana sensed that he was not used to friendship. She sensed that her gesture might have been a rare kindness in his life. Luc smiled seeing the two engaged in banter, hoping for something better from the boy. Then fatigue crossed Luc's face and he moved to the stairwell. "Time for a rest. I'll be below for a while."

Lana handed a safety jacket to everyone, and when she reached DK with his, she touched her hand to the nape of his neck. She felt him relax into her palm. They had made a truce.

"She rides smooth when she has propellers," DK said, smiling at Lana.

It was his peace offering. She responded happily with a dimpled smile.

A n hour later Luc awoke and called everyone together to review more of his documents. "I want to show you some historic information. Where is Sonoteas?"

"Does it matter?" Gusta asked. "I'm just glad to get rid of him. He itches my bones."

DK returned from the bowsprit having tightened a rail. He jumped down into the cockpit. "What's that my friend? Itch your bones? First time I ever heard that one."

Luc shook his head, "Now, now friends, he is just a kid."

Everyone chuckled over the issue, and light radio music accompanied the vessel as it cut through the wind and the waves around them. A familiar tune played on: *Around the world, I searched for you….* The radar screen began to show an atmospheric ripple blooming at its furthest edge. The team's attention was distracted by Luc's instructions. "We may need to explain our connected Arawak and Native history as we meet people in Cuba. So, here is a rundown.

You know that Ponce de León took the *Masque* we seek. Let me show you copies of historic documents from the original Caribbean Island archives in Madrid.

"Juan Ponce de León had been contracted by his king to follow in the footsteps of Admiral Christopher Columbus, under whom he served at one time. Subsequent to the

admiral's discoveries in the Caribbean, several conquistadors were assigned to various explorations for purposes of settlement and aggrandizement to the crown. De León was given the island of what is now Puerto Rico, which he colonized. He was encouraged to explore more islands for conquest. When he reached the east coast of a very large island, on March 27, 1511, he named it, 'La Florida', and claimed it for the Spanish Crown. Ponce de León made copious notes in his ship's log on the local geography, its easy harbor and low coastline.

"In Florida, de León encountered only a few indigenous people at first. He was dismayed to find no evidence of wealth. On his homeward voyage, he identified a discovery of great value: the Gulf Stream. Understanding that these currents were reliable and how they moved was a boon to Spanish shipping. De León saw a bright future for Spanish trade with the Americas, riding 'his' current.

"At risk to himself and his men, de León's explorations of these lands called La Florida took him to a string of sandy spits, so small at that time that you could walk on each and any, from one end to the other; from the Atlantic Ocean mainland to the great sea now called the Caribbean. The sailors named the area, *Little Keys*. De León had also made forays into the mainland, finding a mix of swamp, forest and prairie. He kept logs of his findings later valuable to science.

"In time, necessity called him back to his family still living on their land-grant farm in Puerto Rico. It was not until 1521 when de León lost a political bid for island governorship of Puerto Rico that he decided to seek new conquest. He wrote that he believed Florida lay in a desirous geographic position, mating with Cuba to protect the Florida Straits and the vital cargos from Peru – precious cargo that included ores, jewels and produce. De León offered the Crown his finances to explore, tame and absorb Florida into the Spanish empire for his king, hoping to reap successful agriculture there and a new governorship for himself.

"However, De León attempted to tame Florida's natives in the same harsh manner conquistadors used on other islands; enslavement.

The outcome was disastrous.

(Then, de León's Letter to the Crown...)

...Among my services, I have discovered the island of la Florida, and others in its district that are not listed here, as they are small and inconsequential. Now I return to that island, if it pleases God's will, to settle it, being enabled to carry a number of men who go at my own expense. I also intend to explore the coast of the aforementioned island and onward to the land north...

I set sail to pursue my voyage hence in five or six days. Thus, may the name of Christ be praised there, and may your Majesty be served with the fruits of that land. By my hand Adelanto, Juan Ponce de León

LOG BOOK
El Santiago
Entry excerpt sent to:
His Royal Majesty, Ferdinand – King of Spain.

When first I followed the path described by Columbus and visited the island he called Colba (now Cuba), I agreed with his assessment; "never seen a more beautiful country... covered with trees right down to the inlet...these were lovely... each bore its own fruit or flowers...different from those of Guinea or our Spanish variety. The birdlife is vast and musical to the ear."

In the verdant lands of Colba, I too felt the resources for us would justify settlements and as you will recall, I pressed that it become for us a vast garden of sugar cane, an industry for the whole of Europe. In addition, by its location surrounded by other islands and the Mexican mainland, our stronghold in Colba would be at the center of a large trade. Much gold would pass her shores riding my discovered currents to Europe. With these goals in mind for Colba, I was successful in subduing the natives known as Taino and begin cultivation.

It is with regret that I had since been replaced as governor of Colba but your will has granted my further endeavors into the land I call La Florida. As your majesty remembers, I was excited for the promise of this undeveloped area.

I report now that my men and I faithfully began with the same practices as our past colonization, but in Florida we found an unpredictable turn of hospitality as the natives had word of our colonization ahead of time and prepared for resistance. We explored as far north as a conference of the sea with a great river that the natives call the Caloosahatchee. They called themselves the Calusa.

As we traveled southward again, we found shores laced one after the other with habitable grassy spits. We took possession of that area in the name of San Marco, but while our party began constructing the governor's settlement, we were attacked with poison arrows that fell upon us like rain. Having no medicines against this poison we were forced to abandon the settlement and make haste for help, heading to the nearest Spanish port, Havana.

We had already stored goods aboard before the rebellion: trinkets, objects salvaged by the natives and barrels of various salted meats. I had collected some items of gold, a Masque of Gold particularly, keeping it for my family, as booty in return for the expenses paid by myself.

Now in Havana, the crew is angry at the outcome of injury and failure. They hold the Masque responsible and believe it is a curse. They would leave it here as I lie dying, but I implore Your Majesty to ignore the condemnation they ascribe to it and order it kept safe for my family. May they remember me with honor and live protected. In humble gratitude and farewell, written by the new captain of the vessel Santiago, Ferdinand Banderas.

Signed and under my seal,

Juan Ponce de León,

Former Governor of Cuba and Florida
December 1521

Standing in the *Esmeralda's* stairwell, Sonoteas broke the silence around him with a scoff.

"Umpf! Curse my foot."

Chapter 13

*L*ana folded all the historic documents for Luc and placed them into his satchel. She noticed that everyone seemed drowsy, even the young Sonoteas, massaging his elbow. The group had been through difficulties. A jug of wine sat on the table for them but held no interest.

After a while, Gusta took Luc back to the staterooms and he himself went to rest. DK manned the helm. The trip had grown to three hours so far, and DK's calculations put them another three hours out. An opaque sun fought visibility amidst growing clouds. A spotty moon peered dimly from afar. Lana joined DK who pointed to the radar screen as it populated more and more. He looked at her with a strained look in his eyes.

"Clouds?" she acknowledged. "That's so strange when Sonoteas had told us he knew the weather would be fine all day."

DK's eyes steeled. He studied the screens and then turned up the volume on the radio. Music played. "Whoa, this is not the NOAA channel. Who moved and lowered the dials?"

"I don't know. I didn't touch it."

"Gusta mentioned a New England storm coming south, but that it was predicted to go out to sea, not come this far south. The storm is moving in our direction after all. We should have known about it sooner! We might have been able to out run it."

"Wouldn't FAT ALBERT be keeping an eye on us?" Lana asked looking at DK in the naïve hope of some over-arching protective eye.

"Probably not. That's the National Security Agency and they aren't concerned about those of us who leave the U.S."

She started nibbling her lip.

Silence reigned on the ship as whooshes of wind provided background noise to the NOAA mumbling. Lana watched the Ray Marine, E-series 90W navigation display.

"I have confidence in this equipment to get us through anything," DK reassured her.

"Will a storm hit us?"

"Not sure. It is descending like a long spoon twenty miles out to sea and heading to our latitude. However, the land mass is so flat in Florida that the storm could skate quickly over it and out to the Atlantic. It will depend on the opposing atmospheric pressure. Unfortunately, the screen doesn't show that pressure giving way."

Lana closed the electronic sunroof and pulled down the rain shades. She rubbed DK's neck and he adjusted his head until a vertebra said "crack."

"Why not take this quiet time for a nap," she proposed. "You haven't had a chance to rest like the rest of us, and I can be on watch now. If a storm is coming there is no safe harbor for us, right?"

"Nope. If we are lucky, the storm will pass by quickly and head east. We are just as well to stay the course and run ahead of it. We would run out of fuel if we head west and go off our navigation plan." He checked the dials again. "It isn't here yet, so if I can rest my eyes for thirty minutes, it will keep me on my toes later. Promise that you will get me up if things worsen. I don't like the way the air smells."

"The air?" she answered, spinning full circle looking for a monster, "The air?"

"Are you having fun?" he smiled at her antics. "Please, just come to get me if NOAA refers to the storm moving to this latitude. The waters here are too deep to anchor, and I hope…well, just come and get me."

"Will do," she answered, turning up the radio volume.

Lana enjoyed the captain's role at first, sitting alone, attentive to the elements, noticing nothing more than a blustery breeze. Then clouds built-up and blocked the sun entirely. A white mass filled the radar screen and the waves begin to buffet the ship. Lana turned up the radio volume again only to hear the same droning voice mention coordinates and millibars.

"Some captain I'd make," she replied to the voice. "I have no idea what you are saying Miss Announcer, or how to decipher all those numbers. You have not said latitude yet so I won't waken Dusty. I can handle this," she challenged the wind.

She made a brief concession for help by crooking her head around the console while holding the helm. She looked down the stairwell, but saw no one. In silence, she straightened back up and glanced around the empty deck. In the roll and pitch of a storm, being alone on deck didn't seem so romantic.

Lana checked the *Esmeralda's* speed. Twenty knots per hour had been forced back to fifteen earlier. Now she saw the wisdom of keeping the engine calm at five knots. It was already cooking as the rising sea fought it. Soon the vessel was tossing herself left and right, up and down. Lana knew to keep the vessel riding between the waves, not cresting them where the drop could crack a hull, but it became increasingly difficult to do. Repetitive swells drew the ship up, suspending it like a breath before an exhale, then deflating under it fast. Lana wondered how long the ship could take such punishment as a whining sound increased around the vessel. The stainless fittings strained. Little squeals of unknown origin rose in pitch. Great claps of thunder overrode the radio sounds – great claps as only found during Caribbean storms. Electric charges blasted around Lana like unceasing blowouts of monster tires. Then lightning strikes became more violent, their light revealing only a charcoal, friendless sky. Lana strained her eyes to see ahead and saw only the bow bobbing on a churning sea. She was too busy containing the sway of the vessel to leave the helm and began to feel true isolation for the first time in her life.

Her live choices seemed so different from those of people who report daily to a safe, functional office or cubicle. Their choice gave them predictable protection and a certain comfort; a photo of dad or brother could hang by the computer, mementoes of friendship could rest on a shelf, awards could stand with pride. Perhaps there are even jobs that give permission for Vivie to visit on family days?

"I've traded away devotion for independence and relationships for freedom," she said to the wind.

"I heard that," DK interrupted, coming up the stairwell. Then standing next to her he asked, "How long do you think it takes us to learn a lesson?"

She placed her head against his shoulder. "How long?"

His shoulder was like iron and he wrapped an arm around her shoulder. He tugged gently on her ear lobe, which she loved. His other hand was set on the helm along with hers. She understood their connection at last, more than words could say.

"You love adventure more than anything, and you won't accept my affection because it will anchor you," DK dared to say.

"That's partially right, but I don't want a failed relationship either. I do not want to party for the heck of it, going from one painful encounter to another. I prefer to keep people as friends a good while. Perhaps we will grow sure that we are soul-mates, good for each other on many levels."

"It's a shame that *you* don't see that already."

"Oh," Lana answered.

He smiled at her, "You do, don't you?"

She gnawed her lip. Then she gave in with a smile. "Yes, I do."

"Sometimes people just have to believe in the same things." he shouted over the wind, "Anyway, I'm going down again to get the others. They need to be above decks now."

While the *Esmeralda* heaved and tossed in DK's absence, Lana's naked, wet fingers were getting raw. This was not her first encounter with the forces of Nature, but it was the first time she felt so close to oblivion. It made her accept more deeply the truth of her person, fragility. In the waterway of Ponce de León, Lana was being pulled by forces beyond herself and beyond the great conquistador and perhaps beyond the power of the *Masque of Gold*. She put her head out from under the cockpit's rain-cover, face to the wind. The waves pounded against the hull jolting her. In the strongest conflict with nature that she had yet experienced, the wind and the sea were speaking. A humbled and tired Lana did not have time in life for a locked heart anymore. Her fear of desertion was very old, very tiring. She admitted that it was no longer, if ever it had been, useful. Lana smiled as she let raindrops fall on her lips. She realized how fulfilling it was to be open, to be alive, aware, and part of a pair. As the rain to that night, DK flooded her heart.

Lana waited for the others to appear as the waves grew, the noise deafening her. She held the helm still trying not to ride the crests. The motion was getting to her and it made her wonder how the others could remain below decks so long — *it should be nauseating*. She called out, but no one replied. She became fearful for them. *Sonoteas is below* she remembered. Her instincts told her that something was wrong. Suddenly a hole opened in the sky. The teaming rain removed itself to a perimeter circle around her. The radar confirmed that they were in empty space, a cloudless hole in the middle of the odd winter storm. The *Esmeralda* sighed and stopped rocking. Lana jumped off the seat, determined to go below and find the others. When she threw open the door of stateroom one, Gusta staggered upright, holding and stretching his neck with one hand.

"Gusta! What is wrong? You should be above now."

"Lord I feel queasy."

"You've got a lump growing on your forehead. Did you fall?"

"I don't remember."

"Here take this towel and get upstairs for some ice. Take the helm for me while I find the others."

Seeing his personal objects tossed to the floor by motion, Gusta realized what was making him nauseous. He made the sign of the cross, and he nodded vigorously to Lana, proceeding right up the stairs to face the storm.

Lana entered the other stateroom and looked around Luc's berth only to spot him fallen to the floor on the far side of the room. He was unable to propel himself up with his disabled arm. "My goodness, Luc, how long have you been like this?"

"I don't know. I called out, but no one replied. The noise and motion were too great for me. I think something hit me, or maybe I passed out."

"Sonoteas was in the other bunk, wasn't he?"

"Yes, he was sleeping, but when I called and awoke him, he refused to lift me up. He grabbed my document satchel. He said that we'd be pulling in to port very soon, and he would be leaving us." Luc's eyes welled up, "Lana, I felt that his glance wished me dead."

"Come now, let me help you go above. You'll feel better in the open air."

Lana hurriedly sat Luc above at the galley table. She returned below to seek out DK. She felt panic. Had Sonoteas hurt him too? Suddenly a great slap sounded, and the vessel gave a huge lurch. The storm had slammed in again, and a fierce wind was pushing them against the waves. She was caught off balance and thrown across the stairs. For a minute, she lay there stunned. As her head cleared, she pulled upright against the greater motion and looked to the only door still closed, the engine room.

It was difficult to see inside that space because the overhead fluorescent lights had not been turned on from the cockpit. She was not sure if she heard a human groan because a whoosh of forced air blew through the open doorways. Echo bounced off laminate walls, but with the door open, light did filter into the engine room. Once Lana could distinguish forms, she found herself in the middle of a square and compact space, large enough for five single bunks. The engine and other heavy equipment was bolted down on either side of her. A pathway down the middle went to the rear wall. She could not see anyone standing in front of her and assumed that the missing men had fallen on the floor. She crouched down for a better perspective and a figure became visible, wedged behind the large water tank and the rear wall. It was DK, not Sonoteas.

A step behind her made her turn in time to see two legs at her back and then a man's arm moving upward to strike her. He wielded a pipe at her head, but her athletic, lean frame wheeled around slamming the attacker backward. He dropped the pipe and she grabbed it.

"What are you doing?" she bellowed, rising and pushing his slender body further away from her. She saw Luc's satchel and pulled it off Sonoteas shoulder. Then he straightened-up, staring at Lana with venom in his eyes.

Lana yelled in his face. "Get upstairs!"

"I don't have to listen to you," he replied, his face tilted close to hers and still full of menace. "What will you do, tie me up in a storm when we might get capsized, drowning me? No, I think not. I would do that, but you are all such *good and selfless* people," he smirked, retreating above for lack of any other option. He escaped DK's notice as the agent began to stir.

Lana clambered around the water tank reaching for DK's body, his long frame wedged behind it. She shuddered, "My heavens! DK! Can you speak? Let me look into your eyes – you may have a concussion." She tugged at him until he showed signs of recognition and unfolded his legs to stand, at which moment he banged his head against the overhead pipe.

"I do not!" he boomed. "Find that idiot Sonoteas. He tried to knock me out when I found him looting Luc's documents."

"Yes," she said without argument.

She shrugged her shoulders at the comic yet tragic confusion that betrayed all their planning. She guided him to the passageway with as much care as possible, trying to avoid bumping things and causing anymore bruise to their bodies. With outstretched hands to steady their climb on the swaying staircase, they passed the Co_2 canister, still attached to the wall. Lana passed it, noting something different, but too distracted to understand why.

Topsides, DK sat down next to Gusta at the controls. "Remind me next time to bring an entire law enforcement kit when I go on a vacation with you."

He growled. "Sonoteas! We have your number now. We'll have to tie you up."

Fortunately, for the group Sonoteas was lightweight and no match for DK. Nevertheless, he snickered to test his luck. Luc looked at the dangerous cousin whose legs were intentionally stretched into the aisle.

"We let you get away with too much as a child."

"Maybe you just left me with the wrong parent."

"Were you the one to attack my father and me?" Luc demanded.

Sonoteas just blinked.

"Why must you tear us down cousin? Who is trying to turn you against our good people. For centuries we have been a civilized society, self-sustaining and productive. The finds on Horr's Island prove that. Why don't you work with us as a family and also work to enhance our honored culture?"

Fishing in his pockets for chewing gum, Sonoteas only said, "Ya, ya, and ya. I have friends better than you do. They'll take care of me."

DK studied the young man and approached him. "When we get to Cuba, you will be detained and interrogated. Then the truth you speak will be tested. For now, I am tying you up. You have all but admitted to the terrible attack on Luc. Do you blame me?"

Sonoteas just glared.

"Luc, you created a file with Naples police against the saboteur of your *Esmeralda* and the hit-run driver. We can attest to Sonoteas violence on board. Although we do not have concrete evidence of all his misdoing, an investigation is likely to provide it. In the case that he has additional mischief in mind, he cannot be left free to roam Cuba. The police in Havana will be very interested to avoid that and will either send him back immediately or detain him until we head home."

"I agree, DK. Do what you must."

Sonoteas just kept snapping his gum.

Running a rope from a cleat, looping it around the kitchen table leg and then around Sonoteas's ankles, DK had to struggle with the boy's antics. "We can't let you go around Cuba not knowing what mischief you intend. You behave with malice toward everyone. The ship's rope will have to hold you until the police come aboard."

As he finished his task, DK tried to stand when a jolt of waves bounced the vessel, slamming DK's head against the table corner. Groaning, Agent Cody was seeing stars and depleted of good humor. He turned his face to Lana, "I guess a six-footer has no business in small places."

Lana had been buttering pita-bread pockets at the table for Luc who continued to fill them with ham and tomato slices, but she stopped and put the butter knife down, no longer able to resist her feelings. She walked up and threw her arms around agent Dusty Kern Cody, planting a big kiss on his forehead.

"Ouch!" He asserted, "What was that for?"

Chapter 14

The storm had finally pulled fast to the east, leaving the *Esmeralda* crew wet and shaky. Gusta checked the vessel's condition as DK adjusted the ship's course. Sunlight faded and true night arrived as they neared the great island of Cuba. Everyone took bites of the food Lana and Luc had kept on the table, while Sonoteas remained silent and surly faced, tied at both hand and ankles now, planted on the kitchen settee along with his goods.

Lana was the first to spot it, the Castillo de los Tres Reyes Magos Del Morro. They all recognized the lighthouse heralding the harbor. DK throttled the ship back and Gusta radioed ahead with a request for docking. The *Esmeralda* had arrived at nine in the evening. The officials denied entry.

The vessel had arrived too late, but their reservation would be honored the next day. Gusta received permission to weigh anchor at a commercial holding area, out of the channel. He was assured that they could proceed after daylight and that a police escort would greet them at the pier to detain the accused.

Lana and DK shared a glance of surprise at the delay, but they also shared the elation of success. They had reached their destination—a different country, beautiful and complex. Cuba was before them at last; the furthermost island of the Antilles chain, close to the great Atlantic Trench; peopled by patience and talent, the subjugated and the powerful and change.

Lana opened her reference book on Cuba, and Sonoteas watched her pour over the route ahead. She made some notes to help the crew on its overland journey, closed and packed her books, then studied the waters around them. "It is really clear water here guys. I know that the shelf around the island is rich in coral life. Wouldn't it be fun to fit in a day of snorkeling. Perhaps the future will limit it or ruin the reefs."

DK looked at her as he tugged at the anchor, not sure it was holding. "We could, and it would be fun, but Luc has to decide when we have the time to fit it in. When it comes to saving their environment and the effect on other peoples, I would not lose hope in the Cubans. They are trying to save these important waters by issuing industry regulations and sponsoring scientific research. They know that unchecked development can pollute and starve the sea life crucial to the world's food chain."

Luc stood up, feeling no better than the day he arrived in Key West. He uttered an encouragement to Lana, saying that if they found their objective soon enough, everyone could enjoy the remaining days. "Bring the guide book with us. If we can fit in some fun, we will. You said the waters are steady at about seventy degrees. Is that warm enough for you?"

"No, but I'll snorkel with a wet suit."

He laughed. "I guess we'll miss our great dinner plans, so break out the tins again."

As they ate dinner and stared out at the beautiful nighttime city of Havana, its details seemed blurry in the distance, but its flickers of light revealed movement and life. Along the coast a long highway ran out of their view, to infinity. The length of it wore a sinuous sheen of streetlights, round-cupped and quiet—luminescent like a necklace of pearls, soft glowing like seduction.

Everyone was exhausted from the demands of the trip. They fell soundly asleep, only waking for a turn at watch. Sonoteas had been released in the night to use the head, but had been tied again, hands and feet. He remained that way for hours, preferring to sit upright on the lounge settee. However, as dawn hinted her arrival, Sonoteas moved. He saw that only Gusta was on deck, and as the boat swayed rhythmically, Gusta dozed.

Sonoteas began to twist around. He had secured a thick slab of butter wedged in pita bread, taking it off the table during dinner and stashing it behind him. When he heard the regular snoring of his guard, he squeezed the grease from the bread he had wedged behind him between the cushions. Soon the lubricant let him loosen his wrist bindings. Next, he greased his ankles until that rope also moved up and down.

Once freed, Sonoteas moved across the deck with controlled strides, making no sound. He picked up his backpack and pulled out his body suit. Once he had it on, he plucked a small plastic sack from the inside crotch area. *No one ever checks that spot*, he smiled. He placed the incriminating sack under the settee cushion. Then he reached for a tall Gatorade drink, untouched from his dinner, and looking longingly at the fire extinguisher. He saluted it and whispered, "I'll leave you for later."

The *Esmeralda* was a thoroughbred of vessels and felt the vibration of cruelty topsides. She shied and shimmied in the water, impatient to see him go. He slipped over the swim platform and swam away, but not before he had unclipped the *Esmeralda's* gas cap. The vessel's worst fear was realized as she felt the pinch at her side, then the long, destructive burn of Gatorade.

Chapter 15

23° 5' 18.45" North - 82° 30' 3.04" West

DK came on deck with the rising sun and sent Gusta to shower. He checked the gauges and screens, prepared the vessel and hoisted the anchor. Soft murmurs reached his ears as local fishermen headed out to sea. A few brave boys took to the waters with pneumatic tires, anxious to drag a baited line in hopes of that day's lunch.

Lana appeared on deck, showered and ready to dock. She brought up their duffle bags and joined DK at the helm as he started the engine, steering the *Esmeralda* toward the entry channel. He pointed to the stretch of ocean beside them, "This is the tropic of Cancer and the water running between the Yucatan peninsula and Cuba is more or less steady in winter so swimming is not impossible if we get an opportunity for fun," he told her.

"I still say brrr…," she said back to him.

"Bracing? Well you don't have enough fat on your body to keep warm," DK teased.

"Yes, I should have a wet suit." she laughed again, and shuddered to get the blood moving in her veins. As DK frisked her, she was half distracted, and then startled-stone-still.

"DK! Where is Sonoteas?"

Gusta and Luc had just come up the stairs. They all looked at each other. It was so peaceful aboard without Sonoteas that none of them questioned his absence. They assumed he was under another's care. After all, where could he go? Lana pulled the ropes off the bench. They were greasy. "I see," Lana muttered—showing a wad of butter to the others.

Gusta descended to the staterooms and looked everywhere, shouting out, "Hiding Sonoteas? Time to go! Time to go!" Without any reply and finding no sign of the truant, Gusta shouted up the stairs. "He's gone!"

"I'll tell the Cuban Custom's & Immigrations officers what happened as soon as they boards us. We can't afford to be linked to Sonoteas if he gets up to mischief," DK declared.

"He had a top grade wet suit in his backpack, so he is likely to have made it okay to the shore," Lana said. "Drats. He probably emerged at some empty cove before dawn, safe and free. Remember he had a waterproof backpack to protect his stuff too. We'd better check to see if anything was taken."

They checked all the necessary shipboard equipment, their personal belongings and monies, but everything seemed in order. DK ran the engine to be sure the propellers were still there. They spun. Then he heard something else, an engine sputter. "Here we go," he said, looking over the hull, reaching down to the fuel cap. He brought his hand up to taste the residue he saw around the cap. "Sugar water."

Luc shook his head, "I can't believe that boy. I wonder what he thinks he will do to re-enter the U.S.."

Lana looked at her friend, "Luc don't you see? He does not intend to return to us or to the U.S. When DK stopped him from taking all your official papers, he was denied the permission papers allowing him to be here, never mind leave. Even though he must still have his passport, that will not be sufficient to leave since he is registered with our permissions, not anyone else's. Anyway, once we report him, the passport will clinch his capture. I feel sure he never intended to come home. If it were proven that he struck you and your father, he could be sent to prison for a long time. No, Luc, he wants to be far away from us, in some nowhere land, free from everyone."

"Exactly," DK said, "Whatever his reason to be in Cuba, he has gotten in with bad company and they have evil in mind. Poor kid, he has been convinced of protection, but modern terrorists do not know mercy, only death.

He will have to leave Cuba under the protection of the people he calls friends, and it is possible he could be spirited to somewhere else in the world, but I suspect they consider him expendable."

"If he has money, he might finesse an escape," Lana noted.

"And from whom does he have the money?" Luc asked in innocence.

"Exactly," Lana said.

DK breathed deep. "Don't you see Luc? If he does find the *Masque* ahead of us, it could provide him the funds to escape before his recruiters use him up."

"Say guys," Gusta spoke up. "Engine?"

"Right you are," DK agreed. "Let's report the missing youth and leave the engine to be cleaned out, or we'll ruin it. We've got our pressing goal to find the *Masque*. Our search has competition, dangerous competition."

"My god where is he?" trembled Luc.

Lana scanned the waterfront, musing that Sonoteas might very well be sitting on the Malecon laughing at them. The scenic thoroughfare stretched a curving distance of five miles from Old Havana to the beaches and the modern hotels of Vedado neighborhood. She put a hand on Luc's stooped shoulder. "It's impossible to see him if he is there now, Luc. I see lots of pedestrians at the seawall and cars on the broad avenue, but no Sonoteas looking for us."

"Oh Lana, it's obvious that Sonoteas had an agenda all along. I am sure he attacked my father and me. His build fits and so does his meanness. I should have known. Once a mistreated child..."

Lana had nothing to say, so she pointed to the dock ahead, "Let's all be ready to disembark. We have no time to waste. We've got to stow all our stuff in a hotel as fast as possible and see what business we can accomplish today."

DK suggested that they contact the American Interests Section sooner than later. "You all understand that with Sonoteas complicating the issue we will be under tight scrutiny. I doubt seriously that we will be able to march away with something valuable."

"Yes, yes. I see that more clearly now," Luc answered, "But I can still hope that the government will sympathize with my tribe's Native American plight."

No one responded to that.

Old habits die hard. Local authorities are wary of Americans with political agendas. Therefore, it was normal for them to rifle through the team's extensive luggage. They looked for weapons, drugs, incendiary literature or anything that might pose a danger to the Republic. They were professional in their demeanor, serious, clad in short-sleeved, grey shirts and trousers. They were no less friendly than immigrations and custom's officials in other countries, but the atmosphere of Caribbean, fun-loving, hospitality was cautious. Why not, when one still had dangerous opponents like Sonoteas? The *Brotherhood of Man* has yet to win over the world.

All the professionalism of the customs staff and the pleasantry of some did not offset the fact that officers were wearing weaponry. This is true of many places in the world, but the four Americans felt vulnerable at this point because they had brought a villain to their hosts. Once they explained the missing person on their manifest, DK and the others were brought into a small office and made to wait.

After an hour, an officer of rank arrived. Sonoteas's alleged attack on the Pios happened in the U.S., so the local authorities could not act on that—they had not received any request for extradition. However, the fact that a man listed on the permission manifest was missing did not sit well. The lump on Gusta's head gave some credibility to the team's victimization. In addition, the *Esmeralda's* engine had been sabotaged. The result of all these declarations caused additional levels of authorized officials to enter and leave the room, check the baggage twice, and repeat questions. Since Agent Cody carried proof of his employment with the U.S. Federal Government, this was more cause for suspicion. In spite of his protestations against being there officially, the officials checked and re-checked his identification on various computer screens, and conferred between themselves. Finally, after a total of two hours, a phone call came to the officials and permission was granted for the *Esmeralda* crew to enter the country. At last the team of four felt relief. They grew excited to have made the passage from home in one piece.

Once outside the marina, DK tried to enlist a car from an official taxi stand. The Pio team needed a large one. The little, egg-shaped vehicles called "CoCo" would not take all their luggage. A 1957 Ford appeared and they were assigned it by the taxi administrator. It sat them comfortably.

"Cute," Lana uttered, looking at the 'CoCo.' "Let's try that another day."

Gusta laughed, "I prefer this beautiful classic car."

"You like it for the open top, don't you? But don't consider yourself a gangland leader or a glamorous movie mogul," she teased.

"Oh, no, but it is wonderful to be here as an ordinary person. I can feel the vibrancy of this place. Besides Lana, not everyone in business was a gangster before the revolution. That century saw many legitimate businessmen invest here, like Mr. 'chocolate' Hershey."

"It's a long time ago, water under the bridge. Yes, I suppose some business people were selfless. Let's see if we can be that way on-going."

"Well, Lana, that's true. I wish the world could be a better place, and then I think of my own cousin and his evilness. What can I say?"

"Well, maybe Sonoteas will just disappear and we can be good people and good tourists." Lana stretched her neck to look all around her at the city. "I'm enjoying the beauty of this classic car too!"

The Ford they rode in was in fabulous shape with clean, cushioned leather seats. Its clear green coat shone, having lived through years of polish by loving hands. Lana waved from the open top vehicle at romancers lining the Malecon wall. Those who took a breath from dreaming together looked up to the exuberant American waving gaily at them. Waving back with equal spirit they called to her, "Si, Si, Esta Bien Americana!"

The ride was less than sixteen miles from moorage to hotel. In less than half an hour the luggage-laden taxi had turned into a long, park-like road, past a circular island and up to a palatial entry. They had chosen the Hotel Nacional for expediency sake, as before the Gatorade damage, they had expected to remain on the boat. The sheer size of the famous hotel guaranteed some vacant rooms for the weekend, and searching for something else would take time away from the quest.

"Lana, I thought you'd chosen something more down to earth for us?"

"Don't you like it, DK?"

"As he pulled duffle bags from the taxi, he craned his neck in an arc to take in the spectacular size of the building."

To take the sting out of DK's under-reaction Luc spoke up. "It's very nice, Lana. Besides, from what I hear the rooms are modest, so we will not be glamorized. It's fun to stay in an historic location, so full of history."

"Look, we are facing the sea too," Lana said.

Cody pouted, "I just thought we'd do things authentic, not touristy."

"This hotel is very authentic. It is done in Art Deco style that speaks of the 1940s. It is definitely reminiscent of a bygone and colorful era," Lana insisted, determined to stay there. DK had to smile at her enthusiasm, as she spread her arms to underscore the grandness of the place. "You are staying in a landmark DK. Enjoy it. Even though Cuba is welcoming tourism these days with more new hotels, we will stay in smaller towns where the casa particular is important. You will see. We'll have opportunities to be down to earth."

"I'm sorry. I'll be fine, Lana."

"Good," she said without further coddle.

A porter helped them with the luggage up a long stone staircase to the front lobby. As they checked in, a loud jingle interrupted their conversation. It was DK's cell phone on its satellite connection. He stepped aside from the registration desk, just in case the call was professional, but it came from the Havantur Guide, Angelina. She apologized for missing them at Marina Hemingway, but would meet them in an hour at the hotel. When DK explained their research mission, Angelina assured him that this very day they would meet with a group of living artists who might have information on ancient art pieces.

"She says," he looked up to tell his companions, "Angelina is her name…she will come for us in an hour. She wants to take us to a neighborhood art group where people have long ties to the area. An artist there may have heard of the *Masque*. In any case, then she will then take us to look elsewhere."

"That sounds like such a tentative schedule," Luc complained.

Lana interrupted, "Luc I'm familiar with the issue of meetings and appointments here. Angelina is not in a position to guarantee meetings with anyone, for one reason or another. Most actions require permission from someone up the ladder. We do not want to complain and stir up any feelings against the regime, or us. Remember what that old cigar storeowner told me in Key West? 'Everyone everywhere has good and bad to say about their country, but we don't have to encourage any dissention.'"

"Can't we just move around independently?"

"It's not done that way at present. Besides, we are not doing a straightforward beach and nightclub vacation. Ours will require entré to things and information not necessarily easy to get. It will be very helpful to have a driver for the long distance we plan. You will see. We'll actually get more accomplished than if we were on our own."

The hotel accommodation was spacious and in very good repair. All the small amenities that westerners sought in a hotel were available. The furniture was sturdy but plain and the décor was simple. The colors had yet to be refurbished from browns and cream to the bright colors so loved by the Cuban people. However, like many things for tourists, this was another aspect of life where local incomes could not compete with dollar pricing. Not yet anyway.

Before they began the day's search, Luc opened the treasure map. He pushed his finger along some faded words near the top of the map page. A crosshatch was sketched, a universal cartographer's mark for mountains or even hills. The word "Rio" was one word still legible on the faded calfskin map. "Those marks indicate a beautiful, hilly and verdant region called Pinar del Rio. My ancestors believed that when the *Masque of Gold* was taken from Havana for safety, it traveled first to the nearest dense hills. It makes sense to me, so yes, we will follow the map route, starting there. Based on the treasure map the logical path of the *Masque* went from Pinar del Rio Province all the way to the eastern shore, to the Punta de Mais. We'll go one step at a time until we find the artifact."

"If the treasure was moved around, how did your family know where it was going over the centuries?" DK asked.

"Over all that time our ancestors did voyage sporadically between the islands for trade and adventure. The legend says that a Pio trader would ask about the *Masque* from time to time, but it was never the right moment to take it, or have it. There were wars, subjugations, dispersion and poverty on both sides. A lot of this knowledge was handed down in oral tradition, but the map itself was brought up to date as we could. I believe that my ancestors kept an honest record of what they knew over the years. I know that additional notes have faded from the original hide, but I'm hoping that the people here can help us anyway."

"I see. Where do you think it might be?" DK asked.

"It would have to be out of the elements. Perhaps it is held in a museum or a church, or perhaps it is still hidden in a cave or burial site. If it is buried, I doubt that we will find it this trip and neither will Sonoteas. Neither of us has any clues other than the map and it doesn't indicate an underground location except at the end, with the Taino."

"Luc, how is it that Sonoteas is against his own people?"

Luc was silent. Gusta stared at him and then spoke. "The Pios have a difficult time admitting to a spoiled apple in the family. I told you I have not trusted Sonoteas for years. I love Father Pio, but he has been too lenient as a leader. He thinks that Sonoteas was a dear toddler, but I remember that he could be spiteful. One day his father scolded him severely, and he jumped on his dad's motorcycle, gunned it and lost control. He smashed it up, there and then, out of revenge."

"Is that what caused the scars on his arm?"

"Yes, his elbow required several operations and now it holds a pin."

"His elbow must hurt him often."

"Yes it does Lana. Sonoteas took a hard tumble, but that anger comes from a difficult moment. I remember it."

"Yes?"

"I guess one day before the smashup, tempers were running high at home when the father was repairing a car. Sonoteas scooted under it to play a joke in spite of his dad wanting him out of the garage. Then the father lowered the vehicle. Sonoteas always claimed his father did it on purpose. It pinned the ten-year old's hand. When Sonoteas started to scream in pain, the father wouldn't let anyone help him. Instead, he left him there for a few minutes to suffer. When he finally pulled him up, he shook him and shouted twice, "That will teach you. I always have to teach you, again and again. Do what I tell you!"

"I was his buddy then and saw it all. None of us were allowed to help him. I guess the father had no patience, should not have been a father, I guess. *'Crying are you?'* His father continued yelling, *'Something hurts you? Well... just rub it.'*"

Lana and DK remained silent.

"None of us ever forgot that moment," Gusta said.

"I imagine that Sonoteas never did either," Lana commented sadly.

Chapter 16

They were beginning their adventure on an island called Cuba. An island that is not an island like most on the earth. It is not a stretch of sand and hills, inhabited by relaxed natives, boasting endless palm trees and fruits of the orchard, like the paintings of Gauguin. It is a large and complex entity; a country aware of its long-layered, cultural influences and political struggles. It is a landscape nourished by natural resources, protected by rocky coasts and numerous mountains, but one that de-mands extraordinary labor of its people. Expansive farm-lands roll up to Cuba's smoky valleys, or to her sandy, dry leeward hills, or to an impassable mountain shear. Every corner or industrious town is worked with patience and inventiveness. Without a doubt, Cuba is a land uniquely herself, sprouted by blood, and washed in love.

The team of seekers left their rooms and headed out to meet Angelina and her driver, Luis. DK stepped from the hotel elevator to join Lana.

"You look bright and bushy-tailed, my dear. All ready?"

"We are going after a treasure!" she exclaimed excited about a new adventure.

He acknowledged her, but was not as excited as she to be on Luc's quest. Taking her hand, he said something akin to their first meeting a year ago. The poetry had surprised her then and now it arched straight to her heart.

"We've made it to this exotic country, and I'm happy for Luc. As for me, I would love to enjoy Cuba with you. You see, I *have* my treasure. Right here," and he gently tugged her arm.

Luc chuckled at the romanticism of his new friend and teased him. "You should be Cuban with that persistence."

"Maybe so, maybe so."

"Look," Lana pointed. "That must be Angelina waiting for us."

After introductions, Luis, the assigned driver, drove the six of them down Camilo Cienfuegos to Porvenir Street. From there Angelina led the group into a large square. There many people were dressed in paint-spattered overalls, absorbed by their tasks, painting the walls with images, or standing off to the side, sculpting forms. The artists were intent on creating what they called, the People's Art Gallery.

"The Peña Communitaria improves the old barrio and provides an opportunity for neighborhood unity and a path to self-sufficiency," Angelina repeated, indicating the spot for entrance donation. She interrupted one of the artists who stopped to greet them. His painting held a large face with vibrant eyes. The background was very colorful, and the visitors liked its power.

"We like your work, sir." Lana told him.

"Thank you for taking the trouble to visit us," he said. My friends and I love art, and this is our way to express ourselves and to improve our lives. We do not become rich from this, but as you know, a worker can never get rich."

Angelina stopped him. "Some of us will get rich, Julio. You will see."

Lana looked around at the busy square and asked if Julio had a studio with small paintings for sale. She could tell he was educated and strong. He wore a wedding band, was good-looking and well spoken. He might work at any number of employments, but here he could be what he loved, a paid artist.

"Not I, señorita, but some Cubans do. Many of them live and work in the countryside, but you can see their art pieces for sale during art events along the Malecon. There is a large market fair weekly. You must attend. There you will see many wonderful pieces of all sizes. Our Cuban art is well-received world over. Many artists are in high demand by the Europeans who visit us."

"Thank you," Lana commented softly, but bold enough to broach the subject of a mask. "May I ask if you know about such a thing here in Havana?"

"What kind of masks?" he asked warily.

"We are trying to find a 500 year old Native American *Masque* like this one. It is called the *Masque of Gold*." She showed him her drawing of it.

The painter looked at it and then at Angelina who nodded to him.

"No, señórita. I have never seen this. It doesn't look familiar to our folklore." He paused, "I feel you are sincere people in your quest, so I must tell you something. It is harsh to hear, but after 500 years, I think your treasure is gone. Many people have come and gone in this small country. So, if your treasure hasn't been taken as booty by invaders or traded by citizens for food, then it has turned to powder under the soil."

He handed back the drawing to Lana, and with a smile, he nodded to them all, "Please excuse me now."

They admired more of the art pieces, and then retreated from the square. The van Luis drove was parked near Paseo di Marti.

"So, Lana, what does this mean?" Luc asked her.

"It means we have a lot of searching to do, but I hope we can accept that the *Masque of Gold* may only be a myth, something of time-past, something lost."

Luc shook his head, saying "No."

Gusta remained quiet at his side.

Angelina interrupted them after a short drive. "Luis will drop us off here and we'll meet up with him at the train station."

Luis pulled over.

Angelina explained that they were at the Habana Vieja. "Here is where so many buildings date from the sixteenth and seventeenth century, the era of Spanish domination. You may find your old *Masque* on display, or camouflaged, sitting in a niche, on one of the old walls."

The group chatted about the interesting buildings and the improvements being made for infrastructure as they walked cobblestone streets. They tried to identify which niche or building could have been built on top of a 500-year-old structure. The idea of finding their *Masque* in an area grown up and re-visited by various peoples for centuries was preposterous to Angelina. She held back from her thoughts, but pressed Luc about his obsession, "Is the old *Masque* so important in America? Do people want to go back to something old?"

He nodded. "It has special meaning to my family. It's been our dream to find its blessings again."

"That is so strange, senōr Luc. Here we are trying so hard to look forward, not back. The world is going places without us."

DK spoke in a low voice to Lana, "The Pios may have to accept that the *Masque of Gold* can never return a culture to the way it used to be. Reclaiming what existed in the past is out of balance with the universe."

"I agree, but we have just begun the search. At some point Luc will have to make the decision, whether the clues are valid to push onward or whether the *Masque* has another meaning, another purpose or another future."

"I heard you two," Luc said. "I will make the best decision I can, for all involved."

DK winked at her, "It took a storm to shake some of our old ideas, didn't it?"

"Yes, but I think Luc may learn them faster than I." She winked back. "Where shall we go next Luc?"

He came to a stop. "I'm sorry everyone, but I feel that my injuries are slowing me down. You know my people do not usually take painkillers, so I think it is best if I rest at this point. Gusta can take care of me, and we will leave the old town soon to rest at the hotel. Lana would you and DK be willing to carry on today? Perhaps you'd go to the relevant museums and ask on my behalf."

"Glad to do it," Lana answered.

Luc's face relaxed and he took Gusta's arm. "Come. We will all meet again at the hotel for a quiet dinner together."

Angelina showed dismay at splitting up the group, "I don't know if..."

DK took her aside, arm in hers, producing a wide boyish grin, "Angelina I'm sure it would be easier on you to lead a smaller group. Lana and I will stay with you. Luc can nurse his injuries. Gusta, can you take care of him and stay out of trouble." DK's natural broad smile won over the young girl's dogmatic rules, and she melted before the handsome American. She could believe this American.

"All right. So, Luc will stay out of trouble?"

"Absolutely," Luc confirmed. "You have heard Gusta and I speak conversational Spanish. Even with our dialect people seem to understand us, so we won't be a trouble to them."

Angelina considered Luc a shy, nice person. Coupled with his infirmity, he was no threat to the country. He could wander a bit on his own. She did not expect any trouble, but she was not sure about the burly man Gusta. She would have them watched, just in case. She halted the group to enjoy the Cathedral de la Habana while she slipped off for a quick phone call.

Luc puzzled over the age of the lovely church. "Perhaps the *Masque* was hidden here, maybe under a stone of this plaza?"

"I doubt it, Luc," Lana told him, looking at the guidebook. "The church came two centuries after the visit from Ponce de León. Based on your family's legend, the artifact was moved out of Havana before that. Anyway, it is not likely that a pagan god would have been displayed in that Jesuit cathedral. If it were ever housed here, the valuable gold would have been separated from the skull long ago by one non-believer, or another."

Angelina led Lana and DK along, down the Calle Mercaderes. "We have a number of interesting museums in Habana, but I have never heard that any of them house the unique *Masque*. Only the Museo de Arqueologia would be appropriate."

Lana looked around at the busy city and reviewed a page of her guidebook. "It seems more cosmopolitan here than I remember from my tours ten years ago. There is more entrepreneurship than when I visited before. I see more restaurants and little shops. This is fun. Oh well, we must keep our mind on the goal. Let us go to the antiquities museum and to the Museo de la Ciudad opposite the Plaza de Armas. Maybe we can even visit the "Museo del Chocolate," she concluded with a coy smile at D.K.

"Surely," Dusty agreed, and then registered surprise at Angelina's answer.

"Oh yes, that's a lovely place, an historic mansion displaying Belgium artifacts to do with chocolate making. There are lovely pieces of porcelain; cups, bowls, and many other pieces contributed by England. However, I'm sorry to say, we cannot go there today."

"Oh," Lana said with a touch of regret. "Why?"

"It is just that way. Today it is closed."

Lana walked on without a further word of protest. They passed Calle O'Reilly and then came upon the Plaza de Armas where they rediscovered Luc. He'd found a place to sit opposite the statue of Carlos Manuel de Céspedes, and signaled them over, pointing to the great statue.

"Now there was a brave man, and yet how destiny and change turned on him. In 1868 he started the *Cry of Yara*. He began the fight against slavery under Spanish rule. Later he was elected President of the Republic, but opposed by wealthy landowners which required slave labor, he was assassinated. Imagine that! Change is slow after all," he said despondent. Lifting his head to study the hero's face again, Luc sighed. "It is as if the old warrior looks through me. He seems to say, *considering all the stories of the past and all the yearnings of mankind, of the whole world with its ideals and conflicts, what possible good can your old Masque do?*"

"Luc don't worry. We do not know yet whether there is any limit of good from your *quest*. We must just keep searching while we can. There is more to this now anyway."

"Yes," Luc sighed. "Now we have to stop my cousin."

He stood to leave and waved Adios to Lana. Gusta stayed at his side, and the two ambled up a side street.

Angelina signaled Lana and DK toward another direction and they walked down streets paved with cobblestone, polished round with time. When they reached the hotel Ambos Mundos, Lana recognized it as a favorite hotel for Hemingway before he bought his estate Finca Vigia. "Will we be able to go to the Hemingway estate, Angelina? Perhaps some of the local fishermen there remember Papa's many conversations with them. Perhaps they heard of the *Masque of Gold* from him since both were American in origin. Perhaps in casual conversation we can learn something?"

The guide registered surprise at the desire to question people, but she did not let it throw her. Although authorized to tour the Americans and to provide the tour company car, she had to be careful not to overstep liberties that might appear subversive to the homeland. "With whom would you like to speak, Lana? Remember we have laws that prohibit a person from offending the dignity or authority of the Republic."

"I certainly don't want to do that! Just the opposite. I love it here, and I'd like to meet everyday families."

"I'm an everyday person, Lana. Ask me what you will. In addition, we can inquire from institutions and authorities about the *Masque of Gold*, but getting too personal with Cubans can put them at risk. We don't want to interfere with their work either." Angelina noticed Lana's dismay. "Ah well, things are freeing up now, perhaps you may speak to some people, but I think that it is best to go through me."

"Can we visit Finca Vigia outside of town?"

"Yes. I will arrange it. I do not know if the fishermen your American writer loved are still alive in his little town of Cojimar, but we will see. We will go tomorrow."

"What about something to eat now? We did not have much breakfast on the boat. Is there a place for a late lunch nearby? A place where people chat together?"

"We can go to El Templete nearby for very good food, but this is a business district so people cannot linger for personal discussions. They must return to their offices where there is plenty of work to do. I don't want a fine for exceeding my permissions either."

Lana understood the dangers of her boundless curiosity, but she wanted to learn about the country and find clues to the *Masque*. Anything she did could be misconstrued, but she certainly had no plans to be subversive. Therefore, she decided not to hold back if an opportunity to learn something arose.

The trio had come upon a large open-door restaurant where food would be a perfect diversion for the moment. Fragrant fresh spices lured them inside, and a waiter led them across spotless, dark oak floors, highly polished. Centuries of footfalls were grooved upon the boards. The wood chairs were simple but restful, even for a man DK's size. The three sat facing large windows open to the outside. Skilled musicians sat on the veranda, playing music that filtered around them, filling the place with rhythm and joy.

The scent of sizzling fish filet excited one's appetite, and the three of them turned silent to consume a good meal. However, at one point, the proprietor skirted their table, and Lana stopped him to praise the wonderful food, "It's the best I've ever had."

He made a small sound and lifted his head with pride.

She pressed on, "Are all your guests business people?"

He did not linger to answer, busy with a full house of clientele, but Angelina spoke up quickly, as if to defend him. "Leave him alone, Lana. Why do you push things? Don't you see he has important people here and lots to do."

"I'm sorry. I wanted to be friendly."

"Here, as on any island community, behavior must follow tradition, you understand? You are not a known quantity and people must be careful. We accommodate each other in order to live in harmony. Besides, here we aren't comfortable pushing our own importance."

Lana realized that Angelina's statement was true. Even in a vast country, like home, freedoms required graciousness and tact. Some freedoms held responsibilities that some people chose to ignore. She didn't want to be one of them.

"I'm sorry if I was selfish. I am not usually that way."

"Well, thank you for that understanding. We must support our government and our laws. You see that many of us are still poor, but you cannot appreciate what it was before the revolution. You were not alive to know that in the 1930s a fancy meal at the Casino de Capri would run $350 American dollars a person when the same thing was $10 in New York. It was only movie stars, gangsters and, well, you know, people with connections who could enjoy life here then. Money made it fast and glitzy in Havana while many Cubans were starving." She paused, "We don't want that again, at least with our system today there is order. There is some peace, some work, some food, some education and some medical help. It was bumpy in the early years, but things have gotten better. Now, however, we know that "some" is not enough anymore."

Lana looked at her. "Do you think that everything is fine?"

Angelina rocked her head, stammering, "Well yes, and no. We have a way to go, but it is not like under the former old dictator who was the worst. He struck down voices of protest by spying, wiretapping, hanging, castrating or imprisoning. We live with certain limitations now, but everyone is saying there are opportunities coming." Angelina began to click her fork up and down on the empty plate, as if she would like more to eat, but at DK's offer, she renounced desert. "Maybe things are just slower…slower than I'd like."

Lana sat there worried and unsure how to remove the gloom she had created.

"Is everything in life perfect where you live?" Angelina blurted, extending an olive branch and revealing a sweet expression. "Some have told me so."

"Never mind Angelina. No harm done on either side. This is a lovely restaurant. You have taken us to beautiful places and we've spoken with beautiful people today."

"Including you both." DK pro-offered peace, as he pulled the chairs from each of his companions and led them outside into the clear winter sunshine.

Others in the restaurant seemed in a hurry, not in the mood to chat as Hemingway might have pursued so long ago. Lana looked around again. Times were different from Hemingway's era and she had not built friendships over time as he had. She wasn't an "habitué". She hadn't earned the right to ask personal questions. Her mind snapshotted through a recollection of changes seen in the world over 500 years and she realized that the world's progress was accomplished without any interference from her. She wasn't a fortune teller and did not know how things would flow.

To be sure, she did not see very well into the future: Lana did not realize she was about to be thrown from a train.

----✖----

At the Museo de la Ciudad and then the Palacio de los Capitanes Generales, Luc and Gusta found no clue to an ancient *Masque of Gold*. They walked the shaded corridors of the city's museum and they took the visitor's tour of the old palace. "Keep looking, senór," the museum guard encouraged Luc, "But keep in mind that your dream of history-recaptured is a hope in the past. That artifact may have been taken from us and spirited to other countries long ago. Moreover, if not, why do you want to take something from us now? Maybe whoever has it needs it? Who knows? Not I."

Gusta watched Luc's shoulders slump. Luc protested afterward. "Even at the beautiful Palacio Del Segundo Cabo, preserved since 1780, things are old. Why is it so hard to think that a *Masque of Gold*, a god figure, could not also be preserved?"

"But, it isn't in this place, Luc. Let it go. We can investigate around the block at the Castillo de la Real Fuerza. The guidebook says that this fortress was built around the time of Ponce de León. Perhaps it offers a niche, a display place where the *Masque* has become unrecognizable, covered with moss. In any case, there is hope, Luc," Gusta said with a patient tone. "There are many beautiful places to see beyond the capital. We will just press ahead until we find the valuable *Masque*. Perhaps we will meet-up with just the person who has it and is very glad to get rid of it."

However, they did not find such a person that day. Moreover, they did not notice two men loitering near them. Luc and Gusta were innocents who did not evaluate the harm their personal desires would set in motion.

Chapter 17

Angelina had never met Sonoteas, but she kept a lookout along with Lana and DK. The three glanced down side street after side street, tiring themselves out looking at the interesting facades and the old avenues. Much of the city was under renovation, these days and the clusters of material or machinery that they found here and there impeded some of their search, but they saw many fresh corners and all the important museums in the city's center.

Luis trailed them in the van and would park at appropriate places, then watch out for his charges until the next advance. He did not hear their conversation nor realize that they were also looking for a man called Sonoteas. To DK, Luis appeared disinterested in the little group from America and whatever troubled them, but he did not discount his importance. Luis never said a word to them or to Angelina the entire day. He just drove, and he kept notes in his little logbook.

Angelina related all the historical facts of a city tour as required, and hoped that the strange Americans would acknowledge her sincere efforts to please. She walked with her head high, her long, black, curly hair flouncing around her shoulders and her arms in swing with every step. She grew quiet after a few hours of explaining the city as the serious businessperson that her role demanded. Gradually she revealed her interest in all things modern and would bob her head to some peppy Cuban tune that might erupt from a small shop opening or a residence window. She was shapely and smart, tough and talented. However, she would prove herself too young for a life of intrigue.

As they approached the train station, she remembered to tell her two visitors that her phone call to the tour supervisor yielded no information on a man called Sonoteas. He had not signed up for a guide, or a tour, or a car rental or purchased an airline ticket.

"…But you still seem to worry? Are you sure he is here? He is so bad?"

"He is," agent Cody told her with authority.

"Oh. Then what should we do next?"

Lana studied her guidebook. "We have covered all the old parts of town and only have the archeological museum to visit."

"Sure, Miss Lana," Angelina responded.

Then DK's phone range. "What? …What? …I don't believe it!" he blurted to the caller. "All right. Since you cannot find Luc, I give you authorization. Fix everything."

Lana waited for the explanation.

"Someone broke into the *Esmeralda* while she was at the repair dock. They ripped out the fire extinguisher."

"Why would they do that?" Lana asked. Then she gasped, "DK something was odd about that canister. I noticed that it had been repainted in an off tone of red. I thought that such a miss-match was strange for a boat with all new equipment."

"Huh? Ah, well. Check another one off for Sonoteas. He is the likely culprit because an ordinary thief would have ripped out the new radio and radar screen. Anyway, everything will be fixed. Let's just move on. Now we know there really is some harm planned. The canister must hold something. We also know that Sonoteas is still in town. The theft took place just an hour ago, in spite of the guard. They think that the thief swam under the dock and boarded that way."

"He is fortunate not to be shot," Angelina stated. "Why is he doing these things?"

The three discussed their opponent and answered Angelina's questions about America as they walked the last leg of the day's search. As Lana pulled ahead of them, they neared the train station. Crossing the broad thoroughfare, Lana spotted a bulky backpack 150 feet ahead of her. The man seemed weighed down by it.

She cried out and then bolted into the crowd.

Angelina and DK were startled. They did not follow Lana's garbled remark at first. DK called after her, but she did not stop. By the time DK ran to the train arcade, Lana had dissolved into the crowded station.

DK called back to Angelina, "I believe she spotted the thief. We have to catch him! Wait here for us."

Angelina stood there watching him ever, the agile military man. He swept through the heavy Christmas holiday crowd into the cavernous arcade, sidestepping people as politely as possible. He studied faces hoping to spot Sonoteas, knowing that Lana's golden-red hair would automatically catch his attention. Having no luck seeing either of his targets, he checked the large schedule board looking for the upcoming departures. He had to decipher the Spanish electronic signs as they changed rapidly indicating arrivals, departures and changing tracks. It took him a few minutes to decide which track might be the one for Sonoteas and to run for its platform, but that track was empty. That train had departed. He searched the board again and found the platform for a train to Viñales, in the Pinar del Rio Province, but when he ran up, its wheels had begun to turn and he could not tell if Lana had boarded or lost her prey and returned to Angelina.

Lana had boarded it. She had darted from the arcade into the vast structure, which shielded the train cars, keeping her eye on Sonoteas and following close on his heels. When he boarded a train, she followed suit, not aware of its imminent departure, nor that DK was so far behind her. She kept going, trailing Sonoteas through several cars, looking back between car one and two and then again between three and four, but she did not spot DK. Still, she would not lose the culprit. Four cars along, Sonoteas dropped into a seat. He sat in the middle of the car and Lana had to do a fast turn-around, hiding in the vestibule, balancing her feet on the connected metal floors, pressing her back against a wall. She thought he had not seen her.

She opened the passage outside door and leaned out between the two cars. No one was coming down the platform after her. A few cars back the conductor hung out his own doorway until the train lurched forward. Lana knew that a serious game was in play, but nothing would stop her now. She was on her own again but danger had begun to dull that thrill. The train's large iron wheels turned reluctantly, slowly increasing their effort, as if to object to another day's work. The cars rattled and pulled away from their protective arcade.

Lana hoped the conductor would pass soon before she had to confront Sonoteas. She stayed calm with a plan to have the police called to meet them. She peered back between the cars to see if DK had caught up with her, but still no friendly face appeared, not even the conductor's. The train picked up speed. Lana craned her neck to see around the doorway at Sonoteas's seat just as a bearded man went to join him. *That man is not a stranger,* Lana moaned in recognition, *and he isn't Cuban.* She saw the man say something to Sonoteas, exchange a parcel. He wasted no time to move on. H passed through the opposite door to the car ahead and disappeared. He was carrying Sonoteas's parcel, a fat tubular shaped package, heavy looking like a fire extinguisher. She could not see what he had given Sonoteas in return, but it looked like a solid cigarette package.

The train had yet to reach its full power, so Lana assumed that it was preparing for a track switch. Instead the train maintained a slow speed. She peered out to the tracks, and saw men at work. When she turned back to look inside the car again, she saw Sonoteas moving her way. It was ridiculous to try for invisibility, but she did, pressing to the corner of the open door. *He might walk right by...*

Sonoteas knew all along that she had followed him onto the train and he came around from the car onto the bobbing platform to greet her with a self-satisfied grin. She was cornered in the passageway hoping someone else would pass through to help her, but the clack of wheels and rumble of iron signified more than nothing, it signified a lonely reality. She tried to shove him aside but he had her cornered with walls on two sides, he facing her and open space at her back. The rusting tracks that ran alongside Lana's train began to vibrate. Another train roared by whipping her hair onto her face and pressing her toward the pursuer.

Once past them, the long inbound train made space on its track and after sounds of shifting rails, Lana saw her train enter the countryside. Sonoteas pressed closer to her, enjoying his dominance. Lana turned her head one way and the other, evaluating her possible escape, but there was none within the train cars. That left only the vast world behind her. When a sign popped indicating an upcoming local station, Lana moaned. The sign on her car said, *express*—not likely to stop. She felt her train jerk beneath her. The train engineer was changing again, slowing to pass the passenger platform...just enough seconds for her to think...

Lana realized that escape was now, or never. She leaned out the edge of the open door, hoping to leap onto the mounded dirt shoulders separating the tracks from a parallel road. Her opponent did not intend to let her go without his help. He clutched her waist with both arms and in one swift motion; he lifted her into the air. She was destined to arc off onto the tracks instead of the sandy shoulder. By instinct, Lana threw out one arm to grasp the car's handle, pushing Sonoteas back with the other. Her opponent had the advantage and continued to push her into the void, but she clung hard to the handle so that the thrust from Sonoteas threw her into a semi-circle, slamming her back into the car's outer wall, her feet paddling in the open air. She hung there a number of seconds, reaching the other arm to a window ledge and clutching it for all she was worth. The safari jacket she wore, stuffed with papers, padded her and then snagged on a train fitting. She could hear it begin to tear, her weight pulling Lana down. Her new hat and scarf flew off in the wind, but before she could choose an action, the concrete platform was searing alongside her. Sonoteas reached out to grope at her, slapping and beating her fingers on the handle. Nonetheless, she hung there, her fingers going numb and her thighs cramping.

The platform was coming to an end and before Lana's eyes a rebirth of dirt shoulder loomed. She knew that time was up, while the train stayed slow, perhaps ten miles an hour—she would have to drop. So, with her feet pressed against the car, using every muscle in her legs, her other arm ready to push her outward, Lana focused on the wild, bushy clumps of foliage running fast toward her.

First, she hit a cushion of brush and briars with one leg and a rump, then her body collapsed like a bag of bones and the wind rushed out of her. Lana let herself roll down the slope slowing over a path of stones. She ended up beside the road, in a dry ditch, still.

Sonoteas snapped a farewell hiss at her, and the train to Viñales rumbled away.

When DK found Angelina an hour later, she saw the concern on his face. He was empty-handed and alone, holding a straw had with a green scarf.

"Where is Lana?" she asked, noticing the soiled hat.

"You haven't seen her?"

"No."

"Well then it must be Lana laying along the tracks. A worker reported a women hanging off the train. He had ferried back to the stationmaster with the hat. The police are sending a crew to see what they can find."

Angelina answered, beginning to shake, "We must go to the station police immediately." Neither of them knew whether they would have to face a killer to the bitter end; whether Lana lay dying on the track.

Angelina was seated in the police corridor, wringing her hands waiting. Agent Cody was standing stock-still. After painful minutes, they were told that a body had been retrieved near the tracks. Angelina had never seen a man go so pale. The icy glint in DK's eye contrasted against his ruddy skin. The other worldliness of his stare made her skin crawl. They waited for an hour until railway medics arrived with a woman in a wheelchair, heading toward the medical office. A nurse stood at attention, waiting.

DK and Angelina raced across the lobby to meet Lana whom they could finally hear. She was protesting loudly. "No! No hospital. I have work to do. Let me go!"

Dusty Kern Cody swept down to Lana and gathered her up from the chair, kissing her head repeatedly until Angelina laughed.

"You better get some x-rays anyway," he said. "Maybe you are too numb to feel anything now, but you should be checked for broken bones and a concussion."

"We have to get after him," Lana managed to utter between squeezes. "Easy now, DK. I am very sore."

"Lana," he said sternly, "We are going to the hospital."

She put an arm around his shoulders. "Now be patient with me. Let's see how I feel later. I did not hit my head or my back, and look, ...put me down. I can walk, if I favor my hip and knee." Lana ran her hand through her reddish curls, then rubbed a limp-looking wrist. She straightened-up with a wince, and commanded that they continue. "Oh I hurt, but it isn't serious. I fell on a lot of bushes, so I'm scratched up, but that's most of it. The swellings are not serious!"

The railway medics weren't convinced and sat her down again, wrapping her knee and wrist in ice. Lana was commanded by the nurse to sit like that for twenty more minutes while they doctored a myriad of cuts.

"The real problem is Sonoteas," she resumed. "He's now on his way to Viñales with a head start. I suspect that he stayed in Havana just long enough to determine that we had no leads."

Angelina interrupted her. "He should be traveling with a local guide, you know. I feel sure he will not last without one. Unless he has an inside accomplice, he will not be permitted to question people for days on end. This is considered too much intrusion. This will be noticed and followed."

DK stood tall, swinging his jacket over a shoulder, his arms more tan than at the beginning of his six days earlier, his face concerned with the events. "*Masque* or not, Angelina, this man has harmed people and property, broken the law and continues to do malicious deeds. You must report him again. Ask that police be alerted to look for him along our route. Here, make a copy of this itinerary and have the police forward the information to police stations in each town listed. Maybe they can alert the hotels. Whatever means of travel he plans, he will be following the same route as our treasure map. I know that we are on a collision course. If I am a judge of his terrorist connections, then the end result of their plans is meant to affect one of your cities."

"Oh my, and he will continue to look for the *Masque* like you?"

"Of course. Whatever the artifact stands for, it means wealth. It can be used for good or evil. You must help us gain time over him."

"I can save you some time after Viñales because without an official guide, these bad men may not realize what shortcuts or other corners to take. You told me that his two friends are not Cuban, so they won't know either. Besides, some locations require official permission to enter, and you said he lost his paperwork. I have permission to question at these locations on your map. Without proper documentation, he has to avoid capture, he won't get much help. He will look over his shoulder often and that is suspicious too."

"Thanks for supporting us Angelina. It is sad to miss so much of your beautiful country by traveling on like this, but we have to keep our eye on the goal. Sonoteas must not find the *Masque* to do whatever harm he has in mind."

DK's eyes had returned to blue as he helped Lana into Luis's van. "We will go for ex-rays, my dear. No argument."

Lana knew he meant to do as he said, but pleaded, "Let's try one more museum before closing time? After all, we have to move on in the morning. The Palacio de Bellas Artes has an excellent section of antiquities. Really DK, we *really* should speak to the people there."

DK looked at her winsome face, scratched and still dirty. He straightened her torn and un-snapped safari jacket, looking steadily at her pupils. "You don't show concusion. Oh my, Lana. You are a bundle, but you have always had me at 'go,' he told her gently. After the museum we go directly to the hospital for an ex-ray!"

"We'll see…boss," she uttered with a grin to Angelina.

Angelina studied Lana and did not take the bite of charm from the red-head who did what she wanted, and forced them to her will. "Really? You want to go into a museum now?" She gave a quizzical side-glance to Luis who said nothing. When he too recognized that Lana was firm, Luis pointed in the direction of Empedrado, "We can cut across to Avenida de Las Misiones."

Limping without protest, Lana kept up with the three others to board the van. Angelina relayed the story about Sonoteas in Spanish to Luis, and he nodded without responding. DK noticed his interest and his silence and that once at the museum, Luis personally waited outside the entry for them, standing like a royal guard. Inside, Angelina led them to the administration area, and Lana made a beeline to the curator's office. Keeping up with her, DK tilted his head toward Lana, "You do the talking. I still don't want to act in any official capacity, okay?"

"Sure. We will keep you our national secret."

Angelina listened to their every word, and she kept a mental ledger.

The curator was locking his office for the day, but responded to their breathless entreaty. "…If your question is succinct," he answered in clear English, re-affirming a high level of education.

"All we need to know is whether you have a collection of masks, and if so do you have something like this?" Lana pulled out her drawing of the *Masque of Gold* and turned to show the picture to Señor Alvarez, whose name was on the door.

"No. I do not have this *Masque*, nor have I ever seen one like it." He handed the paper back, ushering them along the hallway. As they walked together out of the museum, Alvarez paused. "I do remember a similar inquiry once, at a seminar of mine a few years ago. A man claiming to be a Taino native presented a sketch such as yours and asked about its provenance. I said then, and I say now, that such a mask is not of Taino origin. Many different peoples occupied the islands of the Greater Antilles over a thousand years. However, I do not recognize this style from any of those groups. I might add that I have never seen nor heard of any other Caribbean Island masks like it. Have you thought that its origin might come from further away?"

"We do not think so, but, possibly," Lana answered. "Thank you for your trouble sir."

"Not at all. It does sound like a very interesting object. The Cuban people would appreciate such an interesting and fine art object in their collection. I certainly hope you don't plan to take it away or extract the gold."

"Not exactly. That's why we are in a haste to find it before others do."

"Well then, I will hope for your success, and to see this valuable in our museum," he smiled with a true curator's mission in mind.

As he darted away, DK turned to the two women. "He didn't really trust our motives which I can understand, but if an informed personage as he, with as important collection as the Bellas Artes, has no knowledge of the *Masque of Gold,* it may be a myth after all."

Lana rubbed her forehead and leaned on DK as they returned to the car. "You know, I still believe in the quest DK. Cuba could still hold an age-old secret."

DK looked at Lana and saw the look of the Irish cross her expression, "Of course we must continue. We must try, even if only to outwit Sonoteas."

She seemed to collapse into him.

"Lana you've gone pale."

"Yes, I am feeling very weary now. Would you mind if I had a brandy? I'm feeling sore everywhere."

DK put an arm around both of the women. "Sure, it's been a difficult day. Would you both like to stop at a favorite Hemingway haunt, La Floridita? It isn't far from here I believe."

"That's right," Angelina confirmed, "and it is only five o'clock. I have time before I report back." She turned flirtatious with a buttery sigh. "Yes, let's go. We will try Hemingway's famous Daiquiri there. I know the bartender, and he makes them terrific." She purred at DK, pressing his arm more and indicating Lana's limp. "I guess there will be no dancing tonight unless you'd like to go with me?" She purred again.

"Oh I can't," he stammered. "Duty calls first."

DK reached for Lana's elbow to help her hobble forward. Seeing Lana's expression, he smiled and then whispered to her, "Not my fault."

As Luis helped Lana toward the van, he smiled at his charges, sensing that some electricity was bouncing between them. Like a knowing uncle, ready to arbitrate family disputes, he spread his arms out to DK and Lana alike, gathering them into the vehicle. He knew that Angelina's flirtation was a problem for Lana, because he recognized jealousy – he had two daughters. Therefore, he tried to provide distraction, joking about the train system still in need of infrastructure improvements. Nonetheless, Lana just sat in the van without comment, the soreness of her body growing. Her spirit also registered discomfort. Encountering insult happens to everyone, but it was not that. Lana's core had grown in concert over one person. She sat behind Luis, and from the mirror, he watched her simmer.

―∞∞∞―

Old storytellers did not come to the Floridita anymore. After sixty years of new government and worldly commerce, the Parque Central had come into its own as a center of international commerce. The country had been modernizing slowly, but with the possibility of America's tourism, many more plans were afoot. So, most people were too busy in this part of town for afternoons of careless banter. Moreover, when they did meet up, it was for moving the economy. Therefore, Lana would not hear anything but business in these quarters, and she was too sore to care. Besides, people here were on the clock. However, she did consider the possibility of a rumor because history creeps into conversations anywhere you go in the world.

Anywhere you go in the world, people have memories that muse over the past. Here, these were not about the *Masque*. Perhaps they would be, but if not, they would be different over time. At some future date, when Cuba was modern, and prosperity reigned for all, it would reminisce as people do now in other major cities of the world. Nostalgia would come at last. Nostalgia for quiet; when mechanical speakers were at low decibel, when cell-phones didn't ring all day, when the pace of living was slower than the flashing pixels of a world-wide-web—when there was calm enough to grow a true friend, not a thousand faces. Those memories would hover like the pleasing fragrance of great-great-grandmother's fresh baking bread. Therefore, even at the Floridita, one day people would speak as anywhere else: They might speak of the present, the future, or the past, but today they would be still wary of personal questions. Present herself as she might, nothing personal would be told to Lana. Eavesdrop as she might, nothing of compromise would slip by the lips of others in this busy, guarded business corner. The lips around her would enjoy delicious, steaming shellfish and swallows of rum and minted sugar.

Newly refurbished, the Floridita was visited by tourists for, once again the CUP earnings were not sufficient. Cuba makes the best rum, but it too is out of reach for the simple wage. So this is not yet a place of memory for the citizens, however those who came were glad. For any visitor who can slip beneath the bold outdoor signage and come through the corner entry with dollars for '*the finest daiquiri in the world*' is treated to the unique experience. With a bronze statue of Hemingway seated at the long, pillared and lacquered bar of the Floridita and the dusky murals painted to capture history a friendly barkeep eases the pleasure. A place for more than fun or amusement, the bar is a place to rediscover the beauty and glow of glories past. Glory is safe now, assured—and reassurance is the best part of good memories.

"Umm, ladies, okay? Let's call it a day for now," DK motioned. "You need medical attention Lana, and Angelina needs to follow up on things for us with her company. Shall we all meet in the morning?"

"What shall I tell Luis?" Angelina asked.

Lana considered the options. "I think that Havana is much too developed after 500 years to hold this *Masque* without historians knowing of its existence. We have checked all the fine old structures. Other than digging the ground everywhere we go, there is no option but to continue to visit other museums, churches and to make inquiries. The other towns and farms are a more likely location having been less re-constructed over the centuries. Let's continue as we planned. Luc would want us to follow his map."

Angelina nodded, "Luis and I will collect you at ten."

They parted; Luis dropping Angelina at her bus stop and taking Lana past the Old Wall Ruins, the Maximo Gomez and Student Monuments to the hospital. Lana and DK sunk back into the leather car seat, jostled to the rhythm of the old, reconditioned shock absorbers. They drove in quiet for a few blocks, and then Lana brightened up.

"Thanks for saving my hat," she said to DK.

"It's a nice one," he said.

He recognized that she was making an effort to overcome her fears of attachment to him, yet she did not move closer to him as he expected. *To what would that commit her?* He just kept his eyes on the sunset. Then spotting what he recognized as the United States Interests Section, he made a mental note. He did not realize that they would return there, sooner than later.

Chapter 18

*G*usta glanced at his watch.

"It's time," he muttered and stood to stretch. Lana and DK had not returned yet from their afternoon of searching, and he was weary of reading in his room. Luc was no real company, drifting in and out of sleep, nursing his injuries. *It would be all right to take a break*, Gusta thought, so he left the room to have a cocktail. At least he could enjoy the company of a friendly bartender at the famous Nacional bar.

"Buenos Dias," he waved to Jorge, a bartender with a ready smile, proud to be in charge of this notable room. Gusta walked by several portraits of glamor-studded movie stars and famous dignitaries, frequent patrons of the past.

Jorge held a bright, clean cloth and moved along the bar toward Gusta, lovingly swiping an invisible spot on the bar top. Several Art Deco objects decorated the counter since the golden days and there were more mementos placed throughout the room. Comical sketches of notable guests had been painted across a far wall.

"Cuba Libre."

"Muy bien, senōr."

After serving Gusta, Jorge checked his supply of cut limes, glancing now and then at a couple at the bar's corner for their needs. He saw that Gusta was lonely, and so rested his arm on the counter. Gusta smiled back, and sipped what he considered a well-earned shot of Cuban Rum and Coca Cola.

"What is that man over there smoking? It smells so smooth!"

"Ahh, that? It comes from our first class tobacco fields of the Vuelta Abajo in Pinar del Rio Province."

"Humm. I will be going that way this week. Where can I see that tobacco farm and purchase their cigars?"

Startled at the request, Jorge said, "Oh no, sir. The exact location is a secret. Tobacco is a proud, major product of ours. You understand."

"What a pity."

"Senōr, if you would like to try one anyway, I invite you." Jorge opened a fragrant cedar box to display several fine specimens of rolled tobacco.

"Muchas Gracias." Gusta said, selecting an Exquisito; a *Seoane,* Jorge called it. Gusta pressed the cigar's middle lightly and then sniffed the five inch length of his aromatic Cohiba.

"Please," Gusta said, extending his hand in offer. "Now I invite you."

Jorge also selected an Exquisito. "I hope you will enjoy it senōr, these are the very best in the world, and not even three-hundred and fifty acres are planted each year to keep the quality under strict control. Of course, that may change these days, who knows?"

Gusta placed the required sum on the bar, lighting his cigar as Jorge instructed. He leaned against the back of his bar stool and considered the smoke. Jorge joined him in the ritual while remaining behind the counter, smiling like a Cheshire cat. With each draught, the men closed their eyes halfway, relaxing into a state of reverie.

"The rich, volcanic soil, the special blend of tobacco, the cut of the leaves, and the compactness of the folds, all these go into the exquisite result." He paused, becoming serious. "Remember Senór Gusta, we are the only ones who have mastered a unique process of fermentation in wooden barrels. This gives our cigars the special aftertaste."

Gusta tapped the ash of his cigar with reverence against the Frank Sinatra ashtray. "Yes," he confirmed, "This is the best. This is the life."

A man seated in a far and dimly lit corner, folded his newspaper, placed a coin on the table and left the famous bar in haste. While discarding the last ash of his cigar, Gusta stood to shake hands with Jorge. He purchased a newspaper, and then nodded good day to the room's occupants.

In the lobby Gusta found no one else, so he settled into one of its soft, deep sofas. His thought went to his travel friends and especially the promise of Lana who was supposed to defeat the Pios' enemy. Luc had underscored his confidence in her. *Well time will tell*, Gusta thought, thumbing through the sports pages until a piercing wail interrupted his concentration.

◆◆◆

The Policia emptied out of official automobiles and marched up the broad and long staircase into the Nacional lobby. It was not long before the desk clerk pointed to the American seated alone. Gusta went rigid, poised to fight. His fist tightened around the newspaper pages until his knuckles went red. Officers encircled him. He saw the desk clerk give him a silent headshake warning, and Gusta also remembered Lana's advice to keep his temper for once. He relaxed his grip on the paper, but he did not put it aside.

"What are you and your friends doing, poking around the neighborhoods, asking questions of Cuban citizens? Today we saw your friends annoying Cubans around the Academia de Ciencias de Cuba. Do you search for secrets of our science? And you? Are you trying to get proprietary information about our tobacco industry? What do you and your compatriots want here anyway?"

Gusta did not have much chance to answer, but he pulled out his copies of the official permissions, verifying his group's purpose in the country.

"Medical supplies, cultural research, really? That is not what you say around town. You and your friends have been asking for an ancient artifact. You must plan to keep it. Why else put such effort into a simple mask?" The captain laughed and pushed a finger at Gusta's chest. "Do you think you will take away from us what belongs here? What belongs to the people? ...Huh? You Americans..."

One of his fellow officers tapped the captain and pointed to Lana and DK now arriving.

Grunting to underscore his intentions, the police captain signaled to his officers. "Ah. Here are the friends. Take them all away!"

As the officer obeyed, Lana pulled her arm from him. "What are you doing?" she asked in Spanish.

"We are taking you into custody," he answered in English.

Then officers reached for Gusta and DK's arms, restraining them behind their backs. DK did not resist, whispering to Lana, "Don't worry."

"No." she said firmly. "It's time I let go of the sweet, but wounded daughter mentality. I got you into this and will stand up against wrong judgement." Then facing the captain, she said aloud, "You cannot do this, this way. What have we done that is so serious you would take us by force instead of asking our help?"

At that moment, Luc was being led from the elevator, still looking shaky and in pain. She turned to the largest officer, who wore significant epaulets and several stars, "I must protest captain! This man Luc cannot be a threat to you. He cannot even speak for himself at this time, he is so ill. Besides, we are innocent of any crimes; we are only bringing humanitarian aid."

"Is that what you have in those large suitcases your companions brought into the hotel?"

"That's right. We went through inspection upon entering the country. We just arrived this morning and haven't had a chance to distribute things yet. We have supplies, like Band-Aids, antibiotics, itch and pain creams, allergy and cough treatments, aspirins and many items for personal hygiene.

These go to your receiving agent for hospitals. Then there are some handy desk and kitchen items like Tupperware containers, tin foil, spoons and a host of desk stuff, like papers and sticky tapes of various types which will be turned over to the churches as we travel here and there…"

The officer cut her off with a tired response, "Si, si, but we will search everything ourselves."

He signaled to another officer to check the rooms. "Give my lieutenant your room keys. I will return them later…if we release you."

"Officer," Lana continued, "We have separate boxes for the native Taino tribe as a gesture of friendship from their cousins in the Florida tribes. No one should object to this. We have the permissions."

"We will see. I think you are smuggling. If we prove that is the case, everything will be confiscated. You will be charged a fine, and if we so deem, you will be detained a long time. Otherwise, you will be sent back to your land immediately. Your country doesn't tolerate drug trafficking or spying. Neither do we!"

"But what have we done wrong?"

"Senorita, you have smuggled narcotics into this country."

The air went from her lungs and Lana could say no more. She saw the shade of DK's eyes had gone steel gray.

"Muy bien, vamos!" He swung up his left arm in a directional move, "Get along with you all."

Lana and DK were led back down the entry stairs they had just climbed and past their own rental van parked along the drive. The officers did not seem interested in it, but Luis was interested in them, and he watched from his driver's seat. He watched the entire commotion from his rear view mirror and saw Lana, taller than she seemed before, certainly redheaded and stubborn. She was not to be pushed easily into any car without her agreement. Then, studying the entire picture; the commotion of other guests driving to and from the entrance, bell-boys with luggage, passers-by and traffic along the Malecon, noisy hellos and farewells, he saw DK make a deft move. DK had turned his back to his captors; slipping quickly into the police car and flipping open his satellite phone. Luis saw him listen to something, then his lips fashioned a reply: *Policia Havana*.

"Ah me... Everyone working at cross purposes," Luis muttered in exasperation.

Once the officer directed his newest captives to the corridor of his headquarters, he took up a stance at his office door. The group of four was led past him down a narrow corridor and through a heavy-framed opening. As the man in charge of this district, he was used to many detainees coming and going from his facility, but he knew that these people were a different lot, and he knew that the real problem was the renegade they spoke of; Sonoteas, a man they could not find. The officer went to his desk and made a call. Someone in higher authority would have to take over, and that someone would have to determine the truth of drug smuggling and the next step for him to perform. Would the group be detained while a search continued for the culprit Sonoteas? Would they be the bait–the center of a trap?

The captain had followed the rules. Now he hoped someone else would finesse the conclusion to this American intrusion. Let them put an end to the silly hunt for some useless old mask. He would wait. He would do as he was told. He would receive his instructions from El Capitan Valdes y Diego.

Like it or not, this officer knew that whatever the instructions from above, they would be part of the country's forward thinking. As a veteran of the old ways, he himself was scared of change, of the many new ideas. Would he still have a job? Would his family be safe? What would the newcomers take from them? What would he and his loved ones be forced to do? He rested his jaw upon his folded hands, and turned away from the blinding sunset.

⊷∞⊶

Trimmed in oak with ornate Spanish carvings, the holding room had only one door, a heavy one. For several hours Lana Bell and her little traveling family would find themselves confined together, milling around, with no further instruction.

"I wonder if they arrested Angelina or Luis." Lana questioned, receiving no answer. "At least we have seats here for us to rest and pitchers of water to drink." She cheered looking around the large, cool room, and recognizing the strong smell of an earth-friendly, green cleaner. She sat down on one of the benches, rubbing her sore hip, and trying to encourage her cellmates with humor. Gusta tried being merry too, while Luc and DK remained pensive.

Overtaking the day, darkness rose. Outside their door, noises set in. Two hours had passed when someone from somewhere had switched on a light for them and romantic Cuban music filtered under the threshold. Luc was the only person dozing with his back against the wall, but comfortable. Lana would have liked to provide him a pillow because his head would fall to his chest, making him jerk awake.

A voice outside in the corridor would be heard now and then.

"It's reassuring that someone is out there, so we don't have to worry about being forgotten," Lana said in a jocular fashion, hoping to lift everyone's spirits. She knew that DK had never been in prison before, and so far, he had been detained twice on this trip. His record with the bureau would certainly be stained. She knew he had fought his entire adult life against those whose goals were evil, and now he felt the unjust sting of such an accusation. Who knew if their next stop would be the law courts and jail?

She walked to the door where her knocking might bring them help to visit the toilet. As she knocked, a clanking noise surprised her, and she jumped backward by instinct. A police officer pushed open the door toward her. Still fiddling with the old, rusted lock, he looked up at them and boomed a command.

"Senōr Cody." He called. "Venga!"

The group of three were left to wonder and worry. Lana insisted that they would be exonerated. They had done no harm to anyone, nor had they smuggled.

By the time each had taken a bathroom break, DK returned. He smiled at the group and waved a batch of papers. "The Chief of Police had us checked out, and was satisfied with our legitimacy. It was a big help that we reported Sonoteas's actions to the customs people at the dock, and that we had an official guide and driver. They had witnessed what happened to Lana at the train, and they had confirmed our presence with them when the theft occurred on our vessel."

Lana made DK sit down and catch his breath.

"The authorities here accept the danger posed by Sonoteas and have identified his cronies. They have been watching the two foreigners who landed here at the same time as our arrival. They showed me their pictures sent by Interpol, and I told them we have the same men pictured in Lana's camera-phone. It will not be easy for these three men and anyone else that might be connected to them to leave Cuba because the Cuban authorities are on watch at every exit point. Even if the devils did get away, they couldn't take the *Masque* with them."

"They could melt it down, DK. Then they could sell or trade the gold for doing harm."

"That's what worries me," DK replied. "This *Masque* must be a tool for terror, a springboard to harm both countries."

"Why did the police arrest us then?" Luc asked.

"Because they think we are smuggling and spying. It must have been Sonoteas who called in a report of contraband on your ship. The police found a packet of drugs just where Sonoteas told them. It was under the personal flotation devices in the settee. It took time and persuasion from the Interest's Section to verify our clean backgrounds in the U.S. and our registered purpose in being here. Anyone would know it is stupid to come into the country with drugs, but that was not enough to exonerate us. I think that Luis and Angelina must have made statements on our behalf. Remember, Angelina had filed reports on Sonoteas, his attack and disappearance, so all our disclaimers rang true. The end game means we are free to follow the map, and go anywhere as long as our driver accompanies us. We just have to read and sign these forms, and then we can leave."

Lana lifted Luc to the table as DK laid down a separate form for Lana to sign. "The police gave me your medical ex-rays Lana. They ask you sign this document for them. Apparently, other than being scratched black and blue, you sustained only a small bone fracture of the wrist. If you keep the Ace wrapping on it each day and don't put pressure on it for a few weeks, it will heal naturally according to the nurse's instructions." He walked up to her, and held her head between the palms of two hands. "In addition, if you give up this wild life you may cure that crazy head of yours."

She laughed, "Never happen."

Gusta opened the door to the guard waiting there and called back, "Shall we go then? Jails itch my bones.

Thank God, your injuries were not worse Lana, and thank God we were not shot for crimes we didn't commit. I guess that coming to Cuba can still be a stressful situation."

"Things aren't that bad Gusta," DK replied. "But there is one more thing. We lose permission to continue through the country unless we leave our passports behind with the Interests Section."

Everyone opposed that idea.

"That's the way it is," he answered with all the firmness of his profession.

"Furthermore, we are permitted to continue only if Gusta remains in Havana. You can sightsee, go beaching and to nightclubs, but you must not try to dodge an observer."

"But why make me stay behind?" Gusta protested, raising his burly shoulders in dismay.

DK faced him, "Since you were fishing for information about the tobacco plantations..."

"Whaaat?"

"Hold on, hold on, Gusta. I am sure it was innocent chatter, but your questions rang a bell with the surveillance people. National security and suspicion is the curse of every nation these days. Lana and I asked too many questions too it seems, but someone has to do the search, and we've been assigned."

"Wait a minute. I'm part of this search, and I have done nothing wrong."

"Gusta, I know that, but I'm afraid this deal was cut with the help of different authorities. You and I have no authority to change it. Be glad you can enjoy the city with a fair amount of freedom, and remain in our comfortable hotel! Use the concierge for any arrangements, and enjoy your stay. However, still be careful what you say and to whom you speak. Don't push your luck with anything." DK took a breath, and then his eyes went steely, "Gusta, if you are careful with what you say, and with what you do, and where you go, no one will detain you again."

"Humf," Gusta complained, turning one way and another like a puppy in a cage.

Luc patted his cousin's shoulder, "Look Gusta, I'm not feeling well enough to travel for another ten days, or whatever it takes. This quest must continue for the welfare of our heritage and we have a lot invested in the quest. I am sure you all see the bigger picture too. Anyway, let me stay behind too. It is best if I remain or my weakness will slow the search. Is that all right with you Lana?"

Lana checked with DK who agreed and she then laughed. "I wouldn't be true to myself giving up before we really began. What kind of an adventurer would I be when a potential good is possible?"

DK put an arm around her shoulder, "Right. What kind of an adventurer would you be? Not my kind." He hugged her, and shook Luc's hand. "We'll continue as far as we can."

The agreement was struck.

As the four took leave of the building, they were stopped by the chief of police. He paused and then re-affirmed his instruction: "Remember you may not leave the country without our inspection. You must follow all our laws. You must report back to your Interest's Section on time."

Each member of the group shook his hand as he warned again. "Honor our people and respect our property."

They would obey.

"I am instructed to tell you to enjoy our country, but stay within the law." With that, he ushered them out of the building, but before his lieutenant closed the door, the captain broke into a sly expression. He grasped his cap, tipped it and smiled at DK speaking now with a mischievous tone. "Remember, we have wonderful musicians for your evening entertainment. Enjoy them... Goodnight."

After showering at the hotel and enjoying a good meal, Lana and DK felt revived and wanted to forget the day's difficulties. They decided to close out the evening on an upbeat note. They started for a dancing club. There is always music to find at a late hour in Havana, and they meant to find it.

They spent the last few hours seated at the Beny Moré Bar in the Plaza Vieja where great music and a very cheerful atmosphere helped them forget the police incriminations and Lana's close encounter with obscurity. Lana only limped a dance or three, but she was determined to enjoy life after all the reminders of mortality.

"I'm happy your bureau and other officials had the clout to set us free. A drug charge is a serious offense," Lana said.

"You are telling me? It could have cost me my career."

"Well I believe that truth would have saved us in the end. I believe it. I will not live with a fearful heart. I always want to move forward. You have done so much good in your military career serving others, and now you are devoted to curing the ills of man. Surely that counts when in the jaws of false accusation."

She stretched taller to reach his face and gave Cody a kiss on the lips, lightly like the touch of a feather.

"You can be proud of your past accomplishments, DK. Take off that frown tonight, and don't worry about the future. Accept that what you have accomplished so far is a lot of good. Isn't that enough to be proud of ? I'isn't that enough for you?"

He turned his head to look at her full on, his blue-eyes still. The corners of his mouth softened with an upturn. "*You* are enough for me."

Chapter 19

The arrival day had been as long as two. Their first night of sleep passed by in peace.

While Luc and Gusta had made their own plans and would go their separate ways, Lana and Cody would continue the search. The next morning found long-framed Dusty Cody stretched across his bed-cover, dead to the world. The other bed held a figure lost under a cloud of tumbled-together, comforter and pillows. Lana fit better in that nest than DK in his, and in comparison, none of her body showed except for a small cluster of golden-red ringlets at the edge of a blanket.

"Room Service?" came a knock on the door. The inquiry repeated several times in Spanish. Then in the desperation that any hotel maid feels under pressure of daily room allotments and expectations of quality, she put a key into the slot and the door banged open. Sleep was one thing, but unconscious awareness of danger over-ruled the mind of a seasoned soldier. DK bounded up, fully awake in a second. He grabbed the bedside lamp with a fierce yank of the wire and would have clobbered the unsuspecting lady if it weren't for the distance of the door from his bedside. It gave him time to see who entered. Time stood still wherein the shuffling cart noises awakened Lana. She blinked at the scene; a maid struggling with her trolley, unaware of the fate she had been spared; a grown man brandishing a simple lamp, arm raised, standing partially nude. Lana kept under wraps, the comforter pulled up to her pug nose where its slight upturn locked it.

When Lana caught DK's eye they burst into the relief of laughter. The maid gave up explaining and questioning, disappearing back out the door, happy to leave the two oddballs behind. Then the phone rang. They stared at it. Another ring of the line, and Lana picked up the receiver.

"Front desk calling. Miss Angelina is here for you."

Lana frowned and looked at the clock. "Oops, please, tell her we are so sorry, but we are late. In addition, we must be elsewhere and will have to meet her back here at…say noon. Please apologize for us and say that a message was sent to us last night. We must visit the Interest's Section this morning. …Humm? …Yes. We are checking out within the hour and oh! And please send up Cuban coffees and toast for two."

DK patted Lana on the head and went to replace the lamp. "Thanks for the coffee order. Shower first?"

"Yes," she said, dashing by him, patting his head too. Then she turned back and planted a kiss on his mouth.

"Are you still teasing me?" he asked, grabbing her hand.

"You know we can't keep the Deputy Chief of Mission or the new Ambassador waiting just for us," she answered with a smile, pulling her hand away. Retreating to the shower, she called back. "After all, isn't it nice to have a little guile in your Mata Hari?"

⸻

They were ushered to an inner sanctum of offices, dusty with lots of folders piled in various corners. The windows gave out to a breathtaking view of the sea beyond the Malecon. The rooms were noisy with the clicking of machines, but only a few muffled conversations. The constant flood of full light had faded the room's fabrics so that the total effect was of grayness-mottled. The general appearance of any business office in the country was far from the luxury known in the 1940s. Lana had once been to see the beautiful, classical style villas in Vedado, still the finest residences in town—architecturally speaking, elegant and detailed. Built in the times of wealthy emigration from Spain and the growing presence of industry barons, both sugar and oil, they now housed more than one family, and showed the wear of time. Even Mafia interests had maintained lovely homes and offices in the Vedado neighborhood years ago, just as did an exponential association of willing and obedient minions. It was a grand life for some, and poverty ignored for others. Who counts the straws weighing on a camel's back before placing the last?

The Ambassador was not available, so a seasoned Deputy Chief of Mission met the two questing Americans.

"I needed to put faces to your names and understand your motives here. Thank you for presenting yourselves to us. If you continue traveling in Cuba, we expect you to keep us in the loop for your own safety and in respect for our relationship with the government here. Now what about this dangerous person you reported?"

"You mean the man accused of theft? Sonoteas?"

"Yes."

They told their story, only to find there still had been no news of his detection.

"There isn't much I can do about the culprit unless the local authorities locate him. Then, and if, he presents himself here for sanctuary, we will have to address his actions. He may end up in prison or deported. I am very concerned at the threat of terror this man presents. If you come upon any leads, get in touch with me immediately. The last thing we need these days is more terrorism. And you have no idea what form it would take?"

They shared a woeful glance. Agent Cody was the first to reply.

"We do know that someone placed an odd fire extinguisher on board the *Esmeralda* and has since stolen it. That person is likely to be Sonoteas because he knew his way around the vessel. Perhaps he placed it there in the beginning. We are worried that there is something harmful in the canister, maybe a special communication device or a bomb. Lana saw Sonoteas receive a small package of something else before she was pushed from the train, and we have no idea what that was or what harm it could do."

"Wait. To what train do you refer?"

They explained the train attack, and admitted that the package Lana saw could have been payment for actions done, or to be done, or another device.

The Deputy Chief of Mission wrote copious notes on her laptop. Several serious men wearing dark suits stood in attendance to the DCM and one of them bent to her ear with whispered information. DK recognized them as U.S. State Department officials.

When Lana finished describing the man she had seen on the train, she handed over her phone with the pictures of the two Key West stalkers, identified as terrorists by the FBI.

"That is the same person we'd seen tail us in Key West. There is definitely some deed in play, and it concerns not only us and the *Masque of Gold*, but some nefarious action meant to happen here, or it would have happened in Florida."

The DCM signaled one of her aides, and he left the room temporarily with Lana's cell phone.

"Now tell me what is so important about *this* mask that you and an enemy would want it."

"It is supposed to have strong spiritual powers, but for the contemporary thief, the goal is likely the gold it contains. The natives have described it as a human skull," answered Lana — "The front half to be exact."

"So it is a skull made of gold?"

"No. It is a skull itself. The Parietal and Occipital regions have been cracked away and filed down smooth so that the back of the head is missing. Native ancestors were masters of working in bone, and you could liken the final shape to a large oval egg, one-half. We are not certain whether the skull is only layered in gold or whether a large egg of gold also supports it inside. There are no records nor recollections of how dense, heavy or full it is, only that it is valuable intrinsically and spiritually."

"Do you mean that the mass behind the bones might be a solid oval of gold?"

"Yes, Madam Deputy."

"Something the size of a human head in solid gold would be extremely valuable, worth a lot of trouble-making. Was it some sort of funerary artifact?"

"In a way," Lana began. "It was created in honor of a loved cacique who died. His successor ordered this spiritual *Masque* to be made. It was entitled with a unique name in their ancient language. Translating the sense of its ancient name over the centuries, it has come to be called, *Masque of Gold.* It was to emanate the cacique's greatest wisdom. It was meant to transmit his golden knowledge. In this way, the tribe might call down upon themselves all the good that the spirits could provide. You would say that it is a god figure, not a god. The supreme creator was said to speak through the great cacique, and he through his *Masque.*"

"I see. And today people want the gold?"

"Perhaps some do, but not the Calusa. The gold is only important in the sense that it is hoped to provide longevity to their artifact. After all, the tropics are hard on wood or shell objects."

"So, do you think the *Masque of Gold* still exists?"

Lana looked at DK, and he nodded. "We don't know, but we think so. It was supposed to hold such spiritual strength that its custodians all these centuries would have felt its power. They would have treasured it, and kept it safe. The Calusa tribe believes that it is still under protection here, now. However, we have not found a definitive clue as to where it is. That is what we seek in our journey going forward."

"Who do you think has it?" the Deputy Chief of Mission asked without hesitation.

"Maybe it is in a museum? If we do not find it squirreled away in one of the country's museums or in a church, we think that it is still protected by its original caretakers, the Taino tribe. We will follow the trail on this old map checking each location. We will inquire where we can, and go all the way to the eastern end of the island if we must – to Baracoa and the Punta da Mais."

"Then what?"

"Well, the Calusa who sponsored the quest would like it back."

"That will have to be decided by the owner, and by the Cuban government. It will not be easy to take such a valuable item away. After all, people in America enjoy certain levels of comfort. You must recognize the needs of the people here for such a valuable find, regardless of its past provenance. We must not be takers. You understand?"

"Yes. We will make fair arrangements for that *Masque*."

"Good. Do not create an international incident, you understand?"

"We understand." DK answered. "We do hope to find it and perhaps renew a blessing on the Calusa, if nothing else."

The DCM remained quiet for several seconds." Describe it again, in detail, for our records."

"It is supposed to be a beautiful head to look at. The workmanship is fine, created by a great shaman or priest of the tribe named Cobalusakayan. It is supposed to measure six inches wide by ten inches high. I do not know how deep the sides go or whether the gold continues on all sides. It is likely that after so many years, some chipping of bone or gold has occurred. The skull surface was applied heavily with gold leaf. Then it was molded in layers all over the skull, from the jaw and chin, to the check-bones and over the nasal arch to the frontal area or forehead. Any parts not covered with gold were to be stained with berry juice, although some say blood. Perhaps the artist did not have enough gold to encircle the piece. Then again, it is possible that the entire cavity is filled with gold, like an egg within a shell."

"Have you ever tried to find it with social media?"

"The Pio clan did reach out, but carefully. The tribe is afraid that such a broadcast would give rise to opportunists and bring sorrow to its protectors. If they call global attention to the *Masque's* existence, evil intent could rain down, much like the men of Sonoteas's gang. How they found out is not clear."

"What about contacting Arawak relatives, the modern Taino?"

"That's what we are here to do on behalf of the Calusa elders. This has been the first opportunity to make such a personal and meaningful contact in many years. We are not sure that the Taino tribe has the artifact or knows where we might find it, but we still hope for time to contact them. Letters have been returned and no contact was possible by phone. Therefore, we hope to make personal contact during this trip. The goal is to bring the peoples in touch with each other for mutual benefit. We have a suitcase with useful gifts from the Calusa."

"I see. Could the *Masque* be encrusted with jewels? If so, it would make the value even more portable, and the authorities will be very interested to know this."

Lana leaned closer, "No, Madam Deputy, we don't think it is. The elder who organized the search never discussed that. He was entrusted with the legend down through the centuries. Jewels were never mentioned. However, the eyes do glisten. They were composed of mica shell, and were intended to reflect the power of the spirit. The Calusa derived most of their sustenance from the sea, you understand. So looking into the mica shell eyes channels the blessings of material life along with the supreme creator's wisdom. The eyes are supposed to shine forever. Their mica inlays were glued by tree sap or melted animal fiber."

"Was large mica so easy to get from the sand five hundred years ago?"

"Certainly." Lana confirmed. "The natives carved slices of it from the Whelk shell which was plentiful then in coastal waters. It is related to the Conch. Of course, it took real craftsmanship to carve out a spherical wafer using crude tools. The ancients were skilled at carving in wood and bone as other artifact discoveries have proven."

The DCM made more notes. "That's a very interesting story. The find would bring added attention to the art scene in Cuba, which is important and growing. Such a find would benefit their industry greatly. Be sure to work with the authorities when you find this *Masque*. I repeat, be sensitive to local feelings because a find like this might really belong in Cuba, provenance or not." She emphasized her remark by standing and lowering her voice, "The need for the past doesn't outweigh the needs of the future. Tell your tribal emissary to judge the highest and best good for the *Masque* as our two neighboring societies move forward."

"Yes, we will pass on your advice to the people concerned."

"Remember, this is a government that has restricted freedom for a long time. It hasn't tolerated defiance either so watch yourselves. Their rules and regulations still bear our obedience."

"Aren't things more relaxed now?" Lana asked.

"They are and they are not. Don't expect change overnight. They still want laws that protect their property and their systems."

In the quiet moment she drew the interview to a close, tapping a pen several times against the desk top. "Well, let me know how it goes. I wish you success. Is there any other feature about this artifact that would help us identify it should some information come our way?"

As Lana and DK stood to leave, they showed the *Masque* drawing to the officials again. "You can see that this face is more humanoid than we would expect for the time period, but then again, the Egyptians, Greeks, Romans and European Renaissance had produced magnificent human-like forms before 1500. Look at the lips. This artifact is different from other objects found in this area from that time. The lips for example are full and normal looking. The legend says that gold was hammered over the tooth area, in layer after layer, time and again, being molded by the application of hot stones. This treatment gave a natural shape to the lips rather than the stylized or puckered look of that period. Many layers of gold were applied over the teeth, giving the lips a bold and sensuous shape."

"The expression doesn't seem warlike?"

"Oh no, peaceful, as if in godly meditation."

"Well, it sounds very interesting, but if you don't find reference to it in any museum here then you can safely assume that it is buried or non-existent. Please do not turn this search into a dig. You don't have permission for that."

"Ah," Lana answered.

As they parted, the DCM admonished them. "Please focus on the international threat in this adventure of yours. Make it your *main* mission to find the culprit, Sonoteas!"

Then she concluded with a raise of her eyebrows, "So, stay out of any more trouble."

Chapter 20

Approved for a tourist stop just nine miles outside of Havana, Angelina and Luis drove Lana and DK to Finca Vigia, the compound of Ernest Hemingway during his last years in the country. Lana had the intention to interview some old time residents of the small town near the Hemingway home. Perhaps they would remember something of legends or the inquisitive, but friendly American author.

Luis drove the van through a pleasing, irregularly shaped village called Cojimar. Angelina pointed out the statue of Papa Hemingway in the small town. They passed the Rio Luyano, which ran alongside the town of twenty-six homes and finally led to the "Finca Vigia" estate.

"And that?" Lana asked.

"That is the hermitage called San Francisco de Paula. It was the Mission church that gave rise to the small town. You can see that this is a very old village. Some of the architecture is Spanish colonial."

DK took both ladies' arms as they climbed the slope to Hemingway's former home.

Lana's voice went wistful. "I like it. I can see Papa Hemingway would too. It is not fancy, but it looks loved. I read that Hemingway wrote *The Old Man and The Sea* and *For Whom the Bell Tolls* living in Cuba. Critics say that these are his best novels. Now I can see the peace he needed to write well."

DK stopped to take in the natural surroundings. "Yes, it is a peaceful and verdant spot. Just what an author needs. He must have loved it here. I know he preferred a life style that is down to earth and this place is that."

They crossed the driveway and peered through the heavy foliage to the pleasing white cottage at the top of a rise. Angelina pointed to the singular tower that stood further back. It could not be missed if one tried. The author had built it next to the house. When they climbed to the top of it, the author's intent was obvious. He could be in the small room and write standing at the tall lectern. He could create his stories in solitude, yet close to home. Opposite his desk, a window had once given out to a splendid view of the sea, now obscured by overgrown forest.

Inside the home they walked the simple, but logical flow of rooms, one to the other, each painted in crisp white, full of light and yet comfortable. Pictures of distant travels covered the walls. Animal trophies, books and little souvenirs filled the shelves. They spelled out the history of a man, both freedom fighter in Spain and wildlife hunter in Africa, both conversationalist and writer, husband and father, fisherman and friend.

Lana studied DK from across the living area as he ran a hand lightly over a mahogany table, staring at a few family photos of Papa's personal challenges and victories. She realized how alike the two men were in their courage against the odds.

"Do you think you might enjoy wild game hunting one day, or take up a creative outlet like writing?" she asked.

He peered closer to the photographs, "I do enough wild-*man*- hunting nowadays, thank you." Sometimes he kept confidences close to his chest, even with Lana. Then, standing upright, he pointed to the fading photographs around him and added, "Maybe I'll take up photography, but not soon." He took her arm and they exited the home. He turned to her with a mischievous eye, "But since I am a man of action, perhaps I'll focus on dancing. What do you think?"

Angelina looked at him with a curious eye. "I thought you were a great man in your country, not a dancer?"

"I was teasing Lana, but I am getting to like it."

"Well aren't you a great man?" Angelina insisted.

He seemed at a loss for words and that made Lana smile. He looked at her but she decided not to bail him out.

"Well I try to be a better person each day. Does that answer your question, Angelina?"

"How?"

"In our country we have lots of opportunities to volunteer for needy causes. I like to volunteer with my military buddies at the local youth center, but that is far from greatness."

Lana waved her arm to encompass their surroundings. "That depends how you look at it, DK. If Angelina and I think you are important to us, then that's true too."

Angelina blushed, and knowing that it gave her away, she changed the subject. "Do you think Mr. Hemingway could have come upon the artifact and maybe bought it? He seems to have collected many interesting objects, although some have been taken away you know. They have been divided between his family, collectors and the state."

Lana replied to Angelina after considering the facts. "I see what you are saying. Maybe he did find or own it, but there is no record of that in his family diaries. Whether the state owns it now, we don't know, or do we Angelina?"

Angelina just shook her head. "I think I would have heard of it. Moreover, since you put the purpose of your quest on the permission documents, I think the authorities would have discouraged you from all this wandering if they already knew of its location. I do not think you would be given such broad permissions to look for something they had already found. However, your country is rich in many ways even without the *Masque of Gold*, so we do think your quest is bizarre."

"We?"

"Well, you know. My people…Luis and me."

DK saw a tension between the women and broke into the conversation. "Ah! your country is rich too Angelina. You are a people with a 'collective unconscious', as Carl Jung calls it. Cuba has seen nomadic tribes cross its landscape and then settle it. Europeans come to colonize it, for better or for worse, and then merge with African rhythms and an industrial age. A lot of discovery, evolution and growth has gone on here."

Whereas Angelina was a grown-up, slender twenty-something woman, with smooth tan skin and a fervent expression about life, she was childlike at the same time. A grasp of history's lineage can be difficult from that perspective, but she was young enough to be eager for new things. "That makes me happy to hear you say. I guess those of us who live here do not always appreciate our heritage because life has been rough for us. I hope we will see a better future soon."

"It is happening, isn't it," he reinforced, "Economic well-being without a violence?"

"Well..."

"Anyway," DK digressed, not wanting to put Angelina on the spot. "This is an idyllic spot. I'm sure Hemingway regretted having to leave Finca Vigia."

Angelina shrugged, "Maybe he didn't think he would be gone long. He was sick I am told. Come," she said abruptly, denying further discussion on the political temper of Hemingway's day. "I can bring us back to the little fishing village for lunch. We have a long drive ahead of us after that. Now, I will take us to the Paladares Cojimar. It is the best family owned restaurant in the village." Then, surprisingly and speaking softly to Lana she added, "There you may find people for conversation."

They strolled the rest of the property and walked down a flowered path, past the pool pavilion and pet cemetery. Beyond that, the beautiful mahogany cruiser, Pilar was moored. She raised her head proudly to them, sitting at the dock, refurbished and lonely. She was still waiting for her beloved master to lead her out on a run to the sea.

Chapter 21

As they entered Cojimar, DK asked Luis to join them for lunch. Luis seemed pleased, first glancing around the dusty and narrow streets. He caught the eye of some townspeople who waved at him—old men, they were sitting at leisure along the edge of the river, telling tall tales as old friends do. They seemed content with their lot now, retired under the State, interested only in fishing. That required just the river's edge, a branch and line. What else would they do? A country club could hardly improve their day in the sunshine, and how would a golf course put food on their plates, or soothe their aching backs?

Entering the Paladares, Angelina and her tourists were warmly greeted and shown a long table in the center of a spotless room. It was a small and plain place, but a colorful wall hanging dressed a narrow wall of the room. Two other tiny tables occupied that side whereas the other side held a simply carved, wood buffet. Bowls of food were set upon it and pitchers of water stood next to a plate of fruits.

The group sat at a table with pretty place mats for each person. Lana could see that it was a luxury for the owner to present matching table napkins and a gloriously decorated breadbasket of fresh-baked rolls.

Luis had said little thus far. He remained his usual calm, happy self, and Lana found him pleasant to be near, both confident and humble. Sometimes Angelina appeared in awe of him. At one point during their lunch, Luis began a calm, but rapid-fire discussion with the Paladares hosts. Sitting next to Cody, with Lana opposite them, he nodded to them during his brief and genial repartee with the owner. Lana did not understand the innuendos of the discussion, and these were not explained, but she could see the deference paid to Luis.

As they exited the Paladares, Luis went ahead to the van with DK at his side chatting amicably. Lana decided to take the relaxed opportunity to press her curiosity and pulled back, nudging Angelina, she whispered, "Those two ladies about to leave the restaurant may know something of Hemingway folklore."

Angelina approached the women with hesitance, but they smiled a welcome to her. At first, the older woman stepped back from the side of her younger companion and kept her eyes downcast; the other woman was perhaps twenty-five—too young to remember the days when dissenters were tortured and held in exile for stating any opinion that might contrary the state. She faced Lana, but with caution. A fresh flower was pinned to her shirt and it was clear that the two women were celebrating something special, proud to enjoy the extravagance of a meal on the town. They behaved conspiratorial with each other, as if their spouses would be shocked at an afternoon away from babies, scrubbing, and miles of walking.

Both women wore simple flat shoes, seemed in good health and moved with a spring to their steps. Lana saw that the younger woman was dressed up-to-date, in fitted cotton slacks and a tight pullover top whereas her relative wore a lightweight polyester dress, somewhat faded, but once top-of-the line, perhaps a hand-me-down from some foreign relative. Beside pairs of dangle earrings that each wore, they could boast only wedding bands and one watch between them.

As Angelina spoke in Spanish about Hemingway, the older woman shuffled her feet on the sand and gravel street, looking shy from habit, but the younger looked Lana in the eyes to speak.

"My grandmother never met this American writer. She was just a baby in the days before the revolution. Things have not changed too much in all the time since, except for a short time, while with the Russians, but even then, we did not see much wealth. We certainly never saw an old gold mask. We have never heard of, or seen any museum piece like you describe." After a pause she added, "Anyway, you don't understand. This is a country full of museum pieces." She let out a big chuckle at her own good humor.

Then, the older woman joined her, emboldened by the comradery, leaning closer to Lana, and speaking in a low voice, "You must understand that things of value are usually controlled by the state, including food. We wouldn't own anything really valuable, like gold." She stood back, ready to depart, but concluding with an old gesture, less needed these days, but often meant to indicate El Commandant—the hand to the chin, a beard.

The young woman tapped the elder's shoulder in good humor, "Oh stop!" They stared into each other's eyes until the younger one said, *"You know we can't complain."* To this the two women burst into laughter at an old bar joke. Angelina stifled a laugh as well, and shooed the two women away, looking at Lana.

"Everyone complains about deprivation, but your U.S. Embargo hasn't been fair to us little people either, okay? What can we little ones be forced to do? Some tried it in '61, and they got dead."

⚬✖⚬

DK was at the van speaking with Luis. They asked Lana to open the Calusa map again for them. As Luis studied the path to follow, Lana studied him. Luis seemed to be in his late 50s with shades of emotion that played on his face at happy moments, but his expression never betrayed inner thoughts. He was muscular, but like most people in this large country, not overweight. He wasn't talkative with her, but broke easily into conversation with his countrymen. Luis had no outstanding features, and could easily blend into a crowd if need be. Whenever he started up the van, a little "tsk-tsk" sound came from his lips as if to cajole it into action. And, so it did act, just for him. And when Luis wanted you to pay attention to something, a gentle "tsk-tsk" would precede the word or the action. Lana likened the habit to former American

President Teddy Roosevelt's "big stick," but a Latin one, more patient and more subtle.

"Tsk-tsk. You want to follow this map, and spend so much time on the road? Why not chose the beaches in between cities? We have such beautiful beach resorts."

"We wish we could relax at the beaches. It is a shame that we don't have the time." DK answered. "At this point, we have no choice but to outwit Sonoteas and his friends. We must stay focused on a quest that has become important to both our countries."

"Then I will be sure that we stop in the heart of the places you note on the map, but it is too bad..." He drove them further and further from Havana. "Your treasure will not be found anywhere on the roadsides, nor stored in homes. It would be impossible to secret the knowledge of a treasure in someone's private possession."

"Could it be buried or camouflaged," DK added, still puzzled that Luis spoke perfect English. He had spoken little up to that point, as if it took a while for him to judge his passengers.

"Sure. However, others would have known it over the span of 500 years. If it has been buried all these centuries, we must wait for some hotel developer to find it during his excavation," Luis laughed. "Or, maybe never. Then what will our terrorists do DK?"

"I would not put it past them to have an alternative and dangerous plot in mind."

"Well, anyway, people gossip, and word would get around if the *Masque* were found, or had ever been found."

"You are a man in a position to hear such things too," Lana added, fishing.

He looked a little startled at the implication, but answered anyway, slowly, "Yes, you are correct. I am in a position traveling the country to hear many things, and I do. So the question is, why has no gossip reached my ears all these years? Perhaps it is because the *Masque of Gold* is long gone, taken out of the country years ago. That is the logical conclusion. It isn't here anymore."

"Do you believe it is worth searching for it?" Lana asked him directly.

"I believe that rushing after treasure destroys, not enriches. A treasure attracts the self-serving from all corners, and so it must have been one day long ago. Beyond its safety in a museum, greed would have wrenched this *Masque* apart. It takes noble men to do what is right with a treasure, and to share it. Most prefer self-gain, like your man Sonoteas. Excuse me for saying it, and I do not accuse you personally, but no, I do not believe it is worth seeking after it. Unearthing the past, possibly causing sorrow with the outcome; seeking quick riches at the expense of others. No. It does not seem a noble effort to me."

Chapter 22

$\mathcal{L}$uis negotiated an erstwhile pothole along the narrow auto route from the outskirts of Havana into the western part of the country. They passed through the town of Saroa. Lana checked her map, "I see there is a vast orchid garden here in Saroa worth a visit. Maybe next time."

"Yes, maybe next time," Angelina repeated lamely. Then she added that the little spa of San Diego was also nearby. "There the spring waters are healing. Or, perhaps you'd go to see Che Guevara's headquarters at La Cueva de Los Portales."

Luis reaffirmed the interest offered by those stops, but said little more for the rest of the drive. He kept his concentration on the road. His driver's skill evident, he slowed down at appropriate times, considerate of people walking along the roadway. Some travelers were pushing bicycles whose baskets were full of necessities. The van passed a parade of live animals, being led to who knows where. Perhaps they were destined for barter, sale or slaughter. Sometimes another car or the country Trans tour coach pulled into the roadway-taking passengers to other parts of the island. Luis would pull to the side, granting them space.

They entered an amazing landscape and Luis pointed to the approaching hills. "Those soft hills are limestone, mini-mountains called "mogotes", he said. They were carpeted lushly from top to bottom with dense foliage and the valley stretched wide between them.

Even with his skill, the drive to their destination took Luis three hours. Finally views of Viñales rose from a small valley. The town reflected pastel colors in the bright sun. Once the van had driven a few streets in the town itself, and found no sign of their enemy on foot, the four travelers parked by the church and strolled the narrow cobbled avenues together. DK and Luis headed off to explore, hoping to see something of their enemy. Angelina led Lana toward the street of vendors. They stopped at a fabric table and showed interest in a square of multi-color cotton. Lana made small talk with her basic Spanish knowledge, asking if the vendor worked every day. The woman told her that she came to market just one day a week and spent her other days sewing cloth or working in the neighborhood vegetable garden.

Angelina added, "Many Cubans grow their own produce here. How else would they eat or barter? Most people work in a garden, either commercial, community or at home."

"Everything organically grown, right?"

"Yes. …Ah! Look here Lana." She pointed to a table of beautifully dyed cloths. "Many ladies like to wear yellow flowers and bright shawls or blouses, especially for celebrations. We like all colors."

"Will this pretty piece of fabric stand up to being carted around with me? I would have to roll it up and crunch it into my duffle bag?"

"Why not?"

After draping the fabric across her shoulders, Lana decided that a sash would be just the touch to wrap the waist and make a proper vest. Then she spotted the tables of straw hats, each with a brim of differing width. "This is perfect for DK," she said smiling with the thought.

As Lana paid for her goods, one gray-haired woman stared at her, mesmerized.

"She wants to touch your hair, Lana. In her dialect she asked if this is your real color and your real curls."

Lana laughed, "Tell her yes, and sometimes not at my pleasure." Then she gently lifted the woman's hand to her head so the woman's fingers could slide through the soft curls. The woman giggled, and those women nearby who had any curl to their hair, laughed with Lana. They all understood the challenge of taming such fine hair in eighty-five percent humidity.

Lana and Angelina said their goodbyes and headed for the steps of the cathedral. This they did at every town on the Calusa map, still believing that these were the likely places for a clue to the long lost artifact. They assumed that Sonoteas would seek no solace in churches and not connect them with the role of sanctuary. Without a guide, he was not likely to seek information in such places. In this, they were correct. In this, they gained an advantage.

Catholicism had been the predominant religion of the island and the churches stood as testament to some people's love of Jesus's words. Even as a communist regime, Cuba's leaders maintained a certain respect for the Christian institutions and had grown more tolerant over the last thirty years. The people would often look to the priests for comfort and guidance. In the presence of their God, they felt a solidarity of faith and purpose; they found strength and wisdom in the face of life's difficulties even if they still felt fear. Although much had come to fill man's mind the world over, nothing had come to replace the spirit.

At the sacristy of the church, Lana asked if the priest was in. He was. He greeted them with graciousness. Lana introduced their purpose and provided some of the supplies they had brought for the people. After a few pleasantries, Lana asked if the priest knew about the *Masque of Gold*, but he did not like the topic. He said that his work was to conquer pagan ideas with the concept of a singular, all-loving creator, not a variety of substitutes. So, he continued with firmness:

"No, I wouldn't have anything to do with idolatry, but in any case, I know nothing of this object. Would it improve the life of my people or bring them sorrow?"

They had not convinced him that the *Masque* was not an idol, but he took a minute to reflect on its spiritual connections. Looking at the cross on the wall, as if seeking guidance, he decided to say no more than thank you. "These supplies are much appreciated. The children need so many things." He bid them farewell with a smile and added, "I will pray for your safety."

Afterward the team of four decided that without a specific lead, there was no further information coming their way in the charming, pastel town. They drove off, leaving the mysterious place behind them. Looking back at the stone church spire, ringing its dinnertime bell, Lana could see people scurrying into doorways. She saw a little trattoria lit-up with candles on its tables. She saw a golden mist descend deeper into the valley. "What a peaceful place," was all anyone had to say, and that was Lana.

As she lost sight of the valley, she turned to see the road as Luis drove. Five farmers trotted their carts past them, heading into Viñales. A driver was seated alone at the head of his simple animal-drawn dray; each had wood slats placed around the sides to keep in any manner of goods. Each ox or mule pulled its load behind the other in a single tandem line, swaying with every footfall to the rhythm of his shifting loads. Each singular man clung to his reins with patience. Each one looked wizened from a long life under repeated sunshine and whipping rains, gangly, with thin arms from years of gathering, tying and lifting harvests, red-eyed, blinking against the billowing road dust.

This was the scene of true economy: not one leaf or vegetable would fall from the carts—not one loose stone would trip the oxen or mules. Neither man nor animal exceeded his belt or yoke, neither in size nor in vanity.

⚬⚬⚬

It was getting late as the van pulled to the top of the mountain. Before they reached it, the travelers had seen signage for "La Sierra del Rosario" indicating the forests at the crown of Pinar del Rio's tallest mountain. A terrain of old plantations caught their attention. Angelina said it was an ecological preserve now, but once it had been a vast tract of coffee plantations.

"It used to be a carpet of rich, dark and striated leaves, which when fruited sent a jasmine-like aroma into the air. Butterfly would fill the valley each spring, but nowadays tobacco grows here. It has little aroma until it is cured and smoked, but it provides a great livelihood for the country. We make *the* most desirable cigars in the world," she added proudly.

Lana had reached a page in her guidebook that spoke of the province and surprised the others with an exclamation. "Oh. This province and its farms were not developed until 1570. De León's men would not have come here with the *Masque of Gold* in 1521. I wonder why it is listed on our map."

"That's true," Luis answered, "unless the natives took it to a tribal enclave. Native peoples moved throughout the island before colonization took its full effect. They could have safeguarded the *Masque* in the caves you will visit tomorrow. One cave is documented to have been the ancient home of Guanahtabey tribe. It is a preserved enclave and very interesting. Perhaps the ranger there will have information. Ah," he added, "Here we are now in the town of Pinar del Rio, but it is almost six so the town is closing down for the night. It is a small place, but you can ask about Sonoteas. Would you like to take a short walk around the main streets?"

"Yes," Lana and DK chimed together.

DK moved with long strides, and Lana kept up, but little Angelina had to jog. She seemed to enjoy the pace they kept anyway and admitted that the remodeling of townships was not yet underway here, to the extent they had seen in Havana. They stopped at a grocer who was just shutting his gate. The man eyed them with hope and curiosity. He seemed happy to greet Americans and asked a few questions of their origins. 'Their country offered him endless things to know,' he said, and would they send him postcards of their towns, one day? Yes, they said and DK added the address to his logbook. Then he purchased some fruits and crackers to be friendly, admiring the simple facades that lined the street, seeing smoke come from some rudimentary rooftop exhausts and recognizing that time rolled slowly through the hills around him.

Lana asked about Sonoteas, but the shopkeeper shook his head vigorously saying that he was sorry not to see more visitors that day: 'Did they think more tourists would come his way soon?'

Luis changed the conversation and the troupe moved on, loading back into the van, weary and happy to head for their casa-particular for the night. As the two Americans turned for a final sweeping look at the village behind them, they saw the hilltop homes scattered low in the foliage, disappearing into purple shadow. Individual rooftops vented a steamy haze as if to welcome them, not say goodbye. The mists lay across the scene, beckoning like frosting on the sweet-cakes of youth.

Down again, entering a valley, the group saw vigorous movement ahead. A large ranch spread before them, alive with fat, grazing cattle, all moving toward their evening shelter and to their troughs of scientifically designed feed. Across the road from them, slender thoroughbred horses played with abandon in fields of waving grass. They would chase and whinny until corralled, tiring themselves out as a farewell to another day.

Angelina introduced everyone to the Hacienda Cortez family. After settling in their room, Senior Cortez insisted that the two visitors see his magnificent horses now in the barn across the yard. He was a genial host and very proud of his stock.

Inside the barn, he encouraged Lana and Angelina to pat the long, silk-coated necks of the calmer horses and whisper to them while handing out carrots. In the meanwhile, he walked DK to the curing barn where the crop manager was introduced. Agent Cody listened intently to the challenges of harvesting tobacco, and to a short history of the ranch, but when the conversation turned to political questions from the crop manager, DK said nothing more. He had put his right hand into his jeans pocket and caressed Lana's smooth stone.

The man was outspoken against a government that had caused them so much affront ever since the time of President Kennedy. It was a time before he was born and yet oddly haunted by the failures of both imperialists and countrymen. "Sixty-four years of failing us senôr!"

Cortez retorted quickly. In rapid Spanish he sent the crop manager inside and tried to smile away the man's ire. "You see, history is not always pretty and we are frail beings. We didn't get this discontented without a prologue of sociological abuse from within and from without," he said. "But that is history. Maybe your being here means we have a truce between our countries. Our leader has done our society some good and we respect him for that. Now it is time for both sides to move on and upward, to respect each other, and yet to help each other."

"So, we all hope Senôr Cortez."

Then, invited in to dinner, DK joined the others in the main building made of stone and timber. The interior living area was a very large open space, and the dining area was a part of it. The house was long and perfectly rectangle, sixty by forty feet, accompanied by a veranda, which stretched the entire sixty feet at the house front. Its covered seating overlooked the vast ranch with a view to the lively horses and contented cattle. The modest but sufficient furnishings were made by hand from various local woods, and the home interior was brightened with Cuban art, painted or sewn in bold colors. The veranda eaves sported little bells that danced in the breeze. It was a home of comfort.

The owner's verbal pleasantries continued. Cigars were offered, and Senór Cortez continued to impress the tourists with an open, conversant manner. He offered some wisdom on raising their prize tobacco crops, and Lana smelled the soft scent of vanilla nearby. As night enveloped the land, only the stars and sparks of insect life illuminated the grounds.

"How long will you stay with us?" Senór Cortez asked Lana.

"We have only enough time to visit the caves tomorrow. If we receive no clues to the *Masque of Gold* then we will leave the next day. I regret to leave your beautiful hacienda however."

"Perhaps the warden has information to help you, and you can stay longer. We will see."

DK made no response, still concerned about the motives of the Cortez crop manager. He was not interested in another political engagement; neither did he want to be taken in custody again for a trumped-up charge.

Sensing something distracted DK Lana stayed with owner's conversation, replying sweetly, "An extended stay would be lovely. By the way, may we also be taken to *Los Jasmines,* tomorrow?"

"Of course. You must visit those caves," Cortez answered. "Perhaps the years have been kind to the hiding place of your *Masque.* The drive and the hike will take you over six hours, and you will need to return before dark, as there are no lights along the road from there to us. Once you travel up the slopes, you'll find heavy mist and water-falls. Now if you go as far as Indian Cove, a boat is neces-sary. Do you have the proper clothes?"

"We have the rain slickers that we needed for our Gulf crossing and we have light nylon coveralls for hiking. We brought our boots too, so we are prepared. DK and I can keep the day's necessities in our safari jackets, so we can move quickly. Each jacket has eight pockets and we have small backpacks. Do we need more than that?"

"I will outfit the van with more supplies, because one never knows what can happen in the woods."

"Just in case?" Lana questioned.

"Well, I mean to say that you might get a lead on the *Masque,* and want to develop it. One is always vulnerable in a vast forest, but if need be, you can camp in some spots for up to a week. If you are careful."

"Oh. I hadn't thought the hike would be dangerous," Lana said.

"My dear girl," he said, standing to leave the table. "It is a dangerous world, no?"

As they all parted for the evening, DK led Lana to the ve-randa for a last peek at the stars. Lana whispered to him "I'm suspicious of everyone now after what Sonoteas did to me."

He gave her a hug, and pretended not to notice her first sign of fear. "Let's assume that Senór Cortez is just being pru-dent. I was not planning to leave the van for so many hours, but we will have to trust Luis. By the way, since he and Angelina don't live in this town, where will they spend the night?"

"The hostess told me there is an addition to the hacienda for drivers and guides because, just like big hotels, the cost is prohibitive for Cubans. However, since we paid for the trip, Luis and Angelina will stay wherever we stay."

"Aren't we staying in other casas along the route?"

"Yes."

"Are they outfitted with more than one bedroom?"

"Some have two, but in any case, Luc arranged all that with the tour company and our guides will stay nearby, in comfortable lodging near us."

"Well, I'm glad that we gave Pio money for our land part of the trip. I would feel guilty to have this trip entirely on his dime. Even as we must face Sonoteas and miss-out on wonderful stops to keep the quest, it is a wonderful first visit for me."

"Agreed."

As the Cortez family retired for the night, Lana whispered to DK, "Isn't it nice to see that some people could make the regime work for them and thrive under it?"

"Yes, very nice, and probably an accident of circumstance. Raising this amount of cattle, and special drought tolerant cattle, that is important and it takes experience. This family must have great skills. Let's hope that moving forward, all will thrive whatever their profession—and not by interference from us or from graft within."

Luis returned to the lanai and commandeered a wooden rocker tucked in a corner. There he sat, again the sentinel of his charges. Lana and DK chose a bench further along the porch, facing a moon-crowned horizon. They sat shoulder-to-shoulder, watching falling stars; freefalls of light rippling in the sky.

Then came a breach in the quiet, a squeak. It came rhythmically from Luis' chair. Back and forth, he rocked. As he rocked, his cigar smoke curled upward and filtered quietly through the little bells along the eaves, as if to supply him several halos. But Lana and DK surmised that he wasn't an angel. His attitude revealed that he knew more of men and more of the world than many others might. Kind as he seemed, Luis was also steady and sturdy, like the rocker; not a run-of-the-mill, poorly made object.

Still, being a trustworthy human was something else.

⸙

The next morning the light was still dim when they left for the caves. The ranger had been alerted to their arrival, and Angelina seemed excited, chatting all the way up the mountain. Luis said little. From time to time, a philosophic word would cross his lips, and he spoke of life in the countryside. "It is a good place, but one must work very hard with their body. Only some reap a generous return."

"Just like our country," DK said with a nod. In the quiet, he grasped the opportunity to mention the crop manager. "Do you know him?"

Luis said, "Not as a friend."

"Ah. Well he seemed very strong in his views."

Luis turned his head around to DK with a look of curiosity, "Oh?"

"Yes, I was wondering if he thought I was a threat. Does he work in an official capacity, perhaps in security?"

Luis shrugged his shoulders a bit, "I'm not sure, Agent Cody, I'm not sure."

DK pulled out his lucky amulet and palmed it for Lana to see. She watched him and shared a slow blink. Neither wanted to get anyone into trouble.

Luis finally spoke up. "Don't worry about the crop manager. He may feel resentful against the pain the people have suffered for so long. It is a pity if he does not recognize that nowadays we can fight with each other, fight against the odds and make positive change. Our two countries share indisputable realities, closer to you than the Bahamas by half as far. Only by working together can we rebuff the insanities of the world, like this man, Sonoteas. Look where we are," Luis gestured around him. "The birdlife alone that moves between Cuba and the U.S. numbers over three-hundred migratory species, not to mention the health of the coral reefs and marine life that swims between us. These are the pollinators of our future and of our mutual survival. Working together to protect them means the world's ultimate supply of foodstuff. Unless we want to survive on soy-powder capsules."

"We also share family ties and common interests in human progress," Lana added.

"That's true," he said more quietly.

Angelina looked out of the windows afraid to speak on such topics.

"Is Cayo Lago on this coast? The place where the treasured green turtles lay their eggs?" Lana asked.

"That's right," Luis answered. "But put the unique sighting on your next trip's agenda. We will not be anywhere near that beach today. Time is short for you, you see.

"I hope that DK and I will return."

"Good. Then and now you will see a host of wildlife in these hills, from snails to eagles. That's treasure enough for most people."

Angelina added, "Yes, anyway, your *Masque* may have been washed to sea if it were stored in a cave here. Over the last five centuries the sea level has risen, riddling the karsts and caves with water. A form like the head could float out to sea. There are red and black mangroves along this particular coast and if something had been washed into them, it could be jammed in the leggy roots forever."

"We can only assume that the *Masque* was moved again to prevent that," DK added, "Or, perhaps its discovery will be left to some young boy in the future as he fishes from the shore."

"Perhaps, but young men here know to be careful in these coastal shallows. They have to avoid the great Pearly crocodile, rare and ferocious." Luis said, and then he laughed to break the frustration on his tourists' faces. "Look ahead!"

A herd of bulls came into sight. They were loafing in a small field.

"Magnificent." DK said.

Luis smiled with pride. "These are just some of our prize bulls which are raised for breeding, but more importantly they are part of a complex agricultural structure. Different parts of our agriculture sustain the other. Every part of an animal, or a plant, or a tree participates in the cycle of organic farming, dairy production, animal husbandry and meatpacking, the exportation of hides and machinery or hand-manufacture. We produce as much as we can here for our population. We waste nothing."

DK watched Luis's hands as he maneuvered the vehicle around a cluster of goats crossing the roadway. "What about the things you cannot make, like medicines?"

Luis hesitated. "We import where we can and have great plans."

Lana noticed Angelina turn her head away from them. Her morning enthusiasm waned in the face of life's truths.

DK went on, "Are you from this province, Luis?"

"No, I was raised in Holguin, land of the orchards, but if one studies in school and gets around the country from time to time, one learns a lot."

"You never did farming by the looks of your graceful hands," Lana added.

"No," he answered, giving only a smile as further comment.

They reached a cutoff and continued upland on dirt roads, bouncing over ruts, lost in glorious canopies of flaming jacaranda.

At last Angelina spoke. "Well, here we are. The warden expects you Lana. I told him that you are a tour director, and he is used to such visitors."

Luis pulled up to a sturdy log cabin where several dogs sat outside ready to face any aggressor. Angelina waited for the warden as he exited the cabin. He subdued his dogs and led the group to chairs on his porch. A well-spoken man, both scientist and ranger, he checked their credentials first, offered water to drink, and then moved to the point.

"So many foreign countries have traipsed across our land since the arrival of your *Masque* that you cannot expect it to be here any longer. At least, I have never heard of it. If it had been here once and has not been destroyed by natural forces, then it is safe to say it was taken for its gold and used up in some way. Archeological expeditions and thievery have taken place in our country over five hundred years. The artifact may have left the country that way. Have you checked foreign records, say Spain, France, and Holland? All those countries have had their hands in our little island."

Lana exhaled and DK was just as embarrassed.

"No, I'm not sure whether the directors of this quest have done that research."

The ranger looked puzzled. "Well you'd be better off doing that before wandering without clear evidence of its existence here," he exclaimed in a clipped tone. "If you'd done your research then you'd know that those countries came, robbed and moved out, one after the other, until the Treaty of Paris in 1898. Then we had sixty years of Americans helping themselves. You can imagine that between the power mongers and the poor, anything made of gold has already been put to good use."

He paused, interrupted by Luis. After a brief word in scholarly Spanish between them, the ranger changed to a conciliatory tone. It was clear that the ranger loved his country and wanted to protect it. DK understood that kind of loyalty and admired the man. He asked him to continue his advice on finding the *Masque*.

"Yes, all right. Well some Amerindian tribes lived in this region after 1499; Havana itself was barely inhabited until that time. To begin, the Spanish settled from the eastern point near Baracoa and moved along the western coast, naming Santiago and more cities heading westward to us. My area was left wild for a long time. I think you will find more clues about the *Masque* with the native Taino settlements in the eastern part of my country, for that was much inhabited at the time of the conquistadors. I know you feel your cause is noble, but there is nothing else I can tell you to help it. Go on. Visit the park. You will enjoy it. And, good luck."

DK accepted the man's brusque attitude. He meant to be of help, and yet they all had to admit that the quest wore a patina of the ridiculous. As they were about to leave, DK went up and extended his right hand. The warden accepted DK's act of friendship and smiled at the handshake. Lana could understand a resemblance of each man to the other. They shared a lifestyle; men living dangerous lives sometimes faced with moments heroic, or clandestine, and sometimes ridiculous.

Later, plodding through thick, low growth and reaching a beautiful glen, the searchers could look below to a secreted valley, carpeted with green tobacco plants. Upright and brave, little yellow flowers bloomed between the elephantine and striated leaves of tobacco. The search through several caves, and a picnic by a waterfall made the afternoon special for the trio, but it was evident that they could never find anything in this vast, overgrown landscape. They would have to wander in caves and underbrush forever. The logic of their treasure map did not support this idyllic spot as home to the *Masque*. As much as they were enjoying the hike. It was time to move on.

On the trip homeward, Lana questioned again the idea that a local household might hide such a special artifact. "That seems the best place for a *Masque* instead of being left in woods or marshes."

"Why Lana?" Angelina answered, "Cubans are honest. Why would they hide it?"

Chapter 23

The next day they continued their journey, stopping at a trattoria along the Carretera Central. It was a one-sided shack with a counter and two seats. A woman stirred rice, keeping the pot constantly filled and the mixture hot. She had chicken pieces sitting in a small refrigerator run by a portable generator. Each order for a meal was cooked on the spot, fresh and tasty with spices. DK drank a beer, sharing a little alcohol with Lana just to kill anything wiggling inside them, but Luis laughed, assuring them of sanitary conditions. "Next time I'll take you to an upbeat trattoria with a veranda and a real kitchen. We have them too, you'll see."

A *Via Azul* intercity bus passed them as they approached the city of Cienfuegos, and Lana turned to look back at it, "I wonder where he is now, Angelina?"

"Who? Oh, you mean that man, Sonoteas. Senior Cortez called my company this morning Lana and I forgot to tell you. Sorry. Havanatur said a bus outside of Pinar a day before our arrival picked up Mr. Sonoteas. He met some men at a coastal town and then he boarded a cross-country bus. He could be waiting for you in Cienfuegos."

"Well, Angelina, why aren't the authorities taking him into custody?"

"I don't know," she wailed and became tearful.

"We *do* know what he looks like," Lana said, exasperated that it was so difficult to get Sonoteas detained. "He is ahead of us now, but if we study the bus schedules we could plan to meet the first bus into Trinidad from Cienfuegos. That gives us two days to catch up with him."

Angelina just hiked her shoulders as Luis answered. "I will get you the bus and train schedules while we are in Cienfuegos."

"Shouldn't you alert the authorities again? Can't they apprehend him?"

DK leaned to Lana. "The authorities must capture the terrorists first Lana. They probably need concrete evidence to hold them here, and they probably want to be sure they know all the players. They are probably waiting for these men to trip themselves up. Don't worry, Sonoteas won't get far without them. We know that he has little monetary resources, and a copy of his passport is in the hands of the Interests Section. These other men can escape more easily and are probably more skilled and dangerous, so I can see that the authorities would want to capture them first. I think a waiting game is in play to understand the scope of the situation and to apprehend the men as soon as they tip their hand."

"I see," she nodded. "It makes me feel that we are the bait."

Luis was listening, but said nothing. He turned the van off the main highway and onto a meandering road until they passed a countryside of bean farming. Farther along, great fields of sugar cane appeared, sprouting leafy green tops. The further they traveled toward the sea, the air became heavier—humid and hazy. Here and there, the colorful flowers of a family garden punctuated the scene, and as the road slid downward to the coast, marshland of rice fields came into view.

"This truly is a garden of Eden," Lana repeated, amazed at the variety of produce and the array of color painting the panorama.

"As long as you like rice and beans," DK chortled.

"Well it's a lot healthier than fat burgers on a pasty bun."

He laughed, "Okay, Lana, you will have your day. I can't wait to see you go wild at a chocolate facility in Baracoa."

Luis broke in with a chuckle, "DK, you do know that tonight our dinner will be a wonderful rice dish, *arroz con pescado.*"

DK smiled, "You guys can't take a tease."

"He's impossible," Lana confided to the guides, but Angelina had become anxious and distracted. Lana followed her gaze as the city came into view. "Oh there we are! Look at the cupolas ahead."

Angelina gave them a bit of history as they drove onto the main plaza. "Cienfuegos was named after a dashing Spanish general, hundreds of years ago, but an old legend claims that the name comes from fires that were lit along the shore to guide fishermen home, *city of a hundred fires.*"

"Take your pick of the stories," Luis spoke up again with good humor, trying to ignore Angelina's nervousness. She began to bite her fingernails, slinking into her seat.

"Is everything all right, Angelina?" DK asked. She shook her head, lost in thought. He had to prompt her down the van step once Luis opened the door for them. Luis called after her about the tour plan. She stuttered a response about proceeding to the center statue and returning in a few minutes.

Angelina walked slowly, leading DK and Lana who were engrossed in the surrounding town. Most of the buildings around the square were erected in beige limestone, or painted in natural cream and white tones, topped by ochre tile roofs. The presence of a large and domed government structure lent importance to the place. Other structures formed an interesting variety of arched, columned or plain architecture, mostly one story high except for the state house and the cathedral.

"It is an interesting city," DK said. "It must be an important one because the architecture is classical. Some buildings remind me of Washington, D.C.

"It is a very important city in Cuba. It boasts this lovely Gothic cathedral and Neo-classical architecture throughout the square. You don't see that in every city of our country." Angelina reported.

"That probably explains the large police presence in the square," Lana stated with remorse, reminded of Angelina's anxiety. "Is the bureaucracy here making you nervous Angelina?"

Angelina just glared at Lana and resumed her speech, as if nothing occupied her concern. "Built in the early 19th century by French settlers, Cienfuegos reflects the European architecture of the time, Beaux Arts." Then, she lowered her head and her voice: "Many back streets in our country aren't nice like this. Some are lined with mildewed walls, sorry for years of no upkeep. Rooftops are strung together with ugly wires and only some places are modernized. We are still poor, you understand."

Lana and DK said nothing in reply. Today's television and movies often assaulted and frustrated the viewer with scenes of wealth and extravagance. They were the stuff of dreams or spawned discontent. There were not many such films shown in Cuba, yet.

From the plaza, they could see before them a wide road that led to the coastline of Cienfuegos Province. It was a day of dazzling yet hazy sunlight where the polished stone courthouse seemed pink, rising at the far end of the plaza. An arcade led down the next side and under its arches, a number of office doors could be seen, as well as a two-story concert hall. A grand cathedral had the third side all to itself, while a line of government offices were strung together on the fourth side. A noticeable columned entry stood among these. It bore medallions of authority and a plaque saying Policia Cienfuegos.

Luis had pulled to an empty corner of the street and kept the van on idle. Moving slowly around the square Angelina spoke of the famous events in the city's history, managing to bring Lana and DK to a white-fenced area in the plaza's center. A tall granite pedestal rose there and upon it the eminent Cuban poet Jose Marti stood to survey his fellow citizens. The statue was bronze, worked with expertise, worthy of the great man.

"He was an inspiration for our independence from Spain," Angelina instructed. "A figure made a hero in his lifetime. Now people come from miles away just to see him here."

"And Cienfuegos is a World Heritage site because?"

"DK could tell you Lana," Angelina relaxed into a purr, talking directly to DK now, "His special work must teach him history, no?" Lana noticed Angelina's second flirtation. How did she know that DK had "special work?" Perhaps the authorities told her when they had been released from suspicion in Havana. What did she have in mind with her tone of voice?

Angelina took DK's arm, brought him closer to the fence around the monument, and whispered to him, "Take this." She pressed a small note into his pocket. Aloud she resumed her lessons. "This town is a prime example of 19th-century early Spanish Enlightenment. That was the era of man seeing nature as a science. Here that translated to one of the earliest examples of urban planning." Suddenly she halted, noticing movement from the police station. Lowering her head, she pulled her two guests around to the other side of the statue, muttering more historical facts.

The strong afternoon glare reflected vapors off everything, blurring one's vision. It was after Siesta yet few people were to be seen in the square. Those visible wore starched uniforms. They began to approach Agent Cody and Angelina. Nothing else moved. DK made a signal to

Lana, and she understood. She separated from him, moving fast toward the van, but with a nonchalant swing of the arms, seeming without care, fluttering her straw hat as if to music. DK slouched, as if tired of studying monuments to please his wife, listening to the chatter of a guide. His manner remained cheery however, and he started to steer Angelina with him to the van. Angelina misunderstood. She held back. Whatever she intended, Angelina was playing a losing game. DK realized he would have to bolt alone.

Luis on the other hand was subdued. He lifted his shoulders from the wheel in slow motion, and staring ahead, he stretched his neck. Then he put the van in reverse as Lana closed the distance between him and the statue. Suddenly, he gunned the engine driving toward her, in reverse. She clutched her hat, standing in his path, trusting destiny. Luis barely stopped the van when he swung open the door so Lana could fling herself onboard.

"Lay down," he barked at her. "Angelina has compromised herself. She will be detained, but we cannot stay."

She heard Luis change gears, increase speed and swirl a U-turn back to DK. The van barely slowed, but DK leapt on board and clung to the open door yelling, "Go. Go!" He glanced back at Angelina who had tried to run, but was now surrounded by officers of the police.

Without further delay, Luis wheeled onto the ocean road, following the seawall. He pulled DK further into the van by his jacket collar. "Close the door now, and both of you stay down."

"What just happened there?" Lana uttered.

Luis only replied, "Later."

He drove them fast and a long way before telling them to rise up. When night fell, he returned to town and drove to a casa particular which he had arranged. He seemed to know the proprietress, and she led them to a private door with its own small patio. Luis thanked her, and she handed a key to Lana.

"Remember to be in by 11p.m. or you disturb my family," the woman said, returning to her own door.

Once she had re-entered her home, Luis gave DK the duffle bags and said, "Come out in an hour, and I will explain everything over dinner. Otherwise, do not open the door to anyone, especially not to Angelina."

"Show us the note, DK," Lana asked.

When they had all read it, Lana shook her head. "She should have known we cannot give her asylum."

Luis raised his eyebrows and shrugged. "The young can be so careless, so impatient," he said, "And for what? Life is good here."

"Will she be safe? Are we safe?" DK questioned.

"Now? Yes. You are all safe." Luis said.

"We have to trust him for the moment," DK told Lana when they were alone. "We are too far from the Interest's Section for immediate help, and if it weren't for him today I'm sure the Policia would have taken us in too. We are innocent of whatever they think of us, but if they think it, we may not be able to disprove it. Luis seems to be our guardian, for the time being. So, let's accept and be glad of it."

"What could we have been guilty of, DK? We were respectful to everyone the entire day. Do you suppose that difficult crop manager said something? Who can one trust here? We said nothing to insult the people or the regime, and we certainly didn't encourage Angelina to defect."

"This isn't the U.S. and maybe we did something wrong out of innocence, but I don't think so. We were in the van most of the day. Let's wait to see what Luis says at dinner, and then we'll decide whether to continue Luc's quest."

"I'm grateful to Luis, but then again, is this a trap to lull our trust and then to have us reveal secrets?"

"Very clever thinking, Lana, but we have no secrets. We have no subversive intents."

Lana frowned, "It won't be the first time in the world that innocent people were made to look guilty, and maybe our quest is threatening someone; someone from somewhere else."

DK enjoyed his plate of picadillo beef.

"This is a delicious dinner Luis."

"Cuban salt and Cuban beef, who could ask for better?"

"And you were spared the beans and rice," Lana said smugly to DK.

"That's for another time, but not to worry. I'm adventurous too you know." They all smiled at that confession. Then DK faced Luis. "Who are you Luis?"

"I suppose our little escape today would make you suspicious of my skills, but I am no one important. I used to be a professor of history in one of our universities until I had to retire for health reasons. When I recovered from illness, my position was not available, but our system makes sure we have work. My higher education, including linguistics skills, comes in handy to instruct visitors about my country. Being handy with mechanical things also pointed me to long distance driving." He chortled to himself, "I guess that my youth tinkering with classic automobiles was well spent after all."

"You speak English so well." Lana complimented with sincerity. "Are you saying that a person as educated as yourself isn't useful to your government in other careers than chaperone?"

Luis just chatted on without commitment to her question. "You see my studies included English, Latin, German and French, and I traveled abroad with my former work. Therefore, since I know my country geography very well, this position is more a natural for me. I like people and do not know of another work that would be as enjoyable. Remember that here salary ambitions do not go very far. One works as one can, and is happy if it fits his nature. This work fits mine." His eyes narrowed on DK. "It didn't take me an hour to realize that you are someone of note. I shall not say the word as the walls may have ears. That assessment came to Angelina too. I could see she was angling for, oh, shall we say, repatriating to your country?"

"Lana and I are here only to help a friend, not influence people."

"Yes, yes, I know that now. However, you can see that some of us love our country and just want it to improve.

Whereas, others? Well, they have no patience, no faith. They feel the need to move on. Angelina is that way. She is young and wants the world, and tries to grab it, but such actions are frowned upon. Naturally, the authorities do not know whether the hapless visitor means to undermine the regime or encourage confidential information from our people. Angelina has such information from her work you see. Someone must have reported her intentions. There are many eyes and ears in the world."

It was DK's turn to look Luis in the eye, "Do you think we are spies?"

Luis pulled back, sitting ramrod straight, splaying his hands out, "I know nothing of that, sir.

"We understand, Luis. You are doing what you can toward peace for all concerned. We intend no harm to you, or to the regime, or to the people. We are just passing through. We are not collecting information for our government. Our mission was to help some native people, and what we thought was a simple task initially, has evolved to be a competition with evil, and a threat to many concerned. We are sorry if poor Angelina misinterpreted my purpose here, and if she is in trouble. I certainly hope that you too are not in trouble because of us. Is there anything Lana and I can do to help?"

Luis leaned closer, dropping his perfectly shaped head, showing off a full crop of pepper and salt curls, his full lips smiling, and a crinkle of crow's feet appearing above his cheekbones. One lower front tooth was missing, the result of many possibilities. "Do not worry for me. I live within the rules and trouble no one. I have seen much in life and

I see the long term of things. I have found myself to be a good judge of character, and I like to make friends. That is enough for me, and very nice of you, if you agree. Isn't it? We each do our respective work, trying to be honest and good, hoping that it revolves well for others. The end will be what it is. That is all. Some people are dangerous people the world over, but I try to side step them, working in the system. That is the best I can do. Angelina is learning. She will be fine."

"Well, thank you Luis for looking out for our safety, especially today."

"I will drive you as far as we can go. It has been sanctioned. Simply, I replace Angelina, who is detained. Do not worry about her. My government does not kill our tour guides."

He quickly changed to another subject, "Oh yes and I have news of your associate, Mr. Sonoteas."

"Sonoteas is not a friendly associate. He has ill will for anyone who is in his way, and I believe he will cause harm if we don't stop him and his partners."

Luis smiled more broadly, "I believe you DK. So let us 'give him a run for the money'. Isn't that what you say?"

DK shook the man's hand, "That's just what we say. So what have you determined?"

"First of all, this man Sonoteas has accomplices, and they are not American or Cuban. My company relayed to me that the two men have been under surveillance ever since their arrival from London. I am not privy to all the information surrounding them, which was obtained from Interpol. They could be from anywhere. That is being investigated. Nonetheless, their behavior here is suspect. They do no business, are not seen at the beaches, and one of them spends a great deal of time scribbling notes, and creating heavy internet traffic. We know that that one met up with your Sonoteas, swapped packages with him on the train and joins him periodically, exchanging materials, traveling parallel and feigning distance from each other. Since Sonoteas is known to cause harm, one must assume his relationship with these men will do likewise."

"Yes, I was on board a train where they met up," Lana confirmed.

"And he tried to kill you. We know that too. They may just be lunatics with some warped idea to gain the *Masque* you seek. Whatever this is about, we certainly do not want terrorists to harm our people, our nation or our international relations. That is my assignment. You can help by continuing your search for him because you know his appearance. We support your effort to find and stop him."

"You mean that we are a handy lure."

"Ah! You have found me out DK. But, it is what you agreed to from the beginning so don't be surprised if we are willing to run with you."

"So the quest that Lana and I pursue is a good cover."

"Agreed," Luis answered. "Finally, I will share with you some good news. The authorities have caught one of the terrorists in a crime. He tried to bribe an official and that was enough legally to take him out of circulation. I do not yet know the results of his interrogations, but at least we are making progress. He is in custody, leaving the other two hanging as threats."

"And Angelina is not a part of that threat?"

"No, DK. She is not. She is haunted by other illusions. It is up to us now to continue the search according to your map, just as Sonoteas is doing. When the Cuban authorities can accumulate sufficient proof of the terrorist activity in play, then the force of law will come to bear on Sonoteas and his friend. We may have the information we need to arrest the other men before the quest is finished, certainly in three or four days."

"Did you get any idea of where the men are now?"

"I think they have left this area and are in Sancti Spiritus. I will choose a detour to gain time. If they are using the bus service, they will go much slower than we will. On the other hand, should they come into possession of a car; they do not know the roads as I do."

"He'll be pulling out of Sancti Spiritus heading for Camaguey, and we are far behind him."

"No time to panic, Miss. I have come to the same conclusion. The car rental companies are on the alert for him. They will notify the authorities because, to rent a car, a person must provide his passport. To slow him further, he will have a flat tire."

Lana startled, "Oh." She began to question how and who, but DK held his hand up to stop her, and she dropped the idea.

"Then should we get on the road tonight?" DK suggested.

"No. The morning is soon enough. These men may play their cards. We have our own."

"Aha," Agent Cody smiled, feeling a kindred spirit. He turned to enter the casa, and took Lana's arm. She turned to Luis, and asked if they should attend the concert in the plaza.

"Won't they be looking for us?"

"Don't worry, things are all right now. Just remain low key. No one will bother you if you arrive at the entry early and sit by yourselves in the back. You see, I have a soft spot in my heart for music, and I do not want you to miss a beautiful cultural event. The Chorale of Cienfuegos is renowned for its concert *A Capella*. Go and enjoy it."

"We'll be discrete, Luis," Lana confirmed.

"I will see you both at seven in the morning. Yes? We will be traveling fast from now on. Esta bien?"

"Esta bien," the couple replied.

⚬⚬⚬

Later, leaving their casa particular, Lana and Cody glanced right and left for anything unusual. The streets were empty and they walked in quiet all the way to the plaza. DK looked both ways at every corner. Once at the open plaza DK Cody broke their silence. "Luis is above his pay grade, don't you think?"

"Yes. I think he is more than a retired history professor these days."

"I've texted home office to update our status. I hope the transmission gets through."

She shot him a rueful glance, "Wow, who would think this would happen on a simple vacation?"

DK thought about the comment, and then put his shoulders back, stopping on the path. "I think we should end this Lana. I do not want to see you harmed. We cannot be sure what lays ahead. Luis could arrange for you to return to Luc and Gusta."

"And what? You go on alone. This is not even your family or friend. How could I do that to you?"

"*You* are my family, and it's my job to keep you safe."

"What? Boy, you are stubborn. If you really want me to be a partner then please realize, *we* are a family."

His expression looked confused, "What?"

"I guess you have to be firm with others in your profession, but you cannot always be right when it comes to our family decisions. You must let me participate in those decisions." She cocked her head, took him by the arm and looked around them at the quiet but lighted roadway. The plaza loomed ahead with its concert hall beaming out its welcome lights. People were beginning to gather at the arcade, busily speaking in soft tones, anticipating the renowned chorale group.

Lana looked him in the eyes, "This is our first full adventure together, and we must make something good of it. That is what brought us here, and that is what brings us together. We share many likes and many interests, but most of all we both are motivated to help others. I feel that is the most important link for us. Now, I am sure of it. You see?"

He nodded slowly, still confused by her.

Inside the hall, they moved with discretion, assessing the innocence of other attendees and finding two empty seats in a back corner. An hour of glorious music passed without incident and their elation over it made worries seem small. They remained in place until the hall emptied.

"Magnificent," DK said, purchasing the last compact disc for sale. They crossed the plaza noticing only a few people still in the area. One person was admiring the statue of Marti, and then moved inside the fence to place a wreath against the pedestal.

"Is that man allowed to be inside the fence, DK?"

"Probably not. See. Now a policeman is chasing him off."

"Humm, he is a fast runner. How strange to lay a wreath at midnight. I think Luis would have mentioned if this were a special holiday."

"Let's move along quickly," DK answered, taking her arm, lifting her along, his longer legs moving faster than hers. They disappeared down the side street as Lana chatted over the quality of the concert.

"My favorite?" he replied to her question. "Variety. Call me eclectic."

"I should have guessed that by your choice of leisure wear."

They both laughed.

"You haven't seen my furniture yet."

"Oh dear."

"Well, anyway, I love Brahms, Vivaldi, Puccini, Fleetwood Mac, Ronstadt, Jerome Kern, Garth Brooks, Lady Gaga, and…" Lana stopped him.

"That sounds perfect. I wouldn't turn up my nose at any of it, in measured doses."

"And that's a little pug that turns up with ease."

"Ha, ha, ha. Most people are jealous of my nose and you are criticizing it."

"Now who can't take a joke?"

She smiled. "I think it will take us a long time to get through all that music together."

"Years and years," he said. Then realizing what she said, color rose to DK's face. He felt Lana pull on his arm, leaning close.

"Wasn't that easy? See you were so impatient before," she said, "and we've only been together eight days."

He grabbed her up, and kissed her on the lips. Then he paused, putting her down, "Now just a minute, don't rush me," he winked as she wrapped her arm around his.

"You know," DK, "All I envisioned for this trip was to help a friend, and visit a great place. Well, with you here too, it has become more than an adventure. That part is good, but I wonder if there are other motives for Pio's quest? Do you realize that the prime mover, Luc, is not on the trail with us. Here we are, you and I, with no personal reason to find the *Masque* except friendship and our idea of justice. After the bad things happening, and perhaps harm happening to others because of our presence, why are we continuing the pursuit of this object? Perhaps we ought to drop it. Perhaps we are being set up, not just by the authorities, but by some devious plot to discredit our own country?"

"Well, that's one for my friends at the CIA, and they aren't within reach right now. I will try to get through again tomorrow and see what clues they have at the Bureau. However, if we dig deeper to see the meaning of *Masque,* it could be something else."

"You mean it could be gold ingots or an international terror scheme?"

He leaned over to her forehead, and gave Lana another tender peck, which she loved. "Yes, maybe something concrete, like a shipment of poisons, weapons, or other dastardly equipment."

Lana just looked at him, eyes wide. "Yes...something more evil than Sonoteas. This is even more reason we cannot give up searching..."

They had reached their casa particular, and opened their ground level bedroom door. It made a healthy squeak in the dark night, and caused the owner to call down from her window above.

"Oh yes, the concert was fabulous," Lana replied. "So sorry to disturb you." DK stepped inside alone to check that the suite was empty. "Oh yes," she continued, "Thank you for the comfortable room. Yes, everything is fine at your casa, very comfortable. ...Yes, we will be leaving at seven. ...Yes, ...yes, well goodnight then and thank you for the comfortable lodging."

Once they had closed the door, DK, and Lana said little other than practical banter, nothing that might be misunderstood if the room were bugged. They bolted the door. Lana propped it more securely with the back of a chair against the door handle.

"How are you going to get out of this room quickly with that chair there, if need be?" DK wondered aloud.

She pointed to the window, "Jump."

"Oh, I see." He crooked his head, and then shook it.

It was easy for the innocents to fall asleep. If an ear were pressed to their key hole, it would hear only a slight snore, and occasionally, a little side whiffle.

Tonight the guiding light of a hundred fires was untended while the steps of one stranger moved in the town's darkness. Counting fifty paces from the Plaza Marti, the man halted his walk, looked back at the stature and around him. The he reached to a brick in the street wall, and tugged it. Something like a package of cigarettes was lifted out from the hole. He grasped it, returned the brick to its place, and ran off into the night.

As morning light crept up the city walls, a loud blast broke her dreams. Lana bolted upright. "Was that an explosion?"

DK was already pulling on jeans with his jacket at hand.

"No Dusty! Don't go out there. I am sure there is nothing you can do now that the explosion has done its harm. From the sound of the siren, the police are on it. They will help anyone who was hurt. We are already under mild suspicion in this country. For a bomb to go off just when we are in town is curious. Wow. It may put us in the cross hairs of suspicion. Stay here. If you don't leave the room, the owner here can testify we haven't left the room since we came in last night."

"How so?"

"That awful squealing door. It has been quiet all night."

"Okay, I'll wait. Let's get ready anyway. Luis is supposed to be here at seven."

Having put their 35 Cuban Pesos on the dresser, Lana went back into the room, and added four American dollars to the pile. *For her graciousness and for her good luck*, Lana thought.

Shifting her backpack to both shoulders, she let DK pull her duffle bag from her hand, saying, "Come on, my dear, it is already seven-ten. We've got places to go and promises to keep." He smiled, shutting the squealing casa door, and prompting her toward the van.

Luis sat waiting with the motor running, "Good morning Lana. Up and ready? Let us get going, no time to waste. We go immediately to Trinidad. If there is nothing there to help find the *Masque*, then we will proceed to the end of the island, the last stop on your map. It may be the most dangerous place of all for you because by then, the terrorist has nowhere further to go. He, or they, will feel the pressure to succeed. Perhaps revenge on you and the Taino Tribe will suit them just as well as finding the artifact. Besides, if these perpetrators are planning a specific crime, it must be accomplished soon, before you leave."

"What about the explosion here last night?"

"A device was planted inside of a wreath at the plaza statue. Someone somehow triggered it." DK detected a bit of distrust in his glance, but said nothing to Lana. "Whatever your Sonoteas and his terrible friends have organized has begun. However, the culprit doesn't have a good opinion of our police skills. We will catch him."

"We?"

"My country of course. An officer spotted the wreath at the statue. He knew that is was out of place. He found a red canister inside of it, and deduced it held explosive, so he protection-bagged it and moved the package to a barrier behind the station. While he was calling the bomb squad, the bomb detonated. It was on a rudimentary trigger, a time mechanism."

"My god, was the officer hurt?" Lana worried, remembering a red canister from the *Esmeralda*.

"No, no. He had wisely put it in the containment sack, and then into a trash bin behind the trash wall." Luis gave a little chuckle, "It is only the trash bin that will never be the same! The wall is not in good shape either, and there is trash all over the back yards, including red metal pieces. Otherwise, all is fine."

"Gee I'm sorry Luis. I wonder if this was done while we were in town to foster that international incident we discussed. I am amazed at the timing. You see when we were coming from the concert we saw a man place the wreath at the statue. We did not know it held explosive. That canister is probably the fire extinguisher that we think Sonoteas robbed. I am so sorry that the quest has facilitated such damage here."

Luis remained expressionless, keeping his eyes on the road.

Chapter 24

rriving at the town's cathedral, Luis stopped and dragged one of the wheeled suitcases to the Sacristy while Lana and DK searched for the church's prelate. Once found, the couple conversed briefly with him to no avail. Luis returned with them to the car and tried to bolster Lana's spirit.

"He was most appreciative of your gift, but he cannot help you."

"I understand Luis," she replied. "He did say that his parish is so anxious for normalization of activities between our two countries. These are people very close to family and they wish to see relatives again, and to come and go freely."

"Yes, that is true, but he will have to wait a while longer. Our government is trying to put rules in place that prohibit an unbridled invasion of speculators; what you call a "free-for-all," correct?"

"That's it all right. I guess such activity would only hurt his parishioners. How does that make you feel Luis? You didn't tell us if you have a family?"

"I don't have much family, just my two beautiful daughters. They are grown now and work in Holguin.

Otherwise, no. My family has died off. I might have liked it differently, but that kind of wishing goes no-where, but bitterness. I believe in kindness and following the law as much as possible. Sometimes, I must be creative, but that is not for you to know."

The couple cast wary looks at each other, but at Luis' insistence they would see a little more of Cuba's "good stuff" to cheer them up. He would make a brief detour to Trinidad and soon brought them to a schoolhouse along-side a lonely countryside road.

"Just a quick stop," he said.

Behind their vehicle, a car lurched and pulled into the trees.

Luis opened their car doors and led the couple into the schoolyard. "I'm proud that you see the high caliber of this little grade school. It is representative of our primary edu-cation, well maintained and pretty. We are family people and take good care of the children."

They entered the small building and stood in the back as the teacher out-lined a continent and asked that each child write one country in its space on the continents. The chil-dren raised their hands eager to apply their knowledge, but soon the recess buzzer rang. With that, the children were excused and twenty of them burst through the front door. Just as eager to play, their voices rose in cheerful calls as balls went back and forth and tag became the dominant game.

The one story building was no bigger than a cabin, but it stood in excellent condition, with trim painted in bright blue to contrast with white clapboard siding. The children filled the large play yard and somehow managed to keep their white blouses clean and the little red ties straight. Agent Cody threw a wayward softball back and forth to a surprised but grateful boy, and as the three travelers departed, DK continued to wave to a group of little girls who giggled and shyly clung together. Lana noticed how unspoiled all the children behaved, and that the man of justice was having fun.

Luis laughed at him too. "Well if it is fun you both like, let me stop again briefly. I have a story to tell you of our universal pastime."

They parked beside an enormous baseball field, and Luis walked them one hundred meters to the entrance. DK took a slow 360-degree look around them, concerned for a car that pulled nearby. Seeing that too, Luis said, "It is okay. We may stop here. We will be brief. We are just peeking in. Go forward a bit."

The couple joined him, peering through the gate to a grassy diamond with benches set at angles to the field. It was an impressive spot and one could almost hear the call of the crowd.

When the trio returned to their van, DK noticed that the other vehicle peeled rubber to race down the road ahead of them. "Who was that?"

"Who?" Luis turned. "No one I know. He did not come near us, you are just nervous. We are leaving anyway. I just wanted you to see this park. We love our baseball and it means a lot to our identity. Thirty-thousand visitors come to this large park in season. You see this development came when we resented Spanish rule. As a consequence, there was also distain for the bullfight, so we adopted our own sport. Our government supports our enthusiasms and the lessons of the game; team spirit and cooperation."

"Yes, like in the U.S., baseball is supposed to be a game of fair play."

"Well, we've played it here since 1805. Everyone plays or follows it. It does unify us, and that is part of our identity. You can speak with any Cuban and enter into a long discussion concerning the sport. You see, we do not want to change our culture like your friend Luc wishes for his. We just need it to have more economic opportunity."

"Do you have a hand in making that happen?" Lana asked.

"He mumbled a single word that she took to mean, yes."

"Isn't baseball a big money earner for the state?"

"It's the same thing in your country, isn't it? Only here, the profit revolves to the people in social services. Your game revenues go to only a few people, perhaps spreading some good from there, perhaps not. Well that's what we are told."

"Luis, the goals are the same, the systems different; each one has plus and minus to it. You cannot say that all the social services are high level here, and you cannot deny that some good done is done by profit. In any case, how to design societies to fulfill the noblest needs of all has been a question for the ages. It may be so for the ages to come."

"Yes. You and I are like mice to elephants. We can only progress in small steps, as it fits our own histories and makeup."

Looking at them, he then glanced around wistfully, as if he were about to miss a game. "We love baseball. Most of the time we are so intent watching a game that no one smokes a cigar! Food is not sold at most parks except by an occasional sandwich or peanut vendor."

"No alcohol either, right?"

"Almost never do we buy drinks at a park! You see we don't really need to change all that peacefulness for gain, do we?"

"But Luis, if there were vendors at each park and people could find things to purchase, jobs would be created and money revolve. Everyone could benefit."

"Americans make everything sound simple. The idea is not bad, but profit leads to greed and greed to crookedness. Cuba is building a new way. Its new path is to build a system that supports profit while minimizing exploitation. It's a dream of the ideal world, but perhaps we can achieve it better than anyone has been able to do."

They re-entered the van in silence then. DK ventured a hope, "Then, maybe there is a game on TV tonight?"

"Not usually, not at night." He turned from his driver's wheel for just a moment. "Electricity is very dear."

———⊗⊗⊗———

They did not notice leaving the park that a cigarette pack had been affixed to the rear bumper of their van.

Chapter 25

Santa Clara was not marked on the Pio's treasure map.

"It is the least developed province, and so beautiful in its natural landscape. You would enjoy it," Luis told them. "There are rolling green orchards and vegetable farms. Several universities are located there, each with a research library." He emphasized his point with a vigorous raise of his shoulders and arms. "Aaii! There is something you should know! The Santa Clara province was a favorite hiding town for 17th century pirates. This is just the place that pirate loot could have been stashed, including the *Masque of Gold.*" He tapped his head hard. "I should have thought of this before. They have a very good university with archives that go back to the 16th century. Perhaps there you would find proof of your *Masque.*"

Lana agreed. "Well, look, we are obliged to follow the map and our time is growing shorter. If we have no luck with the *Masque*, further on, then maybe DK and I will return one day, yes?"

"Okay. That makes sense, and I would be pleased to have you return. We will look forward to it."

Then DK proposed that Luis call the university also to warn about anyone asking after the *Masque*. "Our competition for the artifact could have gone to Santa Clara even though the town is not on our map."

"Being not on your map, and without a formal guide, the terrorists wouldn't connect the dots or understand the history of the place. I doubt they would think of it. From what you tell me Sonoteas isn't a scholarly person."

"I surmise so," DK concluded.

Luis wheeled onto a turn-off, continuing down into Trinidad. "Still, I will make the call, and I will check with authorities here to find out their plan to apprehend these evil men."

"Oh!" Lana interrupted them, "That is such a pretty place ahead. It reminds me of a medieval village."

"That is what it is."

Luis pulled over and parked. "The streets here in Trinidad aren't conducive to driving my van. Most were designed for the horse. It is better if you go on foot to see the town. That will also make it easier to meet people. That's how you'll get a lead."

"Where will you be?"

"The van needs some attention, and I'll visit the police station to make those calls. We shall meet back at this corner after lunch, say 4p.m.?"

"Of course."

As the couple left him, pulling a case of goods for the church, they wended their way through a riddle of narrow passages. Lana tugged at her companion, "It seems odd to me that Luis can go into any police station and be given access to telephones, and how did Angelina become vulnerable? How did he get from chauffeur to investigator? Should we continue to trust him?"

DK raised his eyebrows, and sighed. "I do not think we have an option at this point. We committed ourselves to the path and he has not given us any real reason to mistrust him so far. Luis could be a highly placed government representative, superior to Angelina, who is supposed to monitor us. He could be an energetic citizen who just wants to do well for his country and likes to make international friends, or he could be vying for possession of the *Masque*. In any case, we will know one way or the other, very soon."

Lana cradled her face with both hands.

"I know, I know Lana. This is not what you expected of the trip. I'm sorry, but this is the time for me to add a tough comment: Confusion and danger; they are part of adventure."

She straightened up. "I get the message, Dusty."

"Do you still like the idea of seeking the unknown? Are you ready for what might come next?"

She took a moment before the answer, then nodded with emphasis, "I'm ready."

He took her arm and they walked on, wary of the unexpected, peering left and right down the quiet side streets. Their feet stepped over cobblestones worn tipsy from centuries of footfall by man, horse and oxen. A mystical haze formed of ochre dust and humidity filled the air around them, and time seemed to stand still. A silent charm lured the couple upward toward the provincial cathedral as they emerged from Calle de Cristo into the central plaza.

Standing at the foot of a long, wide stone staircase, Lana and Dusty could understand the former glory of Trinidad. Heavy broad beams jutted out from under tile roofs and thick limestone walls paraded down side paths as far as the eye could see. Iron fixtures gone crusty with rust, oft-times re-touched with resilient black paint, clung insistently to various walls as useful features; lanterns, knockers, horse posts, or balcony rails. Architectural corners boasted statue niches, waiting for the return of their saints.

DK could not resist his own love of humor. He pointed up to the cathedral entrance, "These stairs are for the true believer."

"So, it seems," she laughed. "Which shall we be?" She answered shrewdly, but he refused to label them. He just started to walk them.

"It is easy to think the *Masque* found its home here, amid the grand old 16th century Spanish mansions. They bear elaborate and decorative enamel tiles which underscore the town's former wealth." DK said.

Lana opened the guidebook. "This says that two thousand sugar mills once hummed throughout the area through the 19th century, and that land owners and busy merchants enriched the city. I can imagine a prominent family buying art objects."

DK nodded, "However, the point is still the same. Where is all that wealth today?"

"Used for survival, I expect, or stolen," she answered, her turn to pull DK uphill.

They entered the cathedral just as a middle-aged priest was rising to leave from prayers. He greeted them extending a hand.

"Buenos Dias. I am Father Rodriguez."

Once they replied, he smiled, recognizing the accent. Then he spoke in English. "How nice to see you in our Church of the Holy Trinity."

Lana looked around. Amidst its sculpted pillars, mahogany altars, and exceptional carvings, a small skull could hide so easily. She explained their quest.

"No, senóra. No lo conozco. I have never heard of it."

He told them something of his ministry to the town, recently arrived from Spain, but his knowledge of native history was limited. He reflected a long time, trying to think of something helpful, turning his fingers over the cross hanging at his breast. With a start, he raised his voice. "Ah, I know the name of a man on the Baracoa side. He is connected with the Taino reservation and might be able to help you. His name is Sergei Rojas. He often passes this way and stops for a quick visit because he loves this beautiful cathedral. He is an attorney who has studied abroad and he knows a good deal about the country's history. I know he would help you. Call his office in Baracoa. Everyone knows him there."

Cody had pulled the last wheeled case uphill with them, offering the collection of needed goods to the priest for his people. Then Lana gave him the little box from Key West. "Tomaso sent it."

"Ah, yes. He has a sister who comes here regularly. I will be sure she receives the box. Are all those things in the case for my people?"

"Yes," Lana and Cody said in unison. "Here is another little one for the most needy person you know."

He thanked them humbly and gave them his blessings. He stopped them from leaving the church as he exited.

"No, please. I ask that you stay a while for grace. It is all I have to give in return. Enjoy this church of mine, stay and pray. I would be most happy for you."

They thanked him. Then, grateful for a reason to pray, and feeling uplifted by the encounter, Cody began in silence. Lana hesitated, then following his lead, trusting it the right thing to do. She never let ego get in her way.

Afterward they linked arms and re-entered the bright day outside. They walked with light steps, no longer hindered by the uneven path.

"Let's see if the curator at Guamuhaya Museo knows anything of our lost artifact." Lana remarked. "According to my guidebook the museum houses a large collection of Amerindian artifacts and reproductions of Taino cave drawings. Maybe we'll see a drawing of the *Masque*, if not the real thing."

"That would be a coup on top of a lead," DK answered happily.

They passed the Architecture Museum with its beautiful manicured garden, but had no success seeing the stone drawings. The Guamuhaya Museo did contain several beautiful representations of wall painting, but nothing similar to Luc's drawing. It was assembled only in the last century. An old woman sat outside like a statue, her eyes closed, dreaming of other glories perhaps. She told them that she was waiting for her son's car, but otherwise would not converse. She was suspicious of the couple for they had appeared out of nowhere, without an intermediary and full of questions. This was something to be feared. After all, the golden-red hair did not seem Cuban, neither did Lana's accent.

Lana did understand enough Spanish to realize that the woman knew nothing of the *Masque*, or treasures or of the 16th century. She was firm in those denials, and turned her head away from them. She patted off the dust from her dark cotton dress, clutched her straw satchel with more effort, and looked into the distance, helpless until her ride could spirit her away from them. With a wrinkle of her nose, the woman shook her head to reinforce her response and to dismiss the completely impractical idea of an ancient plaything.

The couple walked on. "Well, I'm beginning to accept that *this* ordinary or exceptional mask may be just too ancient to still exist, or stands for something else. It is hard to believe that it was lifted from place to place and moved all across the country without damage or destruction. Why do the Pios persist?"

"As you say Lana, it's a family holy grail."

"Humm, perhaps. For the terrorists?"

"I wonder. The Spanish brought slaves through this port city in the early centuries. Nowadays, any quiet coastal city of Cuba could become a port of hiding, setting up a post to use against the States. Maybe the *Masque* is the easy first deposit. Such hidden resources could not be traced electronically by international policing activities. A secret cache would be better than banks. And, maybe Sonoteas and his henchmen are an advance team to arrange everything."

"Then again, maybe the word *Masque* is more than a mask. Maybe the *Masque* holds a secret to other wealth, hidden wealth; something to be used against humankind. Remember a discovery like that happened in the U.S. in 2014 when dangerous and forgotten microbes were discovered in an old medical facility."

"Okay, but…"

"Hold it Dusty. There is a large group of men watching us. Let's be calm and stroll over to purchase a beverage at their café."

He laughed. "Maybe we can learn something concrete, beyond our fantasies."

"Oops," she startled. Everyone in the café looked out past the veranda to the township below. "Did you hear that? It sounded like another explosion."

He put a gentle hand on her shoulder, "Well, if it was, we know we are in the same town as Sonoteas, or at least his terrible partner."

The patrons of the café continued to stare downhill at the source of the noise. A small column of smoke drifted into the valley.

"You don't think Luis was attacked, do you?" Lana asked alarmed.

"Or, perpetrated it to leave us stranded?" DK said. "Look, you stay here. I'll come back as soon as I can."

"Sure. Good luck, and be careful."

The old men seated at a dominos table turned away from a problem to which they wanted no part. They pressed closer to each other, silently agreed to ignore the noises of the outside world. They dismissed the curiosity of the crazy American, and they would just put up with the crazy woman who sat near them. They pretended to ignore it all. They pretended that intrigue did not interest them.

Occasionally Lana gave a toss of her red curls to punctuate her presence, continuing to stare on the domino games the men continued to play. The players puffed up a little, proud to have the attention of such a pretty, young woman, but they said not a word to her. After a while, Lana pointed from her waist to a move at the board that would save the play of her seatmate, a thin, patient man. He made the successful move, and turned to Lana with a grin of satisfaction. By the end of an hour, Lana had been allowed a play a turn or two, but was doing very badly at it. Experience and seniority won the matches. This did not displease the players.

After an hour, the camaraderie gave Lana an opening to press her question on Sonoteas. An old man who spoke for the group held his breath for a moment, uncertain of whom to trust in this unpredictable world, but he liked her. Moreover, she was an easy domino opponent. Studying her face for the first time, he spoke to her in broken English.

"We have never seen this man of whom you speak, but if he comes looking for you, don't worry, we say nothing, Nada!" The old man gave her a toothless smile, and her bench mate winked at her, returning to the country's popular parlor game.

Lana thanked them all, leaving Cuban pesos on the bench, saying it was her loss on the bet, but meaning for them to enjoy a festive supper together. She left quickly, pretending not to hear them. They called after her to say that, in their games, no bets are made.

She walked down the stony paths to the meeting place Luis had set for them. A vision appeared from a side street ahead of her. It was a rumpled man, limping closer, his clothes sooty and torn.

"Luis!" Lana called with alarm. "What has happened to you?"

"We must leave here immediately. Our van was exploded. I have rented a replacement car and moved your belongings to it. Your duffle bags are worse for wear, but all your things are still inside and clean. Come, we will dine first. I will explain everything."

"But where is DK?"

"He will be along. He was with me at the police station and stayed to make a phone call."

Lana was relieved, but worried that the culprits were getting bold and insistent. "Luis, I wonder which is the real objective of these people; killing Americans, or getting a hold of the valuable *Masque*?"

"Those are interesting options, but so far, and lucky for us, neither has succeeded."

"No, not so far, Luis. Not so far."

The two of them proceeded to the newly rented car, and when DK joined them, they headed for a small Paladares, fragrant with Creole spices. A group of boisterous locals toasted the newcomers and sat them before steaming platters of food. "Tasajo!" They called out in unison, identifying the specialty dish, and cheering the downcast Americans. By the end of the meal, everyone was in good spirits, toasting the chef, "Tasajo!"

The room had filled with professional singers, dancers and musicians, joining in preparation for their performance of Ballet Folklorico de Trinidad. The gaiety of the group relieved the hurt of the afternoon, but DK kept on alert. Lana pressed to stay for the concert which was influenced by century-old African traditions, but Luis sounded anxious, "No, Lana. We cannot stay."

Lana let the subject go. Luis explained that the music held some connection to Santeria, and that meant witchcraft to many people. In the nooks and crannies of the large island, one might practice several religions at once. That was another mystery, and the people's right, so Lana did not press her questions. Instead, she linked arms with her two companions, and they moved with quick steps to the newly rented car.

"Luis, it is so fortunate that you had stepped out of the van when you did. Are you still hurting?"

"The police station had medication for my cuts, but my ear drums were impacted which may require treatment. For now, I am grateful that the plastic explosive went off during siesta when no one else was nearby, or in the repair shop. They had finished with the van and parked it out on the street for me while I made some calls about our lodging. It went off just as I was returning."

"So, someone was watching and detonated when they saw you?"

"Maybe."

"If you were intimidated enough, you'd leave us stranded, freeing them to capture the *Masque*."

Luis nodded, "That makes sense, but I'm not leaving you. They don't realize who I am." He was angry for the first time.

"Who are you Luis?"

"I am you Lana. I am DK. *Masque* or not, we are brothers. The people who fill the world with hate do not understand that the harm they do eventually rotates back to them because evil is like the worm in an apple. The worm consumes its house until it starves itself, twisting to its end."

"Then our task is clear. We move even quicker now, act on the offensive and take every opportunity to rid the barrel of worms," Lana said to support his philosophic metaphor. She hoped he was on the up-and-up because she liked Luis a lot.

It was dark night when they pulled off the road to park near their lodging. The three grabbed their torn duffle bags and walked through a dark avenue to a lovely torch-lite garden. Set back amidst blossoming jacaranda trees, the patio was under the floral canopy of purple. The three adventurers bid each other a quiet goodnight, but their minds were not at rest.

—⊸⊶—

Sancti Spiritus is part of a string of beautiful beaches along the south-west coast, and when Lana woke before dawn, she could not resist a walk. She quietly moved the chair away from the room door and grabbed a beach towel. Joyful, she watched the sunrise, and splashed in and out of the refreshing surf, mulling over the search ahead. The quest had provided very little knowledge so far, and the couple would have to return to Havana to be debriefed soon. *Something positive must come out of all this harm and trouble,* she repeated over again to herself.

The industrious and prosperous city of Camaguey was next on the journey and it would require their strong focus. Once they checked the usual locations, contacting the Taino scholar was of utmost importance. Lana hoped it would be fruitful for she sensed that the next leg would be their final chance to bridge the centuries and connect the tribes. This would be the final reach for a *mask* and all that it might represent.

She was toweling dry as a voice rose from behind the garden wall. It startled her.

"Lana!"

She wheeled around and then smiled broadly at DK. Somehow his love always found her out.

Chapter 26

Luis headed the van in the direction of Camaguey leaving dust in his wake. The coastal breezes of Sancti Spiritus faded and waves of humidity rose up at the travelers from vast plains ahead of them. An expanse of farmland grew flatter and wider on either side of the long roadway to Cuba's center. Then the car was brought to a standstill.

A congress of animals, trucks and equipment spilled from a ranch alongside them. Upon inquiry, Luis decided it was best to park and let the commotion dissipate. He enquired from a group of people at the farm gate, and they pointed to dignitaries covered in badges who represented all things agricultural. With permission, Luis invited the young Americans to join him.

"The road will be blocked another twenty minutes as all the visitors and equipment move out, returning to their own shops and farms. Anyway, you have been invited to come in. I think is a worthwhile for you, culturally speaking. You see that we consider it an honor to be in the company of such experts and these are competitors for a national prize. You participate in the honor received by this cooperative," Luis told them. "It has won the highest award for production."

The three of them walked to a podium where a group of farmers was listening to the latest ideas on healthy produce. Perfect rows of vegetables stretched before the viewing stand. They were plump and appealing to eat. There was no evidence of insect infestations or miss-watered plants. The soil was rich, deep and black.

The manager of the collective was introduced as Senõr Octavio. Apparently, he had delivered a welcome speech about the newest organic fertilizer blend. DK congratulated him.

"Thank you sir. Yes, we've done an excellent job considering the limitations on us for machinery and funds."

"You mean because of the trickle-down, negative effect of an embargo?" Lana asked.

"Yes, senorita," he chuckled. "Perhaps you can speak on our behalf in your country. We could shine amongst farmers of the world with availability of more tools."

DK noticed the glint of bravery in the man's eye as he lowered his voice to them. "You can see how much we try to be self-sufficient. We have the will and the strength but we are in a circle of insufficient income to purchase machinery and parts from abroad. Therefore, the circle turns; we cannot manufacture what we need to produce what we need, to earn what we need. It is a circle like the Nautilus shell—and we are caught inside."

Passing from the farmland into a lake district, Luis brought them across numerous bridges on the way to Camaguey. By mid-afternoon, they saw the city spread wide before them. Camaguey offered no deep forests like Holguin Township or the Sierra Maestra Province, but it buzzed with industry. This was a place where people wore contentment, relatively speaking. Their hard work in commerce paid off relative to countrymen in other areas, and relatively speaking, they gave the impression of people who dined well, napped well and loved well.

"There is so much commercial activity in Camaguey that your *Masque* would find it hard to stay un-utilized all these years." Luis looked at the treasure map, and scratched his head.

"That may explain its move onward at one point," DK answered.

"Nuevitas is the major port in Camaguey Province and a large trade of nickel, copper, iron and lesser metals supports it. There is wealth here which could have purchased the *Masque* at one point, but it is such a big place that we could never find it in the time allowed. All we can do is ask of the mayor's office if they know anything. However, this location could be the terrorist's harmful objective because of the area's economic importance. All we can do is warn the administration here."

Tiled red roofs and white limestone walls brightened the panorama that threaded the Camaguey landscape. When it came to the finest homes, the architects of centuries ago had encircled the windows with stone embellishments. Some windows were graced with small balconies, framed in iron. However, every century of construction was represented in Camaguey City. Seventeenth century shops built of hewn stone were seen next to square buildings erected in practical plain brick. There were 20th century factory structures built out of aluminum, impossible to miss for their practical lack of beauty. All the structures were jumbled and crowded together, like the days and centuries that fold us fast, one into the other.

Colonial-era churches caught Lana's eye because their towers rose above flat-roofed residential neighborhoods. The greatest of these boasted an enormous painted dome. Walking several blocks to survey the town while Luis went to question the town administrators, Lana and DK headed for that largest of churches, the cathedral.

Townspeople were on the move as the couple passed them. No one stopped to ask what Lana and DK were seeking. People were hurrying—not so much in a hurry, as walking with a sense of purpose. Camaguey is an island metropolis.

After a visit to the museum, where they questioned the curator without success, the couple met the cathedral prelate. He had been gracious discussing the *Masque* with them, but he had never heard a rumor over it nor seen such odd wealth in parishioner's homes. In parting, he did suggest they contact native tribesmen whose Cuban heritage went as far back as the fourteen hundreds.

"Continue to the eastern part of our island. Oral history tells of these ancient people. They suffered dispossession, property by property, century by century, but they still exist. Some of the family names that I have heard are Rojas and Ramirez. Inquire of them what you seek. There are other family names that I do not know, but many of the tribe live along the valley of the Rio Toa. Go to Baracoa in particular. Their customs are rooted in the Arawak traditions, the people who came from the southern continent."

———

As evening descended, Luis drove to their next hotel. On the drive to the edge of town, a white 1955 Chevrolet Impala rolled behind them. When night fell, the Chevrolet remained parked on the street of the hotel, a good ten car-lengths back, if there were that many cars on the street. A small tree-filled corner kept the stalker and his vehicle from view. It was only in darkness, when Lana and DK had left for dinner that the Chevrolet inched nearer to the hotel. The driver entered it and spoke to the desk clerk.

"Special Delivery from Havana for Señórita Lana Bell. Will you get it to her or shall I bring it to the room?"

Wary of the stranger, the desk clerk did not intend to grant him passage upstairs. His eyes downcast he simply shook his head. "I will let her know a package is here, sir. If you'd like to leave it."

"Well, do not hold it long. It is perishable."

Seeing the room key tucked in its mailbox, the clerk said, "We'll give it to her as soon as she is available."

The stranger turned quickly to leave. "Bueno," he called over his shoulder passing through the exit doors.

The clerk raised his wary eyes to the departing figure, curious about his unfamiliar accent. He looked at the plain but large package, and saw that it would not fit in the mailboxes so he slipped it under the desk. He knew the young couple had taken his recommendation and were dining at the Taquito Real on Oriente Plaza. They had ordered a soup be sent to their friend's room, for Luis was very tired of long distance driving and constant duty.

The box remained at the front office until the day clerk left. The night clerk arrived around 9 p.m. He tidied the lobby waiting to lock the doors at midnight. He answered a call from room 310, the one just under Luis in 410, and carried up more towels. He returned to the desk, checked the paperwork and made a cup of coffee. He waited patiently for late arrivals, but there were none, and he became bored. He spotted the shoebox package with Lana's name on it for room 408. He felt motivated to get it out of the way. Besides, what better thing to do than be one-step ahead of a guest. He saw the room key idle in the mailbox and decided to do something nice for his guests—for the couple named Bell & Cody. To please and to feel useful was the Cuban way.

Lana and DK romanced over dinner and proceeded down city streets finding murals and statues of interest. There were many art corners in Camaguey and they paused to enjoy them. Statues representing the everyday scenes of children at play could be found in pocket parks. Heroes appeared on horseback and farm animals stood at small crossroads. All bore the noble mien of people to admire, love and emulate.

Lana kept her arm in DK's as they neared the hotel. "The clues we've had point us in the direction of the Taino Tribe. It boils down to the fact that since no one else can speak of the *Masque of Gold*, the Taino at least have an ancient history that could know of it. Pio told us that the Calusa did contact the Taino, so it is very reasonable to think of them as friends. We have spent a lot of time looking everywhere else, but not trusting the simplest clue—the last place written on the map. It stands to reason that the artifact traveled all the way to its relations."

"Well, let's see if we can speak with the man known as, Sergei. Then, we have to get going because there are only three days left before our visa expires." DK took Lana's elbow to lead her across a wide thoroughfare.

They had just rounded the corner to their hotel when a large explosion reverberated through the street. They saw windows fly out of their hotel and debris scatter around them. Lana's hand rushed to her mouth, and she gasped, "That blew from the fourth floor windows!"

"Luis," DK said gruffly.

They sprinted to the hotel lobby. The clerk held them back from entering, making room for guests who were filtering down from their rooms, everyone in a nervous state. As people waited outside, the police arrived and the crowds became larger. A clanging rose as an ambulance approached. People were peering out of windows.

"Chaos," Lana muttered in despair.

The Chevrolet Impala inched in reverse and pulled far back into the night.

It was late the next morning when the orderly town of Camaguey awoke from the night's unrest.

"Luis, how do you feel?" Lana asked, looking at the face now crisscrossed with small white bandages.

"I have had the wind knocked out of me two days in a row, so I must admit to feeling shaky. My ears are still dull, but I'll be all right. The cuts are all small and unimportant."

"I'm so sorry we got you into this caper, Luis. The night clerk tried to do us a favor. The rooms on either side of us got the blast."

"How lucky that you didn't come in earlier. Was anyone else hurt?"

"No, the blast wasn't strong enough to go through the floors. It exploded outward and that's how it reached your room. It also went through the doors and made a mess of that hallway. It is so lucky that your bed was on the other side of your room. The bulky furniture between us must have absorbed some of the shock."

He grimaced, trying to roll on his side.

"Look, Luis. We do not want you in harm's way any longer. Please let us pay for your flight back to Havana so you can be safe. We will hire someone else to ferry the car back to wherever. DK and I must keep going. This evil group will not deter us, certainly not now. It's obvious by their increasing hostility that we are close to the *Masque* or that the devils are close to their purpose."

"No, no. I am not going back. This is my work, danger and all."

"I'm not sure what you mean Luis. Why should you accept danger in this job?"

"Because I do DK. Now if you can wait one day, I will be released from the hospital and I shall continue with you."

"It's true we have only one town left to visit. However, our time is running out. We can be sure that the terrorists have more damage in mind. You should return home and recover, but it would help Lana and me if you put pressure on the authorities now to dragnet Baracoa. Can the authorities help us there? When we spot Sonoteas, we can point him out. I'm sure he will identify his evil companions if pressed do it."

"I'm not going to let you do this alone," Luis said, trying to raise himself up on the bed.

"Nonsense." Lana added. "DK and I have each other and we'll have your police dragnet, right?"

Luis leaned back against his bed pillows, seeming too weak to argue. "I see. All right. When do you fly to Baracoa?"

"We have chartered a small plane for this afternoon because there is no regular flight between Camaguey and Baracoa."

"Right, Okay. Nurse!" he called. "Go on with you two. I'll call the local authorities for you now."

"Thanks for all your help Luis. We may not see you again, this trip anyway."

"Ah. Well, then, to the next time," he said too nonchalantly for Lana's taste, but he was probably tired of the intrigue, she mused.

DK shook hands with the injured man, and Lana gave him a peck on the cheek.

"You don't mind that we must move ahead? We don't want to quit now, whatever the danger ahead."

"Whatever the danger Lana? You are sure?" Luis pressed.

"Whatever," Lana responded.

—∞∞∞—

It was at the airport that DK finally made satellite connection to the States. He was able to reach the Department of Justice in Washington, D.C. When he concluded the call, DK took Lana's arm, and together they walked the tarmac toward a small aircraft.

"That was interesting."

"Yes?"

"The Bureau has been compiling records on this organized type of terror and they appreciate the information we relayed which helps to pin-point this particular cell. Let me read this to you from my phone."

These individuals form one cell. They are part of a group that travels broadly with one purpose in mind— to seed internal unrest and international discord.

"They are just as Luis said. The worm in the apple. These men plant worms and leave them within a state to destroy it."

They repeat their efforts in one place and another until a society, or a nation, or a group of nations has bloodied themselves. This type of group doesn't use violence directly: They encourage fear and bigotry, faulty logic and the miss-understanding of events and history. They use internet, rallies and brainwashing to influence people, encouraging hate and breach of the law.

"What country do they represent, DK?"

"Country?"

"Success at evil —that is their nation. He looked down, feeling for the moment that all his good effort was and would be futile in the face of such nations. "They are the furthest thing from goodness and brotherhood, Lana."

"I understand," she said, taking his arm and sighing. "This has become larger than we knew, but we must not lose faith in the future. It will be here long after us, and we can only try to make it better."

He folded her arm in his. "I don't like you being here now. Something may happen."

"Dusty…" her tone slid up. "Don't you worry for me. I choose to be here, by your side. Besides, if we are lucky, there are only two of these enemies against us at the moment. So, we are even. If we don't find the *Masque* first, or stop these people, they will only grow stronger."

"Okay, m'dear. Remember we can't be sure of Luis or that we will receive any back up from the locals."

"Ah. Well let's make a plan."

And they did.

The plane took off and Lana looked below at the lush countryside. "So this plane won't fly us over the Sierra Maestra?"

"No."

"It's a shame that we can't stop there at the mountain base of Bayamo and be close to Pico Turquino. I would have liked to see the tallest mountain up close."

He chuckled that Lana had not lost her daredevil personality. "I'm sure that those forests aren't an easy stroll. Their dense rain canopy hid revolutionaries under Fidel for a year, so we would not hike it in a day. Look, don't despair Lana, we will return one day and for now we have challenges enough to find the Taino and enter the Punta de Mais."

"I suppose flying over Guantanamo is forbidden, DK?"

"What do you think?"

"Just checking, just checking. It is so close to Baracoa. Have you ever been to the naval base there?"

"Nope, even though the Marines do the policing, I was never sent during my stint. However, since the lease goes on in perpetuity, I hope we will all see it as friends one day."

Chapter 27

Touching down with a thud at the Gustavo Rizo airport, the small Cessna 170 scooted along until it sidled like a boasting little brother next to the ATR 42-600 destined for Havana with an evening flight plan.

The airport sat at the sea, large rocks breaking the surf. Runway and buildings faced 180 degrees of waterfront. The airport and harbor fronted the city that grew back from its shore, unrolling gracefully to the mountains behind. Bolsas, or limestone pouches, dominated the rocky coast; the harbor itself being one giant hole eaten away by wind and water for millennium.

"There would be no hiding an important Masque, in this town," DK mused. "It seems a petite and simple place. Yet it is important because of its location at the tip of its fatherland and a jump to South America."

"Yes."

"So," he continued. "I like the feel of it, focus on the boating, fishing and small town life. It feels comfortable even if it is not richly endowed like some of the other places we visited. I mean, it doesn't seem a showy place where people might boast and brag with valuables like the *Masque*."

"It is a very interesting geography, isn't it? Look how a thrust of the earth's crust on land runs parallel to the Cayman Trench in the sea. See? It is marked that way on my tourist map. I'm very glad we made it here. I like it too."

They were standing at the customs and immigration desk when a wave of chocolate vapors entered the passageway.

DK saw Lana's expression. "Lana, this place begins to have even more fascination for you."

"I can smell it," she blurted out.

The airport guard laughed at Lana's reaction to the aroma. "You may not be able to purchase it Miss, but this is the day for processing the beans."

"How does that work?" She asked.

"First the beans are separated from the fruit, and then cut, shaved and boiled, then processed into a rich, dense liquor. That is what you smell today. We export to candy manufacturers, spice and flavor companies, and such."

"I can't wait to taste it. My friend, Captain B., told me he loved coming here, for many reasons. Now I understand and get the *scents* of that," she laughed at her pun.

"Really?" DK questioned with a protective edge to his voice. "You never mentioned that man before."

"No? Well anyway..." She changed the subject. "He said the biggest hill here is el Yunque. The forest near town is the dryer section and I can't see hiding a *Masque* in sparse pine forests, but we will see."

Receiving their papers back from the airport official, DK hailed a bicycle cart. "I like these colonial landmarks. The narrow streets look connected at the hip. It makes for a warren of walls where people can spend their lively lives protected. Or, so it seems."

"Look to the left. I think that is the original fort," Lana said. "Ah, here it is marked in my guide book as the Museo Municipal del Fuerte Matachin. This says it houses a lovely collection of art and crafts."

"I believe there won't be time to visit it this trip." He glanced at all their luggage and Lana, still tall, still agile, but not an Amazonian. "Come on let's take a cab and hurry this stuff to the hotel. We will not walk with it all while we have limited time. We've got to find our contact before end of business hours."

Their bicycle cart filtered through the cobblestone paths, over a wider street and finally up a long drive from the bay to the hotel Castillo. The driver knew his way and had strong legs to pull the heavy load of luggage. Beside their duffle bags, there was still a large wheeled case filled with gifts for the Taino.

The hotel matron checked them in and opened a room. She pointed with pride to a view that stretched from the city's eastern forest to the Playa Negra: from a town monument dedicated to the freedom-fighter Hatuey to the cut-off for Carretera Central. That would have been their route into town had they been traveling with Luis by van.

"Could be an escape for us if we miss the plane back. We'd pass Guantanamo then, Lana."

"Don't even suggest such a thing. Are you trying to discourage me?" She objected.

"Just saying; just providing alternatives. Anyway, I would rather stay here. It is a pocket paradise," he said, smiling at her.

They glanced across the wide view, enjoying the flowery and chocolaty fragrances of the town.

"What's that?" Lana startled.

"What?"

"Did you see a man jump from a cart opposite this hotel?"

"Was it Sonoteas? Did he see us?"

"It sure looked like him. He was rubbing his elbow and staring at my red head."

"Let's get going, now! Our concierge may be able to point us to the priest's friend, Sergei. Sergei is our only hope for progress since we have lost Luis. We've got to get ahead of Sonoteas."

Sergei was an attorney, known to most proprietors in Baracoa. So it proved easy to find his office. When they arrived, Lana and Agent Cody found that Sergei had returned from a meeting, but was booked with more appointments. They waited with patience on a bench in the office corridor. Two clients came and went.

"This is nerve wracking," Lana whispered to DK. "After all we have been through to think we are almost done, and then maybe not."

He looked at her amused. "I've never seen you nerve wracked. You won't be like that the day of our wedding, right?"

"Oh. You are pushing it," she scolded.

DK stood and approached the legal secretary who sat at a tiny desk next to one of the doors at that end of the corridor. He tried to impress her about their urgency, and how they had come at the wishes of the prelate in Trinidad.

The secretary spoke to a waiting client who agreed to come back in an hour. Then she led the couple into Sergei's office. It proved to be modest, holding only one large desk, a long bookcase bursting with all manner of printed materials, and several chairs scattered around. The furniture looked sturdy and hand-made out of a light colored wood. The floor was a darker hard wood and shone, polished to a glow. Someone had pulled in the shutters to a half-closed position, shading the room against a brilliant sun. The opening let breezes waft in from the sea. Several crystal ashtrays rested on the wide desk. They were spotless—honored as gifts and inscribed from grateful clients.

The secretary brought in a gift delivery of flowers and she placed them on the bookcase across from another bouquet. She returned with several glasses of water for the three of them, and then stepped from the room in silence.

Sergei entered from another door in the room, and he closed it.

Lana unzipped a jacket pocket and unfolded a sheaf of documents that supported their quest. Introducing themselves to Sergei first, the conversation between them went to the point, subdued, but pleasant. He was curious about their intentions, and patient with the complicated explanations Lana presented. He never expressed mockery at the unscientific quest they were on, or insult at their needing help. He did not rush them along, given their crowding his busy client day.

A man of stature, Sergei was six feet in height with broad shoulders and an attractive head. His face proved the Slavic heritage of his first name and boasted balanced features with a broad jaw. The presence of Russian lineage was evident. Even Taino damsels were not immune to the handsome men who occupied their attentions during the latter part of the 20th century. Although his beard was light, the man's hair and eyes gave him away; dark like his complexion, they spoke of Sergei's Taino heritage. The combination of intense eyes, dark lashes and pale skin lent air of mystery to him.

"I hope our legal papers and Pio's ancient map legitimize us in your eyes. If your contacts know of the Calusa spiritual icon, perhaps they will help us return it to the original owners."

He took a deep breath. "I cannot say. However, I will arrange a meeting with the most important Taino representative of our area. He is *cacique;* a venerable man who decides major matters for the tribe. I know that he does what he thinks best for his people, and although he would like to see them more comfortable, he doesn't want to commercialize them, so he will want to review the ramifications of your, let us call it, alliance. Besides, he may or may not have your *Masque of Gold.* Come."

He showed the couple to his main door. "You shall meet me here tomorrow morning at nine, and I will tell you then if the cacique is willing to meet. Be ready for a hike."

<hr />

Their lodging at Hotel Castillo provided the unobstructed sea-view that any lovers might seek on an island holiday, but the couple felt pressured by the remaining time to accomplish their mission and the sadness of having missed so much on the island. They elected to dine at the hotel under the care of their solicitous host. She chatted freely and merrily with them between courses and they loved her. At the end of the meal, she arrived with her special desert, the Cucurucho. She also proudly served a luxury of hot cocoa.

"This is a nice change from all the strong coffee we've enjoyed," Lana grinned from ear to ear.

"Yes," the matron replied, happy to share with them. "It's a major commodity for us."

"Do you think it is legal to take a box home with us?"

"Senõra, there may not be much available in the shops, you know."

"I see."

"Disappointed? I'll bet." DK remarked. "If we cannot bring any back with us, I'll have to take you to Belgium for a decadent week."

"Deal." Lana saluted him. "That is beyond thoughtful."

"It would make a fun honeymoon, no?" He grinned as he took her hand, but Lana pretended to ignore what he said, gnawing at her lip, still fearful of her commitment. He led the way onto their balcony for a last breath of the evening and a splendid view of the town. "I'll bet it is a beautiful sunset over the mountains behind us, but morning sunrise from our room will be spectacular," DK courted.

Lana replied, still dodging his romanticism, "I wonder where Sergei will lead us?"

"It sounds like we will head for the hills where Taino live, as we were told."

"Maybe there are several enclaves scattered there." Lana said.

"Probably. Lucky for us Sergei will lead the way, to the nearest no doubt."

"At last we will meet someone of importance with knowledge of these artifacts. It's exciting."

"Yes, my dear. I am glad for you and your friends the Pios, but of course, we do not have the artifact yet. By the way," DK added, referring to the guidebook, "It says here that there's no such thing as pure Taino. Not even such a claim of pure DNA for conquistadors. It says that the Spanish conquistadors who traveled even 500 years ago were already a mixture of Moors, Sephardic Jews, Basques, Africans and mercenaries from other lands."

"We've discussed the same thing about Calusa with the Pios, but they still dream of returning to some more perfect state of original culture."

Probably never happen. We cannot reverse time. Things just change," he said softly. "Anyway, our time is up. We are due to report to authorities in Havana. After that, we still need a few days to muster the vessel, motor to Key Marco, and catch flights back to our jobs. We cannot get off mission tomorrow. Let us hope we are given a useful lead to pass on to Luc. Then our assignment is over."

"Look! DK. Look!"

"Ha. Unbelievable...he never stops."

Sonoteas stood across the street watching them. The dangerous man they had seen several times ever since Key West was next to him now.

"That's a pair of double-trouble-makers for you. They certainly mean to get the valuable *Masque* or to involve us in some international incident. What shall we do DK?"

"Nothing tonight. Our room is high up, and the matron is too shrewd. I'll go down and speak with her. Sergei can call for the police cordon once we explain the dangers."

After securing the room, Lana and DK settled in and Lana read some of the Taino reference material in case they would meet the tribe before leaving the next night:

"The Taino culture is similar to the Calusa. They share the same origin and history of Caribbean life. Their belief structure is similar. Taíno Indians believed that being in the good graces of their Zemis protected them from disease, hurricanes, or disaster in war. These figures could be made of wood, stone, bones, or human remains. They were served cassava (manioc) bread as well as beverages and tobacco as propitiatory offerings. 'Yocahu' was the supreme creator. Another god, 'Jurakán,' was perpetually angry. He ruled the power of the hurricane. Another mythological figure was 'Maboya,' a nocturnal deity who destroyed the crops and was feared."

She looked up from the papers, "You know I think that the Calusa *Masque* we search for still exists! It spoke from a very important god, the only god. The Calusa called the *supreme Creator*, 'Ioacahu,' but the Taino said "Yokahu." Since both tribes believe in a supreme creator and worship through similar icons, I'd say that this *Masque* is dear to both tribes."

DK looked at her, moving his head in accord. "I see. Since the gold was only a handy material to make the artifact beautiful, we can hope that the Taino did care for it instead of trade it. The talk of them so far indicates a people who live closer to the earth, simply, but who appreciate their gods. I suppose that trust in a supreme being brought more peace to them than seeking glamourous things."

"Yes. I'm sure that they can tell the difference between the fleeting things and their faith—nectar from God."

Chapter 28

They said little more until they left the hotel the next morning, relieved that this time no bomb had blown out the lovely hotel. Sergei met them as promised and drove them to a long beach.

"We must take the beach path from here because the road would take us longer and I could not get you back for your flight in time. This is the fastest way to go, if you don't mind walking?"

"Oh no Sergei. What a lovely way to start the day." Lana was tugging the last wheeled case behind her. They were gifts for the tribe.

"That was thoughtful of your group. I am sure that all the recipients you met crossing the country appreciated the gifts. I know this tribe will too. Medical items and other useful things are always needed. Give me the handle, Lana. I can pull it since you and DK have backpacks. You know the beach walk is several miles. Then we go uphill, …better that we share the load."

She smiled at the thoughtful man as she and DK stowed their hiking boots into the backpacks. They went barefoot across the sand, and their packs carried water bottles, snacks, windbreakers, a flashlight and a small medical kit. DK was carrying a flare that he had been carrying every day, just in case…

"Sergei, did you have any success with your call to the authorities? Will they be on the lookout for the terrorists?"

"I was told that the issue was under consideration. Sorry, that is all I know. I hope that my people will be kept safe. I have alerted them to certain precautions."

"Ah, Sergei, would we be endangering the Taino if we go up there followed by these terrorists and have no police around us?"

"Leave that to me, Ms. Bell. Once we are on the mountain, no one will pass without my tribe knowing. They will defend us all. Shall we continue?"

He kept them at a good pace as they hiked the beach. They chatted about themselves and about the life in Baracoa.

"My work keeps me so busy that I cannot come to visit the tribe often. Your visit gives me a welcome opportunity to leave the demands of the day for this crossing. Usually I take the road, but it takes much longer and I still must walk to the particular camp we seek today."

He told them he was married and that his children were studying to be bi-lingual like him. "They even speak some Russian," he chuckled.

Suddenly Lana's intuition caused her to glance back down the long beach behind them. "What is that?"

DK stopped to see what she had spotted, "It is a man, but this is too far away to tell who it is. It could be Sonoteas, but I am not sure."

"It could be Luis too, but why wouldn't he have called our hotel to tell us to meet him?"

Sergei stopped for only a second, turned abruptly back toward the hills and kept going. He called back to DK and Lana, "Move on!"

Lana and DK rushed to catch up, surprised at the situation. They also shared a signal, concerned over Sergei's own intentions for them and the vagueness of what lay ahead. Conversation had petered out.

The sun had reached a vertical point above, and they stopped for a rest. They cooled their feet in the surf, drank from their water bottles and soon came to a river's edge. They were at the Rio de Miel, a flow of mountain water running its way to the sea. It formed a barrier between the beach and the people who lived in the hills.

They looked at the honey-colored river with curiosity as Sergei walked them to a narrow, rickety bridge at the narrowest neck of the river. "The river eddies are strong. Try not to fall," he warned. "We will cross one-by-one. It isn't a long bridge, just thirty feet, but you must keep your balance." He directed them across the expanse of roiling water, one-step at a time, each in turn, holding their backpacks aloft. Sergei went last. More accustomed to the narrow bridge he zipped across it pulling the wheeled case of gifts behind him.

Once all three were on the other side, Lana saw that it was time for the hiking boots, and so they proceeded, dry and fully shod. Only two mountain ranges were visible from the low point at the river, but once the troupe began its uphill climb, a mass of mountain tips became visible. It was evident that these scalloped around the island's end, mating the two great seas that flow beside Cuba. Other ranges stretched behind the town itself, and they fled west to the next province and Guantanamo. Seeing the varied jumble of many mountains grown thick with foliage, the naked eye took in the scene as a portrait of sleeping cats, their soft curves rising and falling with each breath of the forest.

Leaving the sandy shore, the scene became fragmented. Scrublands pockmark the rocky ledges and present a host of thorny bushes. Higher up, eighteen-foot pine trees and palms rise. With every gust of the wind, a ballet of graceful treetops dance, cooling the underbrush.

Sergei watched Lana's curiosity with appreciation. "You can see what a unique place this is, both forbidding and sustaining. A varied climate and special soil conditions provide home to a variety of succulent plants and pines. Those are herbaceous plants growing between the rocks," he pointed. "The constant sea spray nourishes them, and salty winds cool all the parched spots along the rocky coast. However, these cliffs are assaulted time and again by the storms and surprises of nature. It is not an easy land, but the Taino have learned how to live here for a thousand years. They make the vegetation work for them, and they fish the sea with success. They have been cornered in this remote place for a long time, encroached upon by civilization. ...Isn't that what it is called, civilization?" he asked.

"Then again, here they are left in peace at last, even if they are still poor."

Lana could not look him in the eyes. She had heard the same thing from Pio and Luc. It was clear that when societies undergo great change, people get hurt. One cannot stop change, so how does one prepare for it? Doing so had been her motivation for years, but she was wondering now if answers were muted in the universe. This was a special place and it would be easy to spoil it with rampant and careless development. For in its raw quiet you could hear a whisper, as if the spirits of a thousand years hung on the wind.

She and DK competed over the names of multiple plants growing on the windward slope. They found crotons, acacia, guaiacum, agave, manzanillo, plumeria and many other plants for which they had no names.

Panting, the three reached a plateau where they turned inland. Then they came upon a sandy clearing, drier than below. Sergei led them past several simple, wooden structures to a secondary clearing. There they paused, studying a cluster of round, hut-like homes, roofed in thatch or brush. It was a compound of sorts, but seemed empty except for a young couple, busy painting cloth. Farther away, down a wide path, several women with gray in their hair, and skin looking leathery, sat speaking in soft tones. A few children were beside them content to watch the older women crush seeds into powder. They all laughed when a bird landed nearby chirping loudly for a handout. Then a group of young men arrived with pails of fresh fish, and some teens climbed up the hill, wet from their swim. Tribal artifacts could be seen on the ground, here and there, but the place was not a land of wealth. Mother Nature and human perseverance were its estate.

The little area slowly became crowded, but Sergei continued to wait. Then he directed his two guests to a circle of stones. He said, "Let us sit and wait here."

At first, Lana felt wary. Just because the Taino were not warlike did not mean that they would treat strangers well. She watched DK, who gave no sign of concern, but she saw that his eyes were steely gray. Then a noise erupted. A group of youngsters burst out of a grove, on the run, playing tag, calling out until they saw Sergei. They quieted down, lowered their voices and formed a little semi-circle around him. Sergei wrapped his arm around two of the littlest ones who hugged his legs.

"This group is one of our family nuclei. We call our family groups, caseríos."

These are family people, Lana thought. *They are not devils.*

It was unclear what happened first but on all sides of the newcomers, individuals filtered through the pines toward them. A population crystallized out of nowhere. Sergei stood. Lana and DK did also. A strong man, bronzed by the years, erect like the pines around him, came into the clearing. He was iron; lean and god-like, not like the thunder of Thor, but indomitable like the wind.

Sergei pushed Lana ahead saying, "Please speak. We are a matriarchal society and so you are welcome. This is our cacique, our spiritual advisor."

She bowed her head. "Buenos Dias, senór."

The bystanders became quiet, and the cacique asked Sergei to translate.

"To what do we owe the pleasure of this meeting?"

Lana let go a puff of constricted air, and pulled out all the paperwork for their trip, waiting for the right signal. Sergei explained the Calusa story to the old man, and he replied with one word. Then, looking at Lana, he accepted all the documents she handed him.

As everyone hung on his response, he leafed through each paper. Some were written in Spanish, which he spoke, some had a smattering of Taino words, which made him smile. He looked up at Lana. Then he studied the drawing of Ponce de León. After a pause, he gestured. With a small backward wave of his hand, he blurted "Eh!"— Understanding that de León was the man who had brought them the Zemi so long ago, he repeated himself with a lifting of the chin, nodding to them with pride in the legend.

After a few more minutes of quiet reading, he signaled Lana, and she stepped forward to take the papers back. The old cacique clapped a hand on Sergei's shoulder. With only a word said, he glanced around him. His expression was like a greeting to the morning, bright and pleasant, full of hope. He lifted his arm away, and with a slight signal to the children, he turned back to the way he had come, down a narrow path lined with fishnets. He plucked a drying fish from a cord suspended on poles while everyone watched. He turned back for a moment and nodded to them with an impish smile. Then he disappeared down the path to the sea. The family of Tainos disappeared in the same way, as fast as they had appeared. Only a rustle of leaves accompanied them into the shrubs.

Then the clearing was empty. Lana and DK said nothing. They waited.

Sergei smiled at their puzzlement. "I'm sorry to confuse you, but our tribe honors the elders. That is our current cacique. He has given me the authority to confer with you on his behalf. I am his son."

Still the couple said nothing, overwhelmed at the revelations and the swiftness of such an important meeting.

"These days he and I speak as one. You are fortunate to meet him. He has guided us wisely for many years. My mother led us before that, and now it is I to help my people."

"It is because you are educated and can do so much for them isn't it? And, you speak a beautiful English, Sergei."

"Thank you. My education was enhanced through the kindness of the Dominican Sisters in Cuba, followed by a scholarship in England. Now I work and live here to assist my people. They do need better living conditions, but on the other hand, we are fortunate to remain intact as a culture, which cannot be said of others it seems."

"Perhaps our cultures can work together to improve everyone's daily life," Lana added.

"Yes, perhaps," he replied, "Perhaps."

"Now follow me," he ordered. He led them on another hike up to a secondary plateau. "Through many centuries we have wondered about this icon, what you call *Masque of Gold*. We have wondered if someone would come again to claim it and by what authority? Now. Here you are, opportunists from the United States. You don't mind if I call you that, senõrita?"

Lana's pulse shot up, but she paused. "Sergei. Sir, we do not mean to offend your people or to take advantage of you. We are here only to help some tribal descendants, not to benefit personally in any way."

He continued to study them, and DK understood that the tribe was still wary of their motives. He and Lana could do nothing more to convince them. Perhaps friendship needed time.

Sergei led them into a large circle of round reed huts sporting pointed straw rooftops, peaking at twelve feet. Larger ones had wide door openings to allow for inside activities out of the elements, but it was evident that food cooking took place in the clearing where stakes and branches created a rudimentary kitchen.

"These are the Bohios of the old way, mostly used now for special events. Elsewhere we have cabins or pre-made buildings. They are more comfortable and sound, except in extreme storms. Then we are in harm's way. Someday we will have concrete homes for everyone."

DK checked his watch. "Excuse me Sergei, I'm sorry to press the subject, but our time is limited." Only the spirits around DK knew how limited time would be that night, but their voice was muted in the wind.

"There is only one flight this evening to Havana and we have appointments tomorrow. Is there anything more we can say to gain your trust? Can you tell us where the Calusa could come to find the *Masque of Gold*?"

A small smile breaking on his lips, Sergei said, "I see you are not a patient man, Senõr Cody."

Lana had to smile to herself too, as she touched DK's hand and intervened, "We are just fatigued Sergei. It has been a long trip." She lifted Luc's map and pointed to a location, where they stood. "You see this mark on our map indicates a pit of stones as the last hiding place for the *Masque*. Was it ever found here or somewhere on your plateau?"

"Everything has its time, my friends," he answered. Then with a signal, and uttering words in a language they did not know, a hefty man emerged from the underbrush. Sergei and the man exchanged signals, then, after a pause, Sergei sent the couple forward. His accomplice led them down a lane planted with cacti, and into a fully outfitted cabin. As they entered, Lana had to rub her eyes until they adjusted to the lack of sunlight. Sergei lingered behind at the door.

When Lana looked up, a vision struck her. On the furthest wall, all in the dark, a head took center place; bursting with its own light—light from within. It was as glistening as the rain and as bright as a cloudless sunrise. Larger than a football, more rounded at the ends, it appeared solid, entirely covered with gold, except for the eye area. The mica eyes that were described in the Pio legend had been lost over the centuries. Now the remaining large, black sockets magnetized an onlooker, as if to promise all the secrets of the world deep within. Above and below the eyes, gold was overlaid with stain, dark and red. The *Masque* would have been frightening except for the mouth, serene and slightly upturned, uttering soft wisdom. Lana and DK stood dumfounded.

"Is this the treasure you seek?" Sergei asked his tone more peculiar than before. Lana felt a tingle up her neck. It was obvious by its presence before her that no one else had taken the *Masque of Gold*, not even Sonoteas. Where were those men of terror anyway? Had they been boiled in oil? Would she and DK meet the same fate, now that they had seen the *Masque?* Was that the curse? She began to step back toward the door, bumping into Sergei.

"Have you encountered any other searchers like us?" Lana mumbled.

"Only once, years ago, some historian appeared to my father, speaking of trust. Now we are wiser in judging who is worthy. That man was not. When the liar tried to run away with the *Masque*, well… you can take it from there."

Lana and DK kept their expressions as blank as Sergei's.

"So this *Masque of Gold* is a vital part of your history?"

"Yes. Each elder safeguarded it down through the centuries. It spoke to our caciques and helped us learn much. It had come to us by chance when a Spanish ship pulled into Havana leaving on the next tide. Their leader was dying, and the people of the ship sought something to help fight the poison he suffered, but we had nothing. They unloaded this bundle, saying it had come from natives like us. The sailors wanted to absolve themselves of the curse, you understand." He paused to chuckle, "Ai! You wouldn't want to throw a cursed object into the sea, no telling what curses might multiply then for men who lived upon the rising waters."

"So your people received blessings, not a curse?"

"That's right. During turbulent times, it offered solace to us. We prayed, and it channeled wisdom. One by one, as our people were diminished by the conquerors, we still received help from the supreme creator through this *Masque* and through our other totems. We moved on to avoid persecution and we took our holy objects with us, out of harm's way. Time has changed some of our customs, but we still honor the great spirit of the universe and we have held this *Masque of Gold* in trust for our distant brothers.

A long time ago, some people came from your tribes, and they said that they wanted to confirm that the *Masque* was still safe. They said that they lived in a period of dispersion and were in hiding. It was not the time to bring back such a prized object. Things changed here for us too. Nonetheless, our ancestors have been expecting someone to return for the icon."

Lana held her breath and stared back at the long sought object.

"Does this mean we may take the *Masque* back to the Calusa?" She asked timidly, adding "Or, is it required here?"

"Of course we would like to keep it. Of course we would like the gods to grant us more blessings, more comforts, but we are careful to shun the kind of greed that rots the body and kills the soul. We hope for Taino survival and greater promise for our children, but we will not hold the *Masque of Gold* as ransom or hoard it. Our ancestors tell us that we can join them only with hearts that live in love, and so the gods will remain with us.

Sergei signaled for the *Masque* to come down, and then he began to wrap it.

"We are people close to the earth, so the generations before and so the generations to come." He handed the *Masque* to DK, standing head high with pride. "You see, our name, 'Taino,' means, *g o o d a n d n o b l e*."

Seeing calm rise to Sergei's face, DK appreciated the tribe's nobility and added that he and Lana would return, "Perhaps we can be of assistance in the future."

Sergei welcomed the suggestion. Then he and his companion led them outside.

"Follow us down to the river. I stay here tonight with my people, and return to the town by caravan tomorrow."

In an unexpected turn, DK felt an object pressed against him. A Glock 9mm sat in Sergei's palm and he whispered to DK, "Take it. It is loaded. The thief you spoke of may try to harm you and the icon. You must not let that happen."

"Thank you," DK responded, shaking Sergei's hand.

Children were gathering for evening song, but they sought Sergei first and shadowed his heels to the river. Lana noticed the Glock hidden in DK's waistband, but just kept walking toward the rising river.

Sergei added his final advice. "Turn the weapon over to Havana customs in my name." He signaled them to the sandbar and pointed. "The River of Honey has risen. It will be over a person's head soon and can wash a man out to sea. The bridge is unsteady at this time, so cross at the sand bar with sure steps and with speed. Darkness falls fast here. Go quickly."

Lana and DK pulled off their jackets and shoes, stuffing them into the backpacks. Lana began to cross the oncoming current, using every bit of her strength, while DK put the *Masque* inside his pack. Both had to ford the river holding the packs high. It took more energy to walk holding arms high, each step growing harder. The water was now at their shoulders, and every footstep was sucked down, clutched by the muddy river bottom. After a long ten minutes, the couple reached the other side.

They pulled their tired legs onto solid ground and DK gave a loud whistle. The Taino family heard it and turned uphill again. Their voices seemed gay to him, but their parting left the couple sad. The children's sounds trickled slowly away. Their bodies became mere moving smudges in the sliding-sun rays.

Lana began to hum a tune, remembering the peacefulness of their tribal encounter. She looked at DK. They made a pact to remember the people.

Standing at the beginning of their trek to town, the couple lingered at the riverbank and DK reached for Lana's hand. Then he turned to her and tugged a little on her ear because he knew she loved that, and he loved her. His kiss drew Lana into a place where thoughts had flown and a sense of joy filled her. She never knew how much time passed during these possessions, but she hung there as long as she could.

"Oh my," she breathed, pulling away, "We'd better squeeze out these soaking shirts, and change to dry shorts. I'll put all the wet stuff in my back pack."

"Don't be silly, girl." He equalized the weight of wet jeans, socks and hiking boots, placing most inside his pack, and then picked up the *Masque* again. Lana tied his and her wet shirts to the backpacks hoping they would dry before boarding the airplane.

"We are covered to the thigh anyway," DK laughed.

"Shush!...did you hear that?" Lana asked, pulling him to a stop.

"What?"

"I'm so sure that I heard a name called."

"Do you suppose a Taino came after us?"

"I don't see why. No," she answered.

They stepped across the beach slowly, laden with wet garments. A mellow breeze picked up, chilling and yet casting moisture from their belongings. Two miles along they were able to pick up their pace, walking side-by-side, watching their footfalls.

Chapter 29

The sky had become dark, as the last licks of sun bid farewell. It arched beyond the mountains behind them. The only thing visible now was a sketch of lights across the distant city of Baracoa. Lana became aware of waves slapping the sand and the scent of salt air off the sea. Now and again clumps of glutinous seaweed caught their feet in a web of seashells, scratching the skin. DK pulled out his flashlight to better guide their steps and they listened to the insistent incoming tide, pushing them closer to the tree line, narrowing their path.

Lana stopped cold again. "I'm sure I heard a rustle somewhere in the bushes."

DK flashed his light into the woods, to the left and the right, but it could only reach so deep, and he saw nothing. "Perhaps it is a bear."

"Just as dangerous as our enemies. Do you think Sonoteas has found the tribal compound?"

"It is hard to say, but it is likely that he is following Luc's map too. He would show up here sooner or later," DK answered. "I'll keep scanning behind us and into these woods, but don't you slow down. Keep moving ahead of me, and keep you're your eyes open looking down the beach."

He assumed an aggressive stride, moving his flashlight in a constant arch searching the woods. He checked that the Glock was still tucked in his belt. "I think we have only a mile to go," he said.

As Lana followed the beach curve DK was twelve or so feet behind when he stopped to listen for a repetitive rustle of foliage somewhere between him and Lana. Then light cast from a moon ray shone on Dusty Kern Cody's back and a figure leapt from the wood behind him. When DK spun around to the noise, he dropped to a crouch, but too late. The aim at him missed its mark, but the bullet found DK's leg. He cursed, felled, fallen on his side, and stretched out with one leg limp and the other of top of it. He groaned, fearful for Lana.

Her response was quick when she heard the noise, and so she turned fast into the wood. She threw herself into a thorny grove, and hid behind a sturdy tree, groping for a heavy fallen branch.

The attackers split up. One went after Lana, while the foreigner he had seen in Key West loomed from nowhere over Agent Cody. With the killer's gun pushed in the wounded man's face, Cody could not pull out his Glock. Preparing to fire, the assailant brought his head to DK's head, and as he did so, DK used his good knee to kick the man's groin. The man wobbled, and then DK used his arms to outwit him, pull him down to his chest. As they grappled with each other for dominance, DK wrapped his strong and trained arms around the terrorist. With a firm and powerful tug, he snapped the man's neck.

Another bullet rang out, and DK gasped, "Lana! Are you all right?"

She slid up to him. "Yes, yes. What about you? I threw stones to send Sonoteas in the wrong direction, so let me take your gun before he gets here."

"No, Lana. Hide in the pines fast. Go."

"No!" she answered, pulling off her backpack.

Another shot rang out, but this time it was closer.

"Sonoteas is just shooting into the void, like a Russian roulette player."

She grabbed her damp shirt and tearing it into strips, made a tourniquet. DK's wound was gushing blood, and his eyes were turning glassy.

"Here." She pulled the tourniquet tight and then lifted him against a tree trunk. She nudged the Glock from DK's waistband and slipped it into her shorts pocket. He reminded her how to use it. Then he tried to move to help her.

"DK, keep low! Are you hurt anywhere else?"

"No," he said, his voice growing weak. "Pull that man's body over and give me his weapon."

Another bullet cracked into the tree trunk. "Drat. Where is our flash light?" Lana swore.

"Under backpack," DK uttered, and lay his arm across hers. "Stay here, where I can help you. Let off a flare instead, the police will see it."

"Are you kidding? We are sitting ducks here. I can deflect Sonoteas from you. Sending a flare will just verify where we are. Besides, a single flare off the beach might not attract attention. I can outwit Sonoteas. I have to!"

"But we don't know that he is alone."

Another bullet flew breaking a flurry of leaves closer now.

"Stay flat DK." She dragged the dead man over DK's body to shield him and grabbed the flashlight, and scooted herself back into the wood.

DK called after her. "Lana, he is a killer, so if you are taking that gun, use it! And remember the firing pin." his words faded as she fell to her knees, edging deeper into the dense foliage.

As she moved through the sand and brush, only night critters met Lana's eye. At one point, she sidled into a clump of mangrove where the leggy plant was thick with little lizards. One forest resident greeted her. At a moment like this, Lana was glad for a friendly living creature by her side. She stared at it, and it stared back with wondering eyes. The prehistoric relative kept his long body stretched with patience. He sat on a branch as if expecting dinner from Lana. She did not move, she stared, listening for sounds. She was so intent that it seemed to her the world was a bubble of silence. The waves seemed asleep, no children called from the hillside and no music drifted from the city. There were no voices of beach lovers filtering through the night and no one to help her. She could see DK laying so still that he seemed invisible. She recognized that once again her self-sufficiency put her at a disadvantage, for weaponry was new to her. She was not a gun expert, but she was fighting for DK's life, and she had to win.

Breathing hard and doubling back to his prey, Sonoteas had closed in on the couple. He spotted the two downed men and realized he had only one opponent left. He smiled hunting for Lana's face amid the scattered trees.

"You won't get away Miss Lana," he called. "And you'll be in for it because I *can* stand pain. My father taught me well."

Crouching and darting like a lizard, Lana weaved through several trees in the direction of Sonoteas voice. *Is he alone?* She asked herself. *Is Luis conspiring with him?* She puzzled at the silence, looking and listening for a clue. *How many people were out there?*

Then she made a decision. *DK cannot defend himself. No matter what, I must stop any villain that appears!*

A glimmer of golden-red hair reflected under the erupting star canopy, but Lana could not see herself, of course. Two shots came at her in rapid succession. They grazed her jacket.

Her wits sharpened, Lana swatted an offending mosquito and spun in a circle. A soft shuffle of feet through the sand grew closer. Once she understood its origin, it was too late; too late to run, too late to shoot.

She thrust her body upward, the flashlight held high now, slamming her attacker's chest, whacking Sonoteas repeatedly, over his hands, arms and other tender body parts. The strikes made him yell and stagger back as Lana reared away to catch her breath. She was shoving one hand into her short's pocket where she fingered the Glock, releasing the safety. Her breathing was fast, her eyes wild under a mop of red hair askew.

Regaining his balance, Sonoteas looked at her with anger and saw her hesitation. She was not a killer and he would take advantage of that. He moved less than an arm's length from her and shaking with fury, he grabbed her by the neck choking the wind out of her. Her right arm still stuck in her pocket, she used her free arm to fight his grip, but having no luck against him, a grin spread on his face. He pointed the gun at her head. She stopped struggling. He aimed his weapon and laughed at his success.

In that instant, Lana did not hesitate. She fired from her pocket.

Spinning around and back, howling from the burning shock to his stomach, Sonoteas began clutching at it, bloodying his gun hand. At last, he stopped swaying. Gathering his venomous will, he turned to face her, again aiming his blood soaked gun level with her head.

Two shots rang out.

With the speed of a light switched off, the night went clammy for Lana. She dropped to her knees and pressed her chest into them. Voices seemed to flow and grow around her. She called softly to DK, but by then Agent Cody heard little. Two arms were lifting him as his mind slipped out of time, without will and without dreams. His eyes saw, but did not register the prowess of El Capitan "Luis" Valdes y Diego.

Epilogue

The American troupe of four were amazed at the skill of all the physicians. Even though a bond was required for hospitalization and treatments, some of the medication came from their own supply and everyone worked together for recoveries. An extension of all their visas had been granted and the day had come for departure. Luis had joined them for a farewell celebration. And while they enjoyed a fine meal at Omar al Palador Toresson on the Malecon, their toasts spoke of hope for a bright future.

As Luc said goodbye, he handed the *Masque of Gold* to a surprised Luis.

"Capitan Luis Valdes y Diego, I believe that the Cuban people and the Taino tribes belong to the *Masque* now—they protected it for so long. My Calusa clan is unified and growing stronger within its own nations of the Miccosukee and the Seminole. It is time for my family to let go of the past, and join our brothers for the future, that all may thrive. We are not happy at the death of a boy who chose greed and terror as his life, but he teaches us that friendship is more satisfying than revenge."

Departing from the marina, Gusta raised the U.S. flag above the *Esmeralda* as she moved beyond the marina into Havana's lighthouse channel. They motored past the Castillo de los Tres Reyes Magos Del Morro and focused on Luis standing along the seawall, waving a long farewell.

Luc sighed, waving back to Luis. "Even with his up-beat attitude, his connections to the powerful, and all the beauty that Cuba offers, Luis has been a prisoner in his own country for a long time. What do you think Dusty?"

DK hesitated. "Well, to read between the lines, I'd say that our friend Capitan Valdes y Diego has told us the future. He would like his people to have better economic opportunities, but to live wisely. He wants them to cross the ocean as he once did, and to have new experiences, to return home invigorated; not for subversion, but to breathe the air of freedom. We all want to touch the stars."

"Yes," Lana added, "But nations find freedom untidy. It isn't easy for old democracies to manage and it is certainly unwieldy for new political orders."

They went quiet, settling in for their own journey. Lana stowed the *Masque*. This one was a plaster copy. "It is a good likeness, isn't it?" Lana asked Luc.

"Yes. I could hear my father jiggle with joy at our safety and the tribal connections we made. He is happy that we left the original. So don't worry. All the photographs we took will attract people to the museum anyway and our written records will enthrall them. My people will understand their rich past better than before. They will know they connect to another vibrant Arawak people like themselves. We will always feel proud that the original *Masque* is where it enriches the life of others."

He took a deep breath. The four friends were standing close together at the helm.

"What else can one say of the *Masque,* Lana?"

"I know what the *Masque* has been for all of us connected to it, and for those who will connect through it; an intent to seek wisdom."

She tugged unconsciously on her ear. "Let us say that the *Masque of Gold* is brotherhood..."

"That's it," Gusta agreed. "We did not come to take advantage of anything or anyone. We joined family."

"Yes," Lana sighed, as they looked back at the sparks of island life. "One cannot visit Cuba, and the people not keep a little corner of the heart forever."

The winds had been fair as they pressed homeward, and DK stood at the helm, his healing leg propped on the settee, Lana nearby. He checked various navigation screens for final tweaks. "We'll make it by dark," he said, giving Lana a small hug.

She looked at him with a large grin, "We've been gone a month, but it made for a splendid adventure!"

Dusty Kern Cody gave a hearty laugh, standing strong and suntanned, doing his best to keep on the Cuban straw hat he wore with pride. Luc and Gusta chuckled to see that the wind had other ideas, and then Luc handed a small sack to DK.

"I have something for you."

"What is it?"

"I brought you several fresh Cucuruchos as a treat for your onward journey."

"I remember enjoying them in Baracoa, Luc, but I've had enough sugar. Thank you. Please share it with Lana."

She nibbled the desert with enthusiasm, getting sugar all over her lips.

"Umm, good," she uttered between bites.

"I'm just happy when you are happy," DK said.

She sighed, then with a smile and a wink to Luc, she said, "Okay, okay then, take care of me, but…"

He bent to kiss her and neither finished their complaints, for a little sugar is not such a bad thing.

To find out what happens next to Lana and Cody and Friends;

Follow the blog from the websites

www.LANAvictoriaBELL.com

www.PenelleOnTour-books.com

Look for the next Lana v. Bell, adventure-suspense novel

LIMELIGHT IN PARIS, *Secrets* ....
Due mid-2016

Acknowledgements

Thank you to the publishing production team at CreateSpace, who know their stuff and worked hard to bring this story to print. In particular I appreciate Kimberly, Kristin, Jamie, Norma, Valerie and Michelle with whom I spoke most often. They were always good-humored and supportive.

Marta Arrojo, artist and wondrous lady whose Cuban birthright provided knowledge and balance to my story perspective, and whose friendship I value.

Thank you to my exacting editor and champion Clarissa Tomlinson of Buscher Consultants who taught me the comma and more. And to Diane Chadwick whose tenacious reads never failed with good ideas.

I cannot understate my appreciation for the first readers who plowed through earlier versions and came up still breathing. They gave me encouragement: Brenda Spalding, of ABC, Inc., fellow author and champion of the independent writer; Susan Hubbard Marketing, Diane and Marta.

A big thank you to Captain Bruce Blomgren of Brandy Marine, without whose guidance the Esmeralda would sink!

My husband Don stands by me with great patience, missing many good meals, and always ready with a listening ear to my flights of fancy and test runs. I couldn't ask for better. My love also goes forth to my kind and generous advisor, Olivia Braida Chiusano, talented sister and artist, author.

To those dear friends who never failed to give me enthusiastic support; Sandy & Gerry Wernovsky, Don Britt at Don411.com, Judy Sherpa, Anna & Joe Acevedo, The Teng Family, Marne McCluskey and my accomplished cousin, Dr. Georgeann Dau, an affectionate greeting and appreciation! I hope that I haven't let you down, nor the reader!

<hr/>

Thank you to the institutional professionals who provided help and information:

- **Cindy Baer, Coordinator of Programs, Randell Research Center, Pineland, FL**
- **Professor Marquardt, Calusa Heritage Institute, Pineland, FL**
- **J. Daniel Rogers, Curator of North American Archeology, The Smithsonian Institute, Washington, D.C.**
- **Museum of Key Marco, Key Marco, Florida**

- **Museum of Natural History, University of Florida at Gainesville.**

To read more about the colonization of the Carib-
bean read the Feature *Heritage
on the website: www.PenelleOntour-Books.com
and the bibliography provided here.

Bibliography

Source material: No blame should fall upon these diligent writers for any miss-interpretation, revisionism or fantasy that I created.

- Brown, Robin C. (1994).
  "Florida's First People, *The Late Archaic Period: Horr's Island"*.
  Sarasota, FL: Pineapple Press. ISBN 1-56164-032-8.

- Chomsky, Aviva, Barry Carr, Pamela Maria Smorkaloff (2003).
  "The Cuban Reader".
  Durham, North Carolina: Duke University Press. ISBN 0-8223-3197-7

- De Cortanze, Gerard. Jean-Bernard Naudin (1997).
  "Hemingway in Cuba".
  France: Editions du Chêne. Hachette.
  ISBN: 2.84.277326-8

- Fuson, Robert H. (2000).
  "Juan Ponce de León. *The Spanish Discovery of Puerto Rico & Florida"*.
  Blacksburg, VA: The McDonald & Woodward Publishing Company.
  ISBN: 0-939923-82-3

- Milanich, Jerald T. (1994).
  "**Mounds,** *The Archaeology of Pre-Columbian Florida".*
  Gainesville, FL: University Press of Florida.
  ISBN 0-8130-1273-2

- Russo, Michael. *
  National Park Service: *"Archaic Shell Rings of the Southeast U. S."* (*Retrieved 10 November 2011 by Wikipedia.)

- Skinner, Penell-Braida (2000).
  Personal Cuba Tour Notes. Havana, Cuba.

- Smith, Martin-Cruz (1999).
  "**Havana Bay**".
  New York, N.Y.: Random House. Random House, Inc.
  ISBN 0-679-42662-0

- Valladares, Armando (2001)
  Against All Hope – A Memoir of Life in Castro's Gulag
  San Francisco, CA: Encounter Books
  ISBN 1-893554-19-8

---

(1) "Historical References," by Jose Barreiro,
The Cuban Reader, p. 31, lines 31-37.

Editors; Chomsky, Carr & Smorkolofff,
Duke University Press, Durham & London 2003.

———∞∞∞———

The United States Cuba Embargo
*To understand the reasons for the U.S. Embargo against
Cuba, its business and nuances over the years, as well as the
cascading effects of food scarcity, immobilization, political
alliances and social harm, read:*

"How the Poor Got More," by Medea Benjamin, Joseph
Collins, and Michael Scott,
The Cuba Reader, pp. 344 to 353
Editors; Chomsky, Carr & Smorkolofff,
Duke University Press, Durham & London 2003.
&
A web blog politically conversant on this subject:
Angelfire.com/nj4/us_cuban_relations/nuka_1.htm

———∞∞∞———

Also

by PENELLE
TRAVELING TO DEATH,
Murder in the Rockies

A Lana Victoria Bell

Adventure-suspense novel